The Bewitching Braid

T0150462

Hong Kong University Press thanks Xu Bing for writing the Press's name in his Square Word Calligraphy for the covers of its books. For further information, see p. iv.

Published in conjunction with

澳門特別行政區政府文化局
INSTITUTO CULTURAL do Governo da R.A.E. de Macau
CULTURAL INSTITUTE of the Macao S.A.R. Government

The Bewitching Braid

Henrique de Senna Fernandes

translated by David Brookshaw

香港大學出版社

HONG KONG UNIVERSITY PRESS

Hong Kong University Press
14/F Hing Wai Centre
7 Tin Wan Praya Road
Aberdeen
Hong Kong

ISBN 962 209 718 9

British Library Cataloguing-in-Publication Data
A catalogue record for this book is available from the British Library.

Secure On-line Ordering
http://www.hkupress.org

Cover images from the film *The Bewitching Braid*, courtesy of Cai Brothers' (Macau) Film Company Ltd.
Printed and bound by United League & Graphic Co. Ltd. in Hong Kong, China

Hong Kong University Press is honoured that Xu Bing, whose art explores the complex themes of language across cultures, has written the Press's name in his Square Word Calligraphy. This signals our commitment to cross-cultural thinking and the distinctive nature of our English-language books published in China.

"At first glance, Square Word Calligraphy appears to be nothing more unusual than Chinese characters, but in fact it is a new way of rendering English words in the format of a square so they resemble Chinese characters. Chinese viewers expect to be able to read Square Word Calligraphy but cannot. Western viewers, however are surprised to find they can read it. Delight erupts when meaning is unexpectedly revealed."

— Britta Erickson, *The Art of Xu Bing*

INTRODUCTION

One of the characteristics of Portuguese overseas expansion in the sixteenth century was the early appearance of mixed populations in the territories that came under some form of Portuguese political or economic control. Most of those who journeyed with the annual fleets that left Lisbon for the Indian Ocean were soldiers destined to defend the forts and trading stations that were vital in Portuguese efforts to gain and sustain a monopoly in the spice trade. More often than not, these *soldados* never returned to Portugal, preferring to settle down with local women, while often involving themselves in trading activity, or continuing to ply their military skills in the service of the Portuguese Crown or even as freelancers in the pay of local rulers and princes. These *casados* (married men) raised families, and their mixed offspring would, in due course, form the basis of distinctive ethnic groups, intermediaries between the representatives of the colonial administration and the native populations that lay within or beyond the political borders of the colony. The Goans, Malacca Eurasians, the Burghers of Sri Lanka, the Topasses of Timor and, of course, the Macanese are all examples of such mixed communities. Interestingly, the tradition of soldiers remaining in colonial territories after completing their periods of service and marrying into the local community, would continue virtually right up until the end of the empire in 1974.

When the Portuguese were allowed to establish a trading settlement on the Macao peninsula in the 1550s, they brought with them women from Malacca and Goa, both of which had fallen into Portuguese hands decades earlier. This is why some of the oldest Macanese families in the territory claim descent from these groups, as well as from the Chinese, with whom the Portuguese later mingled. Down the years, there would frequently be other admixtures — Dutch, French, English, Timorese, Filipino, and even Thai and Burmese — reflecting Macao's importance as an international trading and ecclesiastical centre. Over the centuries, these *filhos da terra* (literally, children of the land) came to be united by a set of common cultural references, which are nonetheless mixed and multiple in their origins. While the Macanese have traditionally taken great pride in their Portuguese, Catholic affiliations, their unique cuisine blends ingredients and flavours from Portugal, India and Southeast Asia with those of Southern China. Their language, popularly known as *patuá* (patois), mixes medieval Portuguese with lexical and even syntactical influences from Malay, Cantonese, the languages of the Indian sub-continent and even Japanese. While *patuá* was, for a number of centuries, the language of spoken communication, domestic intimacy and a vibrant oral tradition, the Macanese (in particular the elite of that group) also cultivated Portuguese, and helped guarantee the legitimacy of the language in the area. For example, it was in some measure at least thanks to the presence of the Macanese that the first independent newspapers in Portuguese were founded in the city during the nineteenth century, in the wake of the liberal revolt that swept Portugal after 1820, and whose effects were felt throughout the empire. But it was during the nineteenth century too that many Macanese left the territory in search of new opportunities. They took with them their language and cultural traditions, establishing 'Oriental Portuguese' diasporas in Hong Kong, Shanghai, Guangzhou and the other port cities of China. In the twentieth century, they would migrate further afield to North America, Brazil and Australia. Most Macanese also had a greater or lesser fluency in Cantonese, and although few could write Chinese, they nevertheless provided a crucial link between the Portuguese colonial officials and the local Chinese authorities.

Henrique de Senna Fernandes was born in Macao in 1923, into a family whose presence in the territory goes back several centuries. After the end of the War of the Pacific in 1945, he obtained a scholarship to study law at Coimbra University in Portugal, from where he graduated in 1952. It was while he was in Portugal that he began to write short stories, one of which won a literary prize. Upon his return to Macao, he set up a lawyer's office, but also worked as a teacher and wrote for the local press, which began to flourish again in the 1950s, after the harsh war years. He was a member of a generation of intellectuals who began to explore and express the cultural foundations of the Macanese and their social predicament at a time when their homeland began to undergo profound changes, and when the Portuguese colonial empire came under threat.

His first collection of short stories, *Nam-Van*, was published in 1978, and contained a selection of his fiction written since the 1950s, some of which had appeared previously in the press or anthologies. Two of the longer pieces from this collection, 'Tea With Essence of Cherry' and 'Candy', feature in English translation in the anthology, *Visions of China: Stories From Macau* (Gávea-Brown/Hong Kong University Press, 2002). Since his first collection of tales, he has published two novels, *Amor e Dedinhos de Pé* (Love and little toes), and *A Trança Feiticeira* (The bewitching braid), both of which were made into successful films. His third collection of tales, *Mong-Há*, was published in 1998.

Macao has, of course, formed the setting for a considerable body of literature over the last century or so, and in particular during the 1980s and

90s, the so-called transition years leading up to the handover to China in 1999. But most of this literature was written by visitors and residents of greater or lesser duration who often had little real interest in trying to grasp the cultural world that surrounded them. This is why Fernandes is a unique figure, for his stories are set in an entirely Macanese world, from which the Portuguese, whether as colonial officials or other representatives of the 'metropolis' are largely absent, and even when they do appear, they are essentially background figures. His fiction evokes not only the relationship between the Macanese and Chinese on both a social and a cultural level, but it also focuses on the internal dynamics of social change among the Macanese themselves, for there are inevitably class divisions and rivalries within this ethnic group. *The Bewitching Braid*, set in Macao in the 1930s, is undoubtedly the work that most effectively includes all these competing interests in the figure of its hero, Adozindo, the product of an old Macanese family, representative of the decline of patriarchal society, who is torn between his attraction to A-Leng, a Chinese water-seller, and Lucrécia, a *nouveau riche* Eurasian widow, whose deceased husband had made his money by migrating to Shanghai at the beginning of the twentieth century. Lucrécia clearly has the capital that Adozindo's family lacks, while the latter has a more respectable social pedigree, originating as it does from Santo António, one of the oldest parishes in the 'Christian city'.

The raw material for Fernandes's stories is often taken from the rich oral tradition of the Macanese, and usually involves a love relationship across social boundaries. His fiction is conventional in the sense that in its intricately woven plots, boldly depicted characters and occasional recourse to theatricality, its eye for local colour and language, and its strong moral purpose, it is reminiscent of the nineteenth-century narrative, especially in its Dickensian blend of romance and social realism. Yet, in his predilection for harmonious conclusions, Fernandes's stories are also eminently compatible with the popular Chinese storytelling tradition. Indeed, his intellectual and literary formation is as complex and multiple as the ethnic make up of the Macanese themselves. Fiction writers in Macao over the last twenty years have, of course, been exposed to the examples of writers like Christopher New and, in particular, Austin Coates, from neighbouring Hong Kong, both of whom wrote lengthy historical narratives about European interaction with China. Indeed, it was Coates's *City of Broken Promises* (1967), a romantic story set in Macao during the eighteenth century, that may have provided a type of 'rags-to-riches' blueprint for subsequent works that were to emerge in Portuguese from the territory. Fernandes, for his part, claims an affinity with English-language literary models, among them the short stories of the popular early twentieth-century American writer, O. Henry. However, there are also echoes in his work of the Portuguese romantics, Almeida Garrett and Júlio Dinis, while his spirited proletarian girl, A-Leng, hovers between the slave heroine of Bernardo Guimarães's nineteenth-century Brazilian novel, *A Escrava Isaura* (The slave girl Isaura), and Jorge Amado's later Brazilian barefoot beauty, Gabriela, in the novel *Gabriela Cravo e Canela* (Gabriela clove and cinammon). Fittingly, both these Brazilian classics, rather like Fernandes's novels, have been turned into television soap operas and films with considerable international success. Apart from this, however, Fernandes's moral objective in *The Bewitching Braid*, is, as in all his stories, to evoke a sense of Macanese identity and to pay tribute to the ability of this resilient borderland ethnic community to survive and adapt to the great social changes of the twentieth century.

For Fernandes, the most profound and long-lasting changes to the social fabric of Macao were brought about as a result of the watershed years of the 1940s, beginning in 1941 with the Japanese occupation of Hong Kong and the ensuing War of the Pacific and continuing through to the communist victory in mainland China in 1949. Portugal's neutrality in the Second World War meant that Macao became the only safe haven in the area for refugees fleeing the Sino-Japanese war, which in turn caused the population of Macao to mushroom between 1941 and 1945. Later, new arrivals fleeing the civil war of the late 1940s and the communist revolution further swelled the ranks of the Chinese population of the city. The increasing influence of Chinese traders in Macao had, of course, been felt ever since the nineteenth century, but it was the wars and political instability of the middle of the twentieth century that intensified this tendency. The huge influx of refugees had a profound effect on the character of the city and on the time-honoured sense of Macanese identity, for the population born in greater China increasingly came to outnumber that of whatever ethnic origin born in Macao itself. At the same time, while many Chinese regarded the territory as a stepping-stone to the outside world, others brought a robust capitalist enterprise to Macao, emerging as a new middle class that tended to ignore old, colonial hierarchies and had little respect for the notion of Portuguese sovereignty over the territory, which had never been formally accepted by any Chinese government anyway. Some of the older Macanese families responded by migrating in the lean, post-war years, convinced that the city's days of Portuguese rule over their tiny homeland were numbered, and that Macao was destined to be surrendered to China at some point in the near future. For those who remained, it was undoubtedly the rivalry between the Macanese and this new, entrepreneurial Chinese social class that would come to a head and, to some extent at least, be reflected in the disturbances of the 1960s, as a result of which Beijing's influence over the Portuguese administration of Macao would become more clearcut.

The Bewitching Braid can therefore be read in a number of contexts. It is, of course, a nostalgic look back at the Macao of the author's youth, at a time before its skyline had been changed by the construction boom of recent decades. In many ways, Fernandes laments the onset of modernization that has made Macao a more global, cosmopolitan connurbation, paradoxically both less Portuguese and less traditionally Chinese than the city he evokes in his fiction. The Macao he recalls with nostalgia is the relatively small town of the early decades of the twentieth century, with its picturesque waterfront boulevard, the Praia Grande, before it was hemmed in by land reclamation, and the less urban pursuits of its inhabitants, such as kite-flying in green areas long since built over, fishing, hunting in Chinese territory on the other side of an easily crossed border, sea-bathing on beaches now swallowed up by the growth of the city. The 1920s and 30s were decades when the Macanese, as the author points out, felt secure, unaware of the great upheavals that were to come, when their culinary arts were still practised by the old families and *patuá* was still spoken among an older generation. At the same time, we must never forget that the novel was first published in 1992, after the Sino-Portuguese declaration of 1987 which had set the agenda for the handover of Macao to China in 1999. Crucially, it is a work that reconciles the Portuguese and Chinese traditions that have given the city its unique cultural characteristics. Adozindo and A-Leng personify these traditions and are the Adam and Eve of what the author conceived as being a more liberal and tolerant, less colonial bourgeoisie, that was an appropriate example of harmonious integration for the Macanese during the anxious years leading up to the territory's return to China as well as for the Chinese majority. Within this partnership, Adozindo never abandons his Portuguese or Macanese habits completely, but learns to respect the Chinese. This is not the case at the beginning, for Adozindo is a young gadabout, who is drawn to A-Leng because she represents a different type of challenge to his usual pursuits, a poor young beauty to be exploited, enjoyed and then abandoned. In time, however, the relationship becomes one in which Adozindo is obliged and enabled to overcome his moral irresponsibility by seeing A-Leng as a fellow human being. Moreover, it is through her that he comes to accept that side of his cultural heritage, the existence of which he, like most Macanese of his age and class, would normally have denied.

A-Leng, for her part, undergoes greater change: as a result of her experiences, she learns Portuguese, becomes a nominal Catholic at least and receives a Portuguese baptismal name, but she also preserves her Buddhist faith, and in due course becomes an elegant middle-class Chinese woman when she swaps her *tun-sam-fu* (tunic) for a cheongsam and her clogs for high-heels. She therefore enters what Homi Bhabha would call the Third Space, that cultural borderland of Macao which defies notions of cultural purity. It is, indeed, through A-Leng that Fernandes demonstrates the dynamics of hybrid cultures in the way they operate through a series of compromises and contradictions: while inner beliefs are sometimes masked by social convention and prejudice, they nevertheless find a way of negotiating obstacles in order to express themselves. A-Leng surely understands this when she approaches the formidable figure of Dona Capitolina, devout Catholic and pillar of the parish of Santo António, and preys on this Macanese matriarch's submerged belief in Chinese geomancy in order to gain her favour. Similarly, it could be said that A-Leng, the former water-seller from the Chinese quarter, has become Macanese by the end of the novel, for she too has added a devotion to Saint Anthony to her former (and now submerged) attachment to the Buddha of the Tou Tei Temple. Nowhere is the co-existence of different cultural habits more apparent than in domestic life, and in particular in the area of food and eating habits, and here, the novel depicts with some sensitivity the contradictions that occur in a marriage between partners from different cultural backgrounds and the compromises and humour that are required to co-exist. In this sense, *The Bewitching Braid* is a very personal testimony to the cultural tolerance that exists in Macao and a homage to its mixed families.

Finally, a word about the translation. It is self-evident that the Portuguese character of Macao differentiates the city from other urban milieu in Southern China, which is why the street names and most place names appear in the original Portuguese. In addition, many terms from the local Portuguese or *patuá*, or from Cantonese, especially culinary names, have been preserved in an attempt to convey more vividly the plurality of the local culture. Where this has occurred, the original Portuguese spelling of Cantonese terms has been kept. On the other hand, where Chinese terms, such as *feng shui* and *mah-jong*, or even *cheongsam*, have become common currency in English, these have replaced the Cantonese rendering used by Fernandes in the Portuguese original. Similarly, the Portuguese *cabaia* has been rendered in English by *kebaya*, a term for 'gown' that has its origin in Malay. Finally, unless it features in a Portuguese name or title, the English (and old Portuguese) spelling of Macao has been preferred in this translation to the modern Portuguese 'Macau', by which this Special Administrative Region is also known. A glossary of Portuguese, Macanese and Cantonese words has been included at the end, some of which were explained in footnotes in the original Portuguese edition.

David Brookshaw

FIRST WORDS ...

Whoever goes down the Calçada do Gaio and wishes to take a short cut to the Rua do Campo, turns the corner and inevitably has to cross a labyrinth of narrow thoroughfares, dominated by an untidy and uncharacteristic mass of dwellings that make up Cheok Chai Un.

It wasn't always like that. Cheok Chai Un, with an area bordered by the Rua Nova à Guia, the Rua do Brandão, the Rua do Campo, and by the rear wall of the Santa Rosa de Lima College, where some of the remains of the old wall of Macao can be seen, was, until about the beginning of the 1960s, an area of unique character that progress subsequently tore down.

In more remote times, it belonged to a tree-covered area, that included the São Jerónimo hillside and stretched, albeit sparsely, as far as the vegetable gardens and the even ground of the Campo da Victória, part of the lowlands of Tap-Seac, an area that was called the 'Garden of Birds' by the Chinese.

As the City of the Name of God developed, attracting people from the surrounding villages in search of better opportunities, the village of Cheok Chai Un was born. Years later, when the wall of Macao was built, it became part of the city, while nevertheless maintaining the characteristics of a Chinese village, without being contaminated by the influence of the 'Christian city' right next to it. Not even when the wall was demolished and it became an urban quarter did it change its peculiar character. The original layout of the grey-stone village was changed as a result of the terrible typhoon of 1874, which all but flattened the quarter, causing much loss of life. It was replaced by a grid of straight streets and alleyways, but the hovels and small houses of two, and less frequently, three storeys remained. And it lasted for a few more decades like this.

Its residents watched over their little world carefully. They were very inward-looking, marrying among themselves, suspicious of and even hostile towards any strange face that lingered there, whether it belonged to a European or a Chinese from another quarter more given to an urban way of life. It had its market and its temple, its little shops and eating houses, its healers and herbalists, its matchmakers and 'worthy men' who *resolved conflicts over money, family quarrels, business disputes and other disagreements. These 'worthy men' enjoyed the prestige of age and white hair or of a more prosperous economic position.*

From its very beginnings as a village, Cheok Chai Un was marked by the stigma of being a place of ill repute. It was dirty, harboured many diseases, a den of rogues and of all the dregs of humanity. Not even when it became a quarter did these labels disappear. Above all, they were applied to the youth, considered spivs and trouble-makers, blood in their gills and their hands ever ready for a fracas. Such categorization was, in huge measure, exaggerated, but they never freed themselves from the shame of such a stigma. So much so that when a young lad misbehaved, or got involved in fights or scams, showing scorn for social norms, he was called, in Macanese slang, an 'a-tai from Cheok Chai Un', 'a-tai' meaning a rascal. It was a humiliating insult!

The population of Cheok Chai Un numbered a few thousand, almost all of them poor people, packed into a confined space that was their world. It is certainly true that there was a small group of hoodlums, but the vast majority of residents were orderly and peaceful, toiling hard for their daily bowl of rice. The men were labourers, joiners, carpenters, messenger-boys, rickshaw coolies, hawkers, dray pullers, and so on. The women were domestic servants, weavers, street-sweepers, hair-braiders, washerwomen, water-carriers, etc. All were people involved in the most humble jobs and few managed to become their own boss.

In many a house and hovel, young girls and old women worked making incense sticks and matchboxes. There were also women who did embroidery or darned clothes, seated at the doors of their houses, making use of the sunlight to complete their work, while they gossiped. Electric lighting would only be introduced much later and I can still remember seeing hovels lit by the flickering flame of oil-lamps.

The conditions of hygiene were abysmal, often mentioned in Health Service reports, the drains were rudimentary and there were no lavatories in the modern sense of the word. The quarter was so closed to the outside world that the passing of time, as if clocks didn't exist, was marked at night by certain men who, every now and then, would bang on metal plates and cry out the hour as they walked through the silent streets.

That was what Cheok Chai Un was like and how it remained, more or less, up until the end of the 1950s. When the old city began to be knocked down indiscriminately, Cheok Chai Un didn't escape either. The construction of multi-storey buildings from reinforced concrete deprived it of its own characteristic features, just as happened, of course, with other neighbourhoods in Macao, and it blended into the rest of the city in an irksome move towards monotonous and unsightly uniformity.

My contact with Cheok Chai Un began when I was at secondary school. I lived on the Estrada de São Francisco, which was then lined with trees and paved in the Portuguese style, and I had a choice of two routes to school. I either skirted the Boca do Inferno and crossed the Estrada dos Parses and then descended the Calçada do Paiol, or I turned into the Rua Nova à Guia. I would get to the top of the Rua Tomaz da Rosa and rush stumbling down the steps straight into the heart of Cheok Chai Un. I would pass the well and the old Tou Tei Temple and come out in the Rua do Campo. From there, I would turn right and in five minutes I would reach the entrance to the secondary school at Tap-Seac. My preference was for this second route.

At that time, the Company had not yet laid pipes for water in the quarter, so that everyone used the well, whose precious liquid, always clear and suitable for drinking, was available to whoever needed it. Consequently, the well, which has now disappeared, was a meeting place from morning till night, especially for the womenfolk, who would assemble there, just as happened at all the other public wells. Here, they drew water, that is, they filled buckets with water in a continual buzz of activity. The well was also a place of social gathering, for people talked and gossiped there, reputations were made or destroyed, and one found out the latest news and heard the latest slander.

When I passed by shortly before nine in the morning, there was always a crowd of garrulous, merry water-sellers, who would fill their buckets with water and carry it to different destinations using a 'tam-kon,' a stout wooden pole over their shoulders to each end of which was attached a bucket with a piece of rope. They earned their living by selling the water from their buckets to houses where there was no spring water suitable for drinking. Apart from Cheok Chai Un, they would sell their water throughout the neighbourhood along the Rua do Campo, the Rua Nova à Guia, the Calçada do Gaio, and the Rua do Brandão. There were water-sellers of all ages, but I was already a tall, lanky boy, and my eyes focused on the young girls wearing a 'tun-sam-fu', a short 'kebaya' and trousers, clothes that although tight-fitting, didn't hinder their movements. Tanned by the sun, without any make-up or face-powder — unthinkable in their line of work — they usually walked around barefoot, come summer and winter. They had an androgynous chest, for they would wrap the curve of their breasts tightly with a strip of cloth, out of modesty and discretion. Their only luxury or touch of vanity lay in their long hair, which was arranged in a single braid that tumbled down to the base of their back. This hairstyle was common to all Chinese girls of the *proletariat. It was pure seduction to watch these shining black braids, their tresses plaited into a thick rope, tied near the end with a piece of red ribbon.*

Apparently uncomplicated, the preparation of this hairstyle nevertheless demanded great care and much discomfort, but they surrendered meekly to their torment. The threads of hair were pulled back and stretched to such an extent that it made the scalp sting. A hard comb would be passed through it again and again, soaked in wood oil, the braiding-woman's hands likewise soaked in the same oil to give the hair the necessary sheen and resistance. The little wisps that were left at the top of the forehead and could not be disciplined, sticking out like skinny, rebellious shrubs, were plucked out with a thread, an exercise in painful pruning that didn't bring the slightest moan of protest from the stoical girl who had submitted herself to it.

In the vicinity of the well, there were also washerwomen who scrubbed clothes on wooden boards, now long gone, having steadily been replaced by washing machines. They also wore the same hairstyles and clothes, and went around barefoot, or on special occasions, wore 'chiripos'. The washerwomen and water-sellers almost made up a separate society of their own. They predominated over men in the area round the well, and would disperse to their various destinations, returning there later to meet up again, living off their earnings and within their quarter, which they never left even in their leisure time.

Not even during the festivals of the Chinese New Year did they feel the allure of venturing outside their quarter. Firecrackers, snacks, incense sticks, everything was sold in the little shops and in the local market. Up until the War of the Pacific, the 'clu-clu' tables filled the streets and alleys, where people could play High-Low and other games, without having to wander off to other thoroughfares beyond the boundaries of Cheok Chai Un.

They clung so dearly to their neighbourhood that they even prayed for good fortune and prosperity in their own temple, the Tou Tei Mio, instead of going to the temple of the Goddess A-Má at Barra, or to the Kin Yam Tóng, at Mong-Há, which were traditionally used for such ceremonies by the Chinese Buddhist people of the City of the Name of God.

During the Tou Tei's own festivities, on the second day of the second lunar month, which almost always fell in early March according to the Gregorian calendar, a bamboo shed was erected, paid for by public subscription or from the profits of the temple, where Chinese opera was performed to large audiences by both professionals and amateurs. This custom is still kept alive today.

The women, whether married or single, were for the most part illiterate, for they were sent off to work early in life. The men didn't have very much more education, for they too were forced to toil, as soon as they reached a certain age. It was a harsh, frugal life, devoid of entertainment and comfort, but the people who had to put up with it seemed content with their lot, or merely resigned, or didn't even ponder the possibility of any other destiny.

This, then, was the scene, at the beginning of the 1930s, onto which Adozindo suddenly burst by chance, the Handsome Adozindo for the romantic young girls of the age, who caused something of a revolution in the very heart of Cheok Chai Un.

PART ONE

1

*A*dozindo hailed from the Largo de Camões, so he was a true son of the Santo António quarter of old Macao. The same went for his parents and his other closest relatives.

He lived in a large yellow house with a long balcony that overlooked the square, enjoying the shade of huge red acacias. In summer, from early morning, it was bathed in the twittering of birds in the Poet's garden, the cry of the cicadas, mixed with the crowing of the cockerel. In winter, the house groaned under the weight of the humidity and with the sadness of an empty, grey and nondescript square, where street-vendors plied their wares with their doleful ditties.

He was an only son in a house full of women — his mother, his maternal granny and aunts, one of whom was a spinster and the other a widow, a female cousin who was the widow's daughter, and three maids. According to some, that was why his father, a former functionary of the Chinese customs house and now the owner of a shipping agency, would shut himself away, when he was at home and after family prayers, to read in his study, exhausted by the chattering and prattling of the womenfolk from daybreak until night time.

From an early age he had heard people say how handsome he was. And this was indeed true. As an infant, his pretty cheeks made folk want to pinch them; he was a light-skinned child, with green eyes, maybe inherited from his Dutch great-grandmother; and with his brown hair, he was the picture of a grandfather from the North of Portugal.

He should have been born a girl, people said. Yet he hadn't turned out a sissy, in spite of his face. On the contrary, he demonstrated manly qualities from an early age, scuffling with fists and footwork, with bigger lads than himself who tried to make fun of his milksop's physique, whether in the Largo de Camões or at school.

And so he grew up among women who doted on him. He was very clean and took great care with his appearance. A mark on his suit, the merest crease in his shirt were enough to produce a crisis. His shoes had to shine like a mirror, without a trace of dirt. He was painstaking in the time he took to wash, springing from the bathtub, smelling like a garden flower. When he did his hair, he would use two brushes and three combs, each for a different purpose, in a ritual that only he understood and carried out to the letter. Nothing would make him shorten the time it took, and he refused to be hurried in any way. He was proud of the silkiness of his curly, wavy hair, of his straight nose, of the roundness of his cheekbones that came from his Chinese side, of his shapely lips and his magnificent row of teeth. In fact he was proud of every aspect of his physical appearance. Having finished seeing to his hair, his clothes and his shoes, he would look lovingly at himself in the mirror, and murmur with heartfelt conviction:

'Oh! God! Thank you for making me so handsome!'

As he grew up, his natural good looks became even more noticeable. He didn't get involved in fisticuffs, which had been such a common occurrence in his childhood, not because he had become a cowardly lad. Far from it. He was just scared that in the heat of a fight, someone might become overzealous in his punching and kicking, and spoil his facial harmony.

A girl would not have examined with such care every aspect of her physiognomy. He even went as far as to assert that he had been born with the most perfectly proportioned ears, 'tender in design'. Whatever the advantage he might reap from this, he never explained.

As an adolescent, he got pimples on his face. He was overcome by panic, gestured wildly, became more and more agitated, and wept profusely. His outbursts sent his afflicted family into paroxysms of despair. Nor was he consoled by the argument that pimples were a common occurrence in youth. They were going to leave his face pitted, prematurely lined, permanently grooved. He took courses of treatment, ran to the doctor's, smeared himself with creams, went on diets and took injections, even went to consult specialists in Hong Kong. To no avail. He aired the possibility of going to Shanghai in order to consult a German specialist in dermatology, but his father Aurélio's spirit of economy put paid to such a wild idea. That was really too much!

A herbalist in the Rua da Prainha, a humble fellow, with little eyes that darted behind thick lenses, suddenly came to the poor lad's aid. He subjected the pimples to a thorough inspection, passed his smooth-skinned fingers over them, and interrogated him in a Chinese he could barely understand. He prescribed a course of bitter teas, made recommendations regarding his diet and dug out a pleasant-smelling ointment to spread over the infected areas. Gradually, the pimples disappeared, and the skin returned to its former smoothness and beauty.

When it came to his studies, he didn't disappoint, but on the other hand, he was never an outstanding pupil. He attended the day school of the São José Seminary, subjected to the iron-fisted but effective discipline of the priests, and with only one failed paper, completed the fifth year of the General Certificate at the state secondary school.

There was no need to proceed further. Neither Hong Kong nor Shanghai beckoned, much less Portugal, so far away. As an only son, cared for by parents and a host of female relatives who idolised him, his duty was to carry on the family name in Macao. As for him, he was relieved, for he went to so much trouble to look handsome that he had no time left for books.

He was a man of limited education, but in keeping with the values of the time, this was enough. Used to being indulged and to his creature comforts, he faced the future with a light heart, for the future would be the same as the present and the past. That was how secure people felt during the 'patriarchal era', an age that was to be shattered by the Japanese attack on China and then, straight afterwards, the War of the Pacific. That was why he had the audacity to cry bombastically, upon completing his fifth year:

'Ah! So much the better! I'm done with studying!'

It wasn't that his father was rolling in money, but he had a comfortable position in life. As a functionary of the Chinese Customs House, he had received a sizeable payout when he retired. He had prudently invested this along with some other savings in such a way as to give him a comfortable return. In addition, he had set up a shipping agency representing the big freight companies based in Hong Kong, from which he made a steady profit. Like anyone weaned in Santo António, he was generous in his hospitality, known for the dinner parties he hosted and for the excellent food that came out of his kitchen.

At the still tender age of eighteen, Adozindo went to work for the firm that he was destined to inherit one day from his father. In effect, this meant that he toiled little and did a lot of swanning around. Time was on his side and something better was bound to turn up, he told himself by way of a justification. His father's employees began to resent him, as they noticed he was more interested in the mirror than in the accounts or getting the work done. This was why they scornfully referred to him as the Handsome Adozindo.

He considered himself irresistible, and indeed he was. He collected hearts, casting amorous glances, flashing his white teeth in a smile and raising his eyebrows in a fashion he practised at home. He was always in the company of beautiful women, was an expert in sweet talk and danced divinely.

For better effect, he always arrived alone at dance parties. He would stand at the entrance to the ballroom, taking in his surroundings with the irritatingly superior air of a bored Englishman, as if he had to fill out a bill of lading. In no time at all, he would be surrounded by the rustling of skirts. The girls competed for him, spared no effort to get his attention. He also knew how to melt the hearts of old ladies and married women. When he waltzed like a professional to the tune of the Blue Danube or the Count of Luxemburg, a space opened up across the dance floor for him and his partner. And so he flirted around, conquered the girls and was the target of consuming passion.

There was no shortage of good matches for him, girls of sound means, willing to go to any lengths. But he skilfully avoided any commitments, convinced in his own mind that he had not yet found a woman who deserved him.

One of his rejects, however, suffered a romantic illness and was hurriedly packed off to Switzerland to forget and recover. Another, more serious and more of a martyr, took the veil, and went to end her days in a nunnery of the Franciscan Missionaries of Mary. These events, rather than sullying his reputation, increased his prestige. With godlike detachment he would brush off all responsibility with the simple declaration:

'They left as virgins. I didn't break any maidenhead!'

He encountered some defect in all of them. This one because she had bad teeth, that one because she was as skinny as a toothpick, another one because she would run to fat straight after giving birth to her first child, and another because she was too intelligent and he didn't want a know-all for a wife. And so on and so forth. In a word, none of them were any good, to the despair of his parents who yearned for grandchildren, and of his granny and aunts who wanted to see him spoken for. Only his cousin Catarina, who was a few years older than him and had a pointed nose, rejoiced in this delay, for she harboured a secret hope that he would at last turn his gaze upon her. This was why she took such care of his clothes, darning his socks and sewing buttons back on his shirts and drawers.

The Handsome Adozindo had a good heart, but vanity and boastfulness got the better of him as the years went by. If only he could hold his tongue a bit! But no. It wasn't enough for him to make real conquests, he had to make a show of them, bragging about them irritatingly in a monotonous display of uncalled for cheap talk. On these occasions, he became intolerable, unconsciously alienating possible friends, making all of them fed up, green with envy and consumed by resentment.

'That one? I've been with her. She's a lousy kisser. Norma? She's got a bigger navel than she has eyes. Esperança? She's got bad breath and cries a lot. Laurinda? My God! What a clingstone! She sticks to you like glue and you can't get rid of her.'

'So you mean you've had them all.'

'How can I help it? They won't leave me alone ... '

His only true friend, Florêncio, another local playboy who openly contented himself with the crumbs left by Adozindo, warned him:

'Be careful, lad ... Don't play around so much.' Adozindo would laugh and reply unmoved:

'Don't worry, I'll find a slipper to fit my foot.'

Around this time, his father, Aurélio, took the difficult decision to move house. For a long time now, he had found the thick curtain of acacia trees annoying, depriving the balconies of a view of the Largo de Camões. They encouraged mosquitoes, May-bugs, moths and other types of insect. And then there was the headlong fluttering of bats that terrorized people. Besides, the old house, rented from the Santa Casa da Misericórdia, was decrepit, full of draughts, gnawed away by white ants, a paradise for rats that scurried ceaselessly across the roof space. It needed sweeping renovation from top to bottom.

He had decided to buy a large new home on the Estrada da Victória, from which a pleasant lane led to a row of elegant houses, each with a garden. Adozindo backed his father in his decision for it gave the family more 'status'.

The womenfolk didn't take to the change. They were used to worshipping at the church of Santo António, to their devotion to its saint, and they had all their friends in the quarter, all their occasions for gossip. There was the bun and pastry seller, the morning and evening cries of the street-vendors, and then they only had to walk down the street to be in the middle of the market where they could do their daily shopping. They put up tearful resistance, arguing that those who had prospered in a house shouldn't leave it, because of the good *feng shui* brought by favourable winds.

But the men of the house shouted:

'Superstitious nonsense!'

They won and the women eventually agreed that they would be much better off in the new residence and the family would improve its social position.

One of the first things the Handsome Adozindo did when he took possession of his comfortable bedroom, was to take out a pair of binoculars and scan the neighbourhood, the Vasco da Gama Garden, the Campal and the houses on the side of Monte Hill, in search of pretty faces, any beauties who, until then, might have escaped his seductive power.

2

Among the water-sellers who 'drew the water' most energetically from the well at Cheok Chai Un, was A-Leng, at the time twenty-two years of age, brimming with health and life. She fetched and carried tirelessly around the well from early morning, filling buckets of water, transporting them, one on either end of the long pole she placed over her shoulder, balancing herself gracefully, her body taut with the weight, her supple hips sculpted in a sensual curve, rolling inside her tight *tun-sam-fu*.

For her, there were no seasons in the year. She was always working, in winter, she wore a woollen jacket, and her *tun-sam-fu* of rough cloth that hardly protected her from the cold, in summer, she wore one of thin cloth, that only came halfway down her arms, and was stained down the back and under the armpits with her perspiration.

Of all her fellow workers, she was the tallest and the most slender. No matter how carefully she swathed her breasts, in her modesty, under her *kebaya*, as was the custom in those days among the humbler classes, her vague contours excited the imagination, like some promise of a hidden treasure. Her almond-shaped eyes, gently curved upwards to a point, made her oval face, with its high cheekbones, irresistibly attractive. When she smiled, two dimples in her cheeks gave her an impish air.

She spoke with a high, musical voice, and had the brisk manners of one who did a hard job, out in the open air, come sun or rain, but most of the time she radiated good humour. She would laugh, revealing an even row of white teeth that she cleaned with the stick of a liquorice plant, chatted non-stop and was the dominant figure in the group. When she was angry, her voice would explode all around the area of the well, her face would glow, and the nostrils of her small nose flare.

She didn't flirt with the boys. She would confront the most daring ones with her tongue, answering their salacious comments in kind. When this wasn't enough, she would face up to them, ready to beat them with the pole she used for carrying buckets. In this way, she had earned respect in the area, in spite of being alone, with no other member of the family to defend her. She had tacitly risen to the position of princess among the water-sellers, given that the queen was a well-endowed woman of about forty, who held sway over the well, the Queen-Bee of all those women, responsible to them as a counsellor, marriage broker, medical adviser and midwife.

The Queen-Bee treated A-Leng as a pupil. She looked upon her as her successor and would have passed on her skills and position to her, if other events hadn't dictated otherwise.

When the Queen-Bee flew into a rage, everyone round the well fell silent, the local householders retreated indoors and the restless children fled in fright. Only A-Leng dared to approach her, serene and self-assured, bravely weathering the first onslaught of her anger and little by little calming her down. As she was the only one never to have been seen assailed by that terrible temper, many people, when they wanted a favour from the Queen-Bee, did so through her pupil. As a result, she was held in esteem in the area and in that peculiar little world.

A-Leng was not without her vanity. The object of this was her thick braid of hair that, when loose, cascaded down the length of her back. She looked after it with great care, allowing herself to linger with her favourite braiding-woman, in whose hands she would stoically suffer torture without so much as a murmur, as docile as the most docile of young girls. But she was fastidious. She wouldn't rest happy as long as the blackness of her locks, bathed in wood oils, hadn't been given the desired sheen, as long as there was a thread of rebellious hair out of place, and as long as the plaits of her braid were not the ideal thickness.

Sitting erect and composed at the side of the road on an awkward little stool in front of the braider's shop, not far from the well, her hands on her knees and her legs drawn in, she would take as much time as was needed for her hair to be combed. Of all the heads of hair consigned to the braider's care, hers was the most well liked because of its copious black abundance, and because of the sensuous pleasure her hands felt as they pulled the tough, resistant threads of hair. As she got on with her combing, the braider would smile and tell stories, soon attracting an audience who would squat around her, like the ladies-in-waiting of a princess.

A-Leng's world was the area where she lived and to where she had been taken as a little girl by an old woman she called granny, without her being so. She didn't know who her parents were, which was why she adopted the family name of the old woman who had treated her with homespun affection. She knew no more than that about her kith and kin.

As a young girl, not yet strong enough to carry buckets, she began by making matchboxes, experiencing in the raw, like all her contemporaries, all the privations of childhood, in her granny's foul-smelling, airless hovel. She grew up skinny, but with an iron constitution, unlike so many others who succumbed to tuberculosis, dysentery and other diseases that were so easily picked up by the destitute in a poverty-stricken ghetto.

She benefited from the Queen-Bee's motherly interest. When she became a water-seller, thus escaping the tyranny of the matchboxes, she jumped for joy for being able to work in the open air. She had no ambitions beyond what her own quarter could offer. When her granny died, she would inherit the hovel. In due course, she would take the Queen-Bee's place when she too died or abdicated her position of her own free will, for this was what she was being prepared for. She earned enough for her daily bowl of rice, had a few coppers to buy her clothes and get her queue braided, and considered herself happy. In her condition as a water-seller, she couldn't contemplate flying any higher, nor did such things worry her. She wasn't interested in involving herself in anything outside the work she was familiar with. She didn't feel at ease in the Rua do Campo or in the Rua do Hospital,[1] neither of which was far from Cheok Chai Un. The Praia Grande and Avenida Almeida Ribeiro led her into a completely unknown and even hostile city, where she couldn't see a familiar face, and where even the water-sellers and maids looked different and haughty. The Inner Harbour and Mong Há were so out-of-the-way that she thought of them as if they were remote lands at the end of the Earth.

The *kwai-los*, as all the Portuguese were called, regardless of whether they were native sons of Macao or had come from outside, were viewed with suspicion. None of them lived in Cheok Chai Un, and if she supplied any of their houses with water from the well, contact with them was almost non-existent. She found them gruff and lacking in manners, speaking a gobbledegook of obscure, inaccessible sounds, insolent and forward in the way they stared shamelessly and intensely at women, as if they were undressing them in their thoughts.

As for the women, they were dolls who lacked any inhibitions whatsoever, showed off their legs and the weight of their bosoms, and some of them were yellow-haired and blue-eyed, something spooky and to be wondered at.

The few times she walked along streets and through squares where she knew she would come across them, she lost her customary self-confidence and put on a falsely arrogant air as if to protect herself. But she compensated for her fears when she was in a group. Then she would stamp forcefully on

---

1.   So called because it contained the São Rafael Hospital. Now called the Rua Pedro Nolasco da Silva.

the paving stones with her clogs, and her companions imitated her, as if they were issuing a challenge. Whenever she left the area where she worked, she wore her clogs.

The ones that scared her most were the African soldiers from the garrison because of their pitch-black colour, and their height and military demeanour that imposed natural respect.

The pretty water-seller from Cheok Chai Un didn't have many distractions. She didn't know what a cinema was, for she had never had occasion to see a film. In fact, the picture houses where Chinese films were shown, were in the vicinity of the Inner Harbour, and therefore at the end of the earth. And so she spent all her days in toil. Her only leisure time came after her evening meal and when she had washed herself, for then she would squat by the door of the Queen-Bee's little house and take part in all manner of conversations. The Queen-Bee knew how to tell marvellous stories better than the braiding-woman. Legends of old, macabre odysseys of spirits and ghosts, epic tales of love and hatred. The prominent position she had managed to achieve in this society was not only due to her personality, but to the fact that she had learned to read and write. In the midst of those illiterate women and young girls, it was inevitable that she would reach the top. To listen to her and absorb her wisdom and experience was the greatest pleasure A-Leng possessed.

The girl would look forward to the annual festival of the Tou Tei Temple, which broke the unending routine of her days. She would sit, spellbound, through sessions of Chinese opera, attentive to every change in the programme. She had a special *tun-sam-fu* for such occasions, which she would lovingly take from the bottom of her trunk. And wearing a woollen blouse over it, another luxury she took great care of, she would settle down in a seat with a good view half an hour before the show began, talking excitedly all the while.

Her hair glowed, and her jet black braid was coiled, decorated with a comb studded with beads at the top of the nape and the beginning of the plaits. Outside her own neighbourhood, A-Leng would always be a pretty proletarian girl. But there, among the raucous audience in the large shed where the show took place, she was indeed a princess because of her upright physique and the way her own awareness of her beauty gave her just a hint of arrogance.

She also looked forward, with excitement, to the feast days of the Lunar New Year, the only three days of the year she allowed herself to take a real rest. Then, she would deck herself out in full, white powder on her face, droplets dangling from her ear lobes, and gold and jade ornaments in her hair. She would begin at midnight, amid the noise of firecrackers, by going to kneel in the temple and touch the floor with her forehead, asking the gods for a new year full of prosperity, good health and much money. After that, she would go out into the night to have fun, burning fireworks, visiting her friends who would meet up to eat fried snacks and titbits in the their local yard.

Later, she would venture out of her area as far as the Bazaar. Delighted, she would walk along the Rua dos Mercadores and the Rua das Estalagens, jostling her way through the festive crowds, stopping here and there, at the *clu-clu* tables to put some money on the High-Low. In the Largo do Patane, she would amuse herself and make admiring comments as she watched the acrobats and jugglers, the puppet theatre shows and listened to the story-tellers, recounting the deeds of the heroes of old and of immortal warrior maids.

She didn't dare go into the Hotel Presidente,[2] the main gambling centre, for it belonged to a class of people she couldn't rub shoulders with. She limited herself to standing at the door for a few minutes, peeping at the crowds of people coming in and going out, her eyes resting on the dazzling cheongsams of the women, secretly yearning to wear them, but knowing full well that her condition as a water-seller would never allow such an opportunity.

When the festive days were over, she went back to carrying the buckets, without complaints or lamentations, indifferent to her fate, but happy for her good health and the strength that enabled her to work hard.

---

2.   Nowadays known as the Hotel Central, on the Avenida Almeida Ribeiro.

3

*I*t was a beautiful autumn day for fishing, the sky was limpid, the scenery all lit up in metallic tones, something that only happens in October and November. The Handsome Adozindo had sneaked out of the house early, so as not to bump into his father. It was half past seven and he was making his way down the Praia Grande, where he would board a sailing boat with some friends for a few hours' fishing in the waters off Macao. He was carrying his fishing equipment, a rod and new lines, hooks from a specialist shop in Hong Kong, and bait in his basket. He was dressed up to the nines, certainly not according to the casual standards this type of trip demanded. It would, of course, be absurd for him not to behave naturally and spontaneously, for he was incapable of doing anything else. The greatest conqueror in town had a reputation to keep. One could never be sure who one might meet, even at such an early hour.

He breathed in the morning air. The Estrada da Victória was completely empty and there wasn't a rickshaw in sight. It didn't matter, and he cut through the Vasco da Gama Garden, skirting the fountains, where silvery threads of water danced like restless children. He took a short cut at the first corner and turned into the Cheok Chai Un quarter.

Up until then, he had always avoided the area because of its bad reputation, but he was sure that in broad daylight no one would harm a peace-loving man innocently going fishing, the only thing preying on his conscience being the fact that he was taking time off work. But it didn't take much to placate his enraged father.

Without further ado, he reached the well when it was a hive of activity, with water-sellers and washerwomen pulling up buckets or forming queues, amid a merry hum of voices. He wouldn't have given it a second thought and would have soon forgotten the otherwise unusual scene, had a youthful peal of girlish laughter not risen up into the air nearby at that very moment. He paused, curious and then with sudden interest at the rustic beauty behind the laugh. He liked what he saw. He had never set eyes on such an attractive, barefoot lass, and he would never have guessed that a quarter known for its criminals and ruffians could harbour such a beautiful jewel as that. Nor had he ever seen such a braid, its blackness accentuated in the sunlight.

A-Leng, for it was indeed she, was the focus of interest, and she had the unpleasant feeling that she was being scrutinised from head to foot. She wasn't used to being examined so blatantly, above all by a stranger, and even more so by a *kwai-lo*. More perturbed than irritated, she decided to get rid of this insolent fellow right there for all her companions to see.

As she picked up her bucket brimming with water, she pretended to lose her balance and the water flew out, splashing the ground, and wetting the Handsome Adozindo's shoes and carefully pressed trousers. She didn't apologise, but instead turned to fill her bucket again. There was laughter, and this hurt the boy more than her clumsiness, which had been deliberate anyway.

Without uttering a word, Adozindo went on his way, burning with anger. For the first time, a woman had dared to treat him with disdain. Instead of falling languidly for his irresistible beauty, the girl had dared to soil his well-polished shoes and his trousers, without even saying sorry. What was more, she was a water-seller or washerwoman, even below the rank of a servant. The cheek of it! There was an example of the famous bad manners of the inhabitants of Cheok Chai Un. It was the last time he would set foot there.

The sunshine, the refreshing breeze that stirred the evergreens on the Rua do Campo, the dry warmth of the best month of the year, soon dissipated his irritability. He wasn't going to allow his good mood to be eroded by futile anger, all because of a water-seller.

He turned his thoughts to the widow from Baixo Monte, the gorgeous Lucrécia, his latest conquest who hadn't even waited for her period of mourning to end before surrendering to his embrace. If she was well endowed materially, she was even more so in bed, with a pair of breasts like plump white doves. As long as she was in mourning, she wouldn't start making demands and he could take full advantage of her. After a year, then the moment of truth would arrive. But that date was still far off, and he had many months to plan how to get her off his back.

He skirted the São Francisco Garden, where chattering children, accompanied by maids, ran along the paths between the flowerbeds, and drew near to the rampart that separated it from the sea. The bay of Praia Grande, from the São Francisco Fort to the curve of Bom Parto, was packed with junks and *lorchas*, in the hazy sunlight. He walked along in the modest shade of the pagoda trees, whose rustling murmurs were a musical background to the lulling sound of the incoming tide, as it foamed on the granite boulders of the Praia Grande.

Women wearing *dós* passed by, their faces veiled, on their way from church. The large houses still had their shutters closed, for it was still early morning and girls preferred the afternoons for watching the world from their windows. Street-vendors advertised vinegary snacks and Chinese pickles. The knife sharpener toiled wearily, turning his little machine, while further on, the shoe mender called his customers, hammering his iron bar with its unmistakeable 'toc-toc'.

He glanced at his watch and hurried up. His friends would complain, for he was late. But when he arrived at the sloping stone quay, at the beginning of the Avenida Almeida Ribeiro, they were drinking their *tau-fu-fá*, which was still hot. The stallholder asked him if he wanted any, but Adozindo declined. He cast his gaze at the building of the Banco Nacional Ultramarino, which was still closed, and then at the Hotel Riviera, both of which were in front of him.

On a second-floor balcony, a blond woman was combing her thick tresses that fell over her shoulders. An Englishwoman! He'd never tried an Englishwoman. It would be a truly unique specimen for his collection. She looked down at him indifferently from on high, as she continued to slide the comb through her hair. Down below, he immediately adopted his seducer's pose, without judging how ridiculous he might look.

'Don't tell me you've had her too.'

'No, but if she comes to live in Macao, I will.'

'You won't get very far with those dirty shoes!'

Hell, he'd forgotten all about them! With the drops of water, his shoes were streaked with dried mud and dust. It spoiled his romantic demeanour. All because of the water-seller's mischief! The impudent girl needed a lesson.

————

It was a magnificent trip, with plenty of fish caught to compensate for the trouble, and they had lunch in a clearing among the Sete Tanques on Taipa Island. With his success as a fisherman, Adozindo forgot his tiresome boasting, to the relief of his companions. They even got to know him better, especially the simpler, more charming side of his character. It was already night when they got back, and on his way home, smelling of fish, he suddenly decided to cut through Cheok Chai Un.

He passed few people, for folk went to bed early there, and he saw no sign of any water-seller. At home, he listened to his father's endless remonstrating, but didn't pay any attention to it, and was supported by a chorus of women who tried to justify his behaviour. When he went to bed, the figure of the water-seller came to him, like some thorn pricking his pride.

For a week or so he forgot Cheok Chai Un. After all, it was a thing of no importance and didn't warrant concern. Nevertheless, when he saw an exhausted, middle-aged water-seller coming down the road, he remembered the blackness of that other braid. Once again, he was filled with bitterness. Unwisely, he decided to walk the same route he had taken on the day of the fishing trip.

The busiest hour at the well had already passed. When he drew near the place, he saw how quiet it was, with just two women calmly pulling the ropes at the end of which small buckets hung. But then, next to a wall, he saw two braiding-women, around whom, squatted a handful of water-sellers and washerwomen awaiting their turn, in garrulous and light-hearted banter.

One of them was in fact plunging her comb into the black mass of the rude water-seller's hair, pulling it back and forcing the young girl to raise her chin and reveal the slender line of her neck and the graceful contour of her breasts. How pretty she was!

He stopped to have a better look. It never even flashed across his mind that he was in Cheok Chai Un, an area of ill repute, which one entered in order to take a hurried short cut, and never to visit or stop there. Nor did it occur to him that his behaviour might be taken as an affront for being ill-mannered and insulting. He even found it perfectly normal to examine that group of barefoot women, as if they were part of some exotic scene.

The loose, uninhibited chatter stopped. Their faces hardened, the girls, who were more timid, recoiled, while the braiding-women muttered indignantly.

The *kwai-los* who appeared in the area withdrew swiftly. This was the first time one of them had turned to stone right there in front of them, with unjustified insolence, A-Leng was the only one to exercise any authority. Her nostrils began to flare. The boy was the same one who had appeared the other day. Here was proof once again that the *kwai-los* had no manners. That was no way to look, as if she and her friends were mere chickens displayed in the market.

'What are you looking at? Haven't you ever seen a woman before?'

'I was admiring your hair,' he replied, in a heavily accented Chinese, but that was perfectly understandable.

It was certainly astonishing that he spoke the language. But she controlled herself and said harshly:

'Well you've done enough admiring. Be off with you ... '

Her high voice sounded threatening. He wasn't going to belittle himself or show fear before those present. A loose cobblestone appeared in the girl's hand. If he persisted, she might well throw it and shout at him, and there would be uproar. He blushed and obeyed. He left behind him a chorus of jokes and bursts of laughter.

Once again, he had been chased away like a mangy dog. A barefoot young girl, a creature even more lowly than a servant, had the courage to humiliate him, the Handsome Adozindo. Evidently, the petulant girl had not been impressed by his appearance or his gentlemanly bearing. And to think that there were so many women dying for him to go and plant himself in front of them.

A-Leng's prestige grew. She had stood up to a *kwai-lo* and he'd taken to his heels. The news spread through the lanes and alleyways of Cheok Chai Un, stoked by exaggerated descriptions. By nightfall, there were those who even claimed that the 'devil' had retreated under a hail of stones, trembling with terror. The Queen-Bee's attentions were all the more eloquent that night. There was no longer any doubt that A-Leng was the princess.

4

*A*ll afternoon, Adozindo chewed over this latest offence. In his injured pride, he felt as if a large thorn had penetrated right through his self-esteem. It was a case of impertinence, and she needed to be taught a lesson! The Handsome Adozindo had been made a fool of by a nobody. The jeering laughter, the raised stone, tormented him to such an extent that not even the promised rendezvous with some plump, dovelike breasts was enough to sweeten his mood. He wasn't used to being humiliated by a woman. No, he wouldn't allow the incident to go without an answer, unpunished. People couldn't make fun of the Handsome Adozindo like that.

At dinner, he ranted on about the scum of Cheok Chai Un, and how draconian measures should be taken against them. Even the barefoot girls were insolent, foul-mouthed, brazen hussies who showed no respect for a peace-loving citizen who ventured into the area. He described Cheok Chai Un as if it were a huge, shameless whore house, comparable only to the Beco da Rosa.

The family, enjoying a mouth-watering meal, agreed with him, as did their guests. In the comfort of a well-laden table, covered in a white lace cloth, with glittering cutlery and the tinkling of fine china, it was easy to be critical. Not a single generous voice was raised in defence of folk who only had themselves to rely on, abandoned as they were to their fate in a ghetto.

Tales were then told of knife fights, the arrogance of the *a-tais* among the dark, narrow streets. A story was recounted of a Portuguese who went there to settle a score, but was the victim of such a savage attack that he'd been left with a broken leg, and lame for the rest of his life. No one knew what had happened to his assailants.

His tirade at dinner failed to unburden his spirit. When it came down to it, he was a hypocrite, reeling off so much nonsense, all to cover up his wounded pride. The girl's chin, her slender neck and above all her glowing hair wouldn't leave his mind's eye, even at that rich dinner table. He felt his dignity demeaned for caring about a high-spirited, ignorant and illiterate woman, who earned her living by delivering buckets of water from house to house. But it was a fact that he did indeed care.

He mulled over plans for revenge. Only then would he rest, his pride restored. Suddenly, he had a brainwave that left him rejoicing. The only fitting lesson would be to seduce her, apply the due corrective and then, when she'd been used, cast her off as refuse. In fact, the girl was no rotten fish, far from it, she was even quite pretty. Her splendid braid gave one the urge to plunge one's hands into her hair.

Such a plan was not for broadcasting to the four corners. This was his own special secret. The girl's behaviour had besmirched his reputation as a ladies' man. He would even be ashamed to admit that he had focused his thoughts on a water-seller, he who had been master of the widow from Baixo Monte, a woman so fought over for her wealth and beauty.

He dressed elegantly, for it never crossed his mind that such clothing would not impress a working girl, accustomed to other standards and another way of life. On the contrary, it might scare her even more, given the differences in education, mentality and fortune.

He would have to avoid the well so as not to have to put up with the chorus of women who, on two occasions now, had laughed at him. He wanted to catch her by herself. For about two weeks, he scoured the place to no avail. He never got a glimpse of her, one disappointment followed another. He was even surprised by her tenacity as he followed her trail. He didn't talk to anyone, and trod the streets quietly, never giving rise to any incident. He even began to recognise many faces. He knew she was somewhere in the quarter, but her movements escaped him, and he was never in the right place at the right time. In his obsession, he continued his act of supreme folly.

A-Leng had, of course, been warned. The 'devil' was wandering the streets, rummaging in every nook and cranny. Intuition told her that she was indeed the object of his search. She was infuriated by his intentions. Her friends' tittle-tattle had altered her peace of mind. She was now the target for teasing and suggestive jokes. Now, when she went to the well or carried her buckets along the streets, she looked both ways, ever alert for the hateful man. She guessed it was only a matter of time before they came face to face.

She confided everything to the Queen-Bee, beset by an anguish in which she sensed that her good name was threatened. The older woman advised her and all those around her to remain calm. The 'devil' wasn't importuning anyone, and was even going about his business in a quiet, well-mannered way. Other measures would be taken if his behaviour changed. This provisional solution was of little comfort to A-Leng.

Adozindo was getting tired of searching, and had all but decided that the girl must have moved when, one afternoon, upon turning into the Rua Tomaz da Rosa and passing the well, he noticed the silhouette of a water-seller with her back to him, walking towards some steps with two full buckets. He recognised the fateful braid before he even identified the girl, and began to follow her, blind to all else.

Her entire frame, in all its slenderness and vigour, was outlined in the rhythm with which she walked with short steps. The weight of her load and the need for balance required her to proceed stiffly, leaning slightly forward. Her *tun-sam-fu* accentuated the curve of her waist, the dancing roundness of her buttocks, her long, well-proportioned legs, firmly set in her flat, shoeless feet. The buckets swayed without spilling any water, in an unchanging rhythm. And her thick braid swung, raunchy and pendulum-like.

He followed at some distance. She climbed the steps leading to the Rua Nova à Guia, without pausing for a rest, which showed how fit she was. He puffed after her, climbing hurriedly up the steps, but when he got to the top, she had disappeared. She can't have gone far, she must have gone into one of the houses nearby.

He decided to wait for her, and walked up and down. He felt at ease, for he was unlikely to run into any of 'his folk' there. He was still among Chinese people. On the other hand, he was oblivious to the girl's situation, who would be seen by 'her folk'. In his selfishness, Adozindo only followed his own interests.

She eventually appeared. She saw him the moment she came through the doorway of the house where she had been delivering the water. She didn't doubt for one moment that he was there because of her. What an affront! What opinion did he have of her? What would the people in the streets and houses say when they saw her with a *kwai-lo*? She was seized by shame, mixed with fury. He had already given her a lot of trouble, and his intentions were surely not honest.

She didn't retreat or shake with fright. As long as he didn't open his mouth, everything would be alright. She would only act if he barred her way. She came straight towards the steps, with her pole over her shoulders and her buckets empty.

Adozindo had prepared his opening words, putting on his most seductive smile. He said:

'So, you're still working at this hour?'

That was as far as he got. A-Leng, furious, swiftly undid the string of her pole, which then became a formidable club in her hands. Adozindo put up a hand as a gesture to calm her, but she unleashed a blow that whistled past him. The boy stumbled backwards with an instinctive leap, while she raised her pole once again. A second's delay, and the weapon would crash down on him.

He turned and fled. He heard another menacing hiss and a violent thud on the ground. The girl, nervous and elated with her victory, leapt after him down the steps and would have thrashed him without mercy, if he hadn't put on a burst of speed.

All this was witnessed by passers-by who applauded and supported his assailant. He reached the first corner with his heart thumping. He only stopped when he no longer heard her steps, but merely imagined them. He leant against a wall and took a deep breath, his shirt soaked in sweat. Such were the depths to which the Handsome Adozindo had sunk, chased away by a water-seller who cared not a jot for his beauty, his fortune or his seductive power.

When he got home, his ashen face gave everyone a fright. He excused himself for suddenly feeling unwell. They gave him some cordial to drink, and as that wasn't enough, Cousin Catarina prepared a homemade tonic for him. He would like to tell her the truth, but he couldn't. He had run away from a woman like a pack-animal in flight. He was just relieved that no one he knew had seen what had happened, to spread the story of his disastrous adventure. The Handsome Adozindo, his tail between his legs, scuttling away from a young girl below the rank of a maid! What a tasty dish for any gossip, his entire reputation as an irresistible womaniser in tatters.

Now he really couldn't set foot in Cheok Chai Un again. He had been seen by many people who would no longer have any respect for him. They would laugh at him openly, the cowardly custard, wetting himself with fear. He couldn't face such shame. What a stupid idea anyway to go and mingle with the scum of society! He'd also run the risk of a broken leg. The riotous incident would have to go down as an unmitigated disaster, the first in his history as a ladies' man. Too bad, what was important now was that 'his folk' shouldn't know about it.

If he could have entered Cheok Chai Un that night, he would have felt his humiliation even more acutely. A-Leng was feted and praised. She had to repeat the story a number of times to captivated audiences. The Queen-Bee was so happy that she offered her a supper of crabmeat, to which all her friends were invited. She was the princess of the quarter, a brave spirit defending her honour. And having given her abuser, the *kwai-lo* a good lesson, there was indeed cause for celebration. When she retired to her hard bed, A-Leng gave herself up to a well-earned sleep, once again calm and at peace. The 'devil' had vanished and would never come back.

5

e didn't have the courage to risk a fourth unbecoming incident. A stain had blemished his reputation and he was astonished at such an unusual display of resistance, an aversion so unequivocally demonstrated. He had suffered a humiliating rebuff.

For some time, he went around anxiously, his ear to the ground, to try and detect any insinuating comment recalling the unhappy incident. But he concluded with relief that nothing had filtered through to 'his folk'. He avoided Cheok Chai Un and when he left his house, he would walk down the Calçada do Gaio before prudently catching a rickshaw.

The rigours of winter came, the humid months of February through to April, and then summer arrived in May, with its heat and its crickets and swallows. All this while, he maintained his reputation. He finally added an Englishwoman to his conquests. She would arrive on Saturday and leave on Monday, and would stay at the Hotel Bela Vista, not the woman he had glimpsed on the balcony of the Riviera, but another even more appetising one, all rosy and with hair the colour of old gold.

At the same time, he kept up his affair with the widow from Baixo Monte, who was beginning to trouble him because she thought she now had a right to get married. She was a real match, with a solid fortune left by her husband, who had taken good care of his profits, and any other man, less fussy and less of a libertine, would be only too happy to settle down with her. She gave him moments of indescribable pleasure, but then, once the passion had subsided, she would moan and weep, complaining tearfully or flying off into sudden fits of rage, asking him when he was going to make up his mind, for she couldn't keep things quiet for much longer, and her reputation as an inconsolable widow was at risk.

His father had already had a long talk with him. It was now time to come to his senses. He would, of course, prefer another daughter-in-law, but he had no objection to the widow. She had money, was beautiful and presentable, maybe a bit too impulsive for his liking. The rest of the family raised objections, especially Cousin Catarina, who was particularly vicious. His mother wanted a virgin bride, a woman who hadn't belonged to anyone else, and in this she was supported by his grandmother and aunts. Adozindo didn't give anything away, distancing himself from the incessant discussions, as if nothing of it concerned him. Only he knew how overbearing and tiresome the widow could be.

In spite of everything, he had not forgotten the water-seller although he told himself that he had banished her from his mind as a bad memory. The thorn of his defeat was still present, needling his pride. If even an Englishwoman, a chosen and cherished daughter of the British Empire had fallen into his arms, how was it possible for a water-seller, without shoes or education, to have the nerve to reject him? For the sake of his vanity, such a fact was simply intolerable.

Whenever he saw a young girl carrying buckets or baskets, with a pole over her shoulder, his heart would race and the now hazy image of the girl dance before his eyes, her gleaming braid shaking this way and that. He adored that braid, felt a fire inside him when he imagined caressing it, a feeling he never experienced with other women's hair. For that reason alone, he would willingly return to Cheok Chai Un. But he was scared of the pole.

One night as he slept, with his hand on his chest, he dreamt he was voluptuously undoing the braid, but the girl had got annoyed and turned against him, raising her pole, which took on the thickness of a huge iron bar. He woke up with the sensation of having been given a beating. His ribs, arms and legs hurt, his body was bathed in sweat. He interpreted the dream as a warning and, out of superstition, he resisted any temptation to go to the area. But he remained obsessed with the braid.

Early one afternoon towards the end of May, he woke up refreshed from the siesta he had taken, before going to his father's agency. He jumped out of bed and went to the bathroom at the back of the house. From the little window that looked over the yard, he could hear the voices of the maids chattering away during their hour of rest after lunch. There was nothing unusual about their daily banter, mixed with the cry of the crickets, and it didn't arouse any interest on his part.

Suddenly, among the voices, he heard a different type of laughter, but one that had already surprised him once before. Smitten with curiosity, he leant over the window-sill. He recoiled instinctively, his heart leaping. Could he have been mistaken? With great care, like a thief trying not to be seen, he peeped again. There was no mistake.

The water-seller of his dreams was down there, squatting, talking animatedly and sipping a bowl of tea. She was wearing her black *tun-sam-fu* for work and, as always, she was barefoot, her toes dirty from the mud and dust of the roads. As she was among the servants, she had unbuttoned her collar to be more at ease. Her trousers, as her knees were bent, had ridden up to reveal her ankles and a shapely stretch of leg. Her sensuous braid was coiled over her breast, maybe so as to avoid dirtying it if it touched the ground. On the curve of her head, her hair seemed to let off flashes of blue, like a raven's wing in the sun.

The girl had entered the wolf's den without realising it. She had replaced a colleague who was ill and broken by age. He now remembered his mother mentioning the new water-seller who was delivering good, clear water straight from a spring. It was the water from the well in Cheok Chai Un! This had been happening for a month. And all that time without him knowing!

He avoided making so much as a sound. She might look up and see him. The shock would be too great, she might run away and after that refuse to deliver water to that house. And he didn't want that, when he had discovered another gift of hers. She had a warm, modulated voice that provoked flutters in him beyond words.

Down below, A-Leng stretched. How nice it was there, so peaceful, and how hard it was to go back to the well to fetch another load to deliver somewhere else. With her hand, she fiddled with her braid, taking it up to her nose to smell it, passing her fingers over it again and again, and tidying the knots.

She was a flower among weeds! It would be such a pity if she fell into the brutish hands of some *a-tai* who would fill her with children, ruin her body and tear her braid to shreds. A few more years of arduous journeys, yoked to those buckets, dragging herself along the streets in the sun and rain, winter and summer, and she would be a shadow of what she was now, a hymn to unselfconscious sensuality and youth.

When she stood up, he didn't move from the window. If he rushed forward too hastily, he might damage his chances in the future. He waited for her to leave and went downstairs to the kitchen, and asked for a glass of water. He asked the garrulous maid who had talked most to A-Leng where such clear, thirst-quenching liquid came from. The maid gave him all the details. So the Handsome Adozindo found out what time of day it was delivered. He didn't ask any further questions and left, whistling to himself.

Two days later, a Saturday, he didn't have lunch at home, and at the appropriate hour he began to wander around the neighbourhood, having worked out the route she would take, and he wasn't mistaken. He caught sight of her from afar, balancing her buckets by taking even steps, with all the nimble skill of her profession.

He waited on the narrow pavement, but stepped aside for her to pass. Her face registered surprise but she didn't react, because she was away from her familiar surroundings. Adozindo smiled at her and bowed slightly, but was not acknowledged. He waited for her to get some way ahead, no longer afraid of the pole for he was on his own territory, and then set off after her.

He was on his way home, and no one could accuse him of molesting her. With the weight of the pole across her shoulders and her hands holding it so that it wouldn't slide off its natural support, and unable to spill any water, the fruit of her labour, she couldn't turn round. All she could do was cast a sidelong glance and the rest was gut feeling.

She stopped at the back door of the house. She disengaged herself from her pole, but didn't brandish it. She turned towards him as he approached, and asked him bitterly, without raising her voice:

'What do you want of me?'

'Are you talking to me? I ... I don't want anything. I'm going home.'

He pointed to the door, and in a dulcet tone said: 'Isn't it here you are going? Me too. It's my house ... '

The girl was thunderstruck. A faint blush tinged her tanned face. With an unctuous gentility, Adozindo showed her the key and opened the door. In a gesture of gentlemanly manners no one had ever shown her before, he said:

'Please come in, *siu-tche*.'

That *siu-tche* directed at her for the first time and unheard of for a water-seller, accustomed to rough treatment and rude words, left her even more confused. She still hesitated, but at that moment, the garrulous maid, A-Sam, appeared from inside.

She wasn't surprised to see the Young Master. More often than not, he would enter the house by the back. There were some steps from the yard straight up to the first floor, and when he came home at night, he didn't need to disturb anyone.

What astonished her were the delicate manners of the Young Master, who allowed the water-seller to enter before he did. A-Leng's cheeks were bright red, and her throat was dry. As she let go of the buckets, she spilt a bit of water.

'I'm sorry ... I'll clear it up right away.'

She'd only wetted the floor, but for her it had been a humiliating error. Adozindo cut in:

'Never mind. It doesn't matter.'

With his most disarming smile, he climbed the steps without a backward glance. But not so fast that he didn't catch A-Sam's proud comment:

'The Young Master's such a gentleman. He's got such nice manners.'

There was no need for him to stay by the window. The girl would get too much of a fright if she saw him peeping out, and she might never go back there again. It was a master stroke, his patience had finally brought him triumph. He had made the most of his opportunity and the sparkling black braid and lithe body would soon be his. He even forgot that at that very moment the widow was expecting him, burning with lust and consumed with jealousy. He took his time combing his hair and only then did he make for the front door on his way to Baixo Monte.

In the yard, A-Sam, unaware of all that had happened, was an innocent accomplice in her little master's plan. Noticing A-Leng's confusion and attributing this to the Young Master's politeness, she began to praise him, and the other servants lent their voice too.

The Young Master was good, he never shouted at the household servants nor ever had an unkind word to say. Whether they were just taking him a pair of socks or a glass of water, he always thanked them straightaway. He never made them feel humiliated for being servants. If she could see all the clothes and shoes he had. When it came to those things, he was very fussy. He wanted his trousers well pressed, shirts without the slightest stain, his shoes always polished. But he never raised his voice. He stated what he wanted in a friendly way, and there was no need to repeat it. Everyone did their best to satisfy his tastes.

Then, in hushed voices, they continued in unison. The Young Master was a jewel, unlike the others. The women were sharp-tongued, impertinent, always seeking and finding fault. They were all bone idle and even expected the servants to stop whatever they were doing to go and pick up a handkerchief they'd dropped on the floor by their feet. And the Boss was a similar fish, gruff in his orders, which had to be carried out to the letter, under pain of harsh censure or immediate dismissal.

By this time, A-Leng had recovered from her discomfiture and was full of curiosity. She had even forgotten about her other orders for water. She asked questions, was receptive to their rambling talk, including their exaggerations. Out of some inner sense of prevention, she didn't reveal that the Young Master was pursuing her. She drank two bowls of tea instead of one, and ate a slice of cake, made the day before and distributed to the servants by the mistress of the house. When she left, she was truly perplexed. Her opinion of a man up until then seen as perverse, had changed.

She didn't confide her experiences to anyone. Not even the Queen-Bee, to whom she went for counsel and advice. At night, her friends were puzzled by her. She didn't usually have that vacant air, as if in distant thoughts. She didn't join in their conversation, instead remaining quiet and distracted.

All night long, the boy's image tormented her. This left her in despair for she was really thinking too much about him, his gentle treatment of her as a *siu-tche*, and the fact that he had stood aside for her to enter the house. He had a different type of face, but he wasn't ugly by any means, unlike what she had first thought.

When it was time to take the 'spring water' to his house, she had got all nervous. What would happen that day? Nothing, and she came away feeling disappointed. To her surprise, she found she harboured as many other disappointments. Could it be that he regretted making her acquaintance, now that she provided water for his home? Was he scared she might make some complaint? But if she were to complain, she would have done so on the first day. What she didn't guess was that everything had been planned. Adozindo, with admirable patience, wanted her to reflect on him.

On the fourth day, she had had her hands full with work. Despite all her efforts, she wasn't going to get to the boy's home on time. She walked along with a steady step, her body taut, her hips swaying in time to the rhythm of the buckets. There were large patches of sweat down her back and around her armpits. Mud caked the hem of her trousers and her feet. Her only clean, presentable feature was her black braid, her source of undoubted pride.

At the junction of two narrow streets, she stopped in a small area of shade to catch her breath. The June sun burned implacably. With a handkerchief that hung from her hip by the opening of her gown, she rubbed the perspiration from her face, thus heightening the arteries in her temples. Suddenly, she heard a voice calling her from behind:

'Good afternoon.' She quivered. So he hadn't forgotten her after all. There he was all spruce and clean, wearing a crisp white shirt, his face smelling of perfume that she later learned was 'eau de cologne'. In his right hand, he held two velvety blood-red roses. His well-being was patently obvious. For the first time, she was painfully aware that she was grubby, covered in dust, her body sweating profusely.

Adozindo offered her the roses, saying:

'Take them. I picked them for you. They're from my garden.'

'I can't accept them. My hands are full.'

'Do you want me to throw them away then?'

'No, they're very pretty.'

She'd been told 'devils' offered flowers to the girls they liked. None of the boys from Cheok Chai Un had ever thought of being so genteel to her. It was the first time.

She couldn't stop there for any longer, exposed to the curiosity of anyone in the street. Speechless and clearly embarrassed, she didn't accept the roses. She crouched down in front of the rich boy, placed the pole over her shoulders, straightened her body and adjusted herself to make sure the buckets didn't tip. Adozindo then placed a rose on each full bucket and they floated, lending the water a burst of colour and joy.

Off she went, without objecting to the flowers. He didn't need to accompany her. Her resistance was crumbling, like a house of cards collapsing. His patience was paying off. He roamed around the vicinity of the house, keeping to the cover of walls or hiding behind trees. He wanted to be sure of one thing, and this didn't take long to be confirmed. When A-Leng left the house, she had in her hands the two roses, the flowers of love and of lovers.

6

hat triumph over the water-seller's distrustful heart made the Handsome Adozindo jubilant and fed his bravado. At night, over billiards, he was profuse in his rejoicing, and bought beers for everyone, even those he hardly knew.

His friend Florêncio, the one who was happy to feed off his crumbs, guessed there was a woman behind this. He was astounded. With a wealthy widow, the coveted Lucrécia, passionately in love with him, what more did he want? What better slipper could he find for his foot? He really was sailing too close to the wind.

'So who is the new "she"?'

Adozindo shrouded himself in an air of mystery, amused by his friend, who was making a mental list of the gadabout's potential victims. He couldn't own up to the fact that the object of his desire was a rustic, barefoot beauty, who hurried along the streets under the yoke of a water-seller's *tam-kon*. It would tarnish his reputation as a womaniser, and Florêncio wouldn't understand anyway.

Now that he was about to enjoy the supreme satisfaction of getting what he wanted, Adozindo was no longer content with fleeting meetings, words hurriedly exchanged. He wanted more time with her. The braid was driving him crazy, and the desire to possess her was blinding him to reason and good sense.

A-Leng, for her part, lived in a state of constant mortification. The boy's image had engraved itself on her mind. Such a thing had never happened to her before. She was illiterate, she'd never had time or money to go to school. But she wasn't promiscuous or cheap, and she knew the difference between good and bad.

The inhabitants of Cheok Chai Un were her people. For those outside, the quarter was a den of iniquity, a lair for prostitutes and hoodlums. But for those within, they had a code of honour, there was a way of life and standards of behaviour, traditions and local customs that had to be observed, under pain of general disapproval. Indeed, there was no such thing as a whorehouse there. The folk that dwelt there were like her. She had grown up believing that her whole life, like that of her companions, would be led within the quarter.

The *kwai-lo*'s intrusion into her simple life had complicated its pre-ordained course. He belonged to a social circle that was diametrically opposed to her own, above all in the question of language, religion and customs. Their differences were overwhelming.

She had been dumbstruck one day when, while the owners and the rest of the family were away, and at the insistence of A-Sam, proud to show her where she worked, she had been led round the inside of the house.

The bedrooms, the bathroom, the room for receiving visitors, the dining-room, the Master's study, stacked with books, the furniture, carpets, curtains, all things she had never seen before, had reduced her to humble silence. She had never stepped on such a shiny floor, smelling of wax, and was ashamed to soil it with her muddy feet, while the maid rubbed the dirt off so as not to leave any traces. The frightening telephone attached to the wall, the gramophone with its huge, gaping speaker, the fans, the refrigerator, the sofas and soft beds, everything that her sight and other senses had never experienced.

And the Young Master's room, so tidy and perfumed, with its softly sprung bed. The bold A-Sam had obliged her to try it and she blushed at the voluptuous sensation as she touched the fresh sheets. So there was really no possible point of comparison with any of the boys from Cheok Chai Un.

Logic dictated that she should forsake any truck with a man that wasn't going to lead anywhere, avoid him, maintain her initial hostility, for the sake of her own safety. But she grew sad just thinking about it. Her resistance was collapsing. She felt like a defenceless moth, irredeemably attracted to the light of a lamp where she would burn, but unable to fly away.

His persistence, however, removed any misgivings she had. When he stopped her as she walked down the road in sight of passers-by and a suspicious A-Sam, she agreed to meet him alone for the first time.

For the want of a better place, this occurred in the shadows of the Vasco da Gama Garden, where there were no lights, on a bench set between thick bushes that would shelter them from prying eyes.

A-Leng appeared, trembling and anxious, looking this way and that. She was not at ease, the slightest sound made her jump, as if she were being followed by young roughs from Cheok Chai Un. They sat down, she at one end of the bench and he at the other. At first, she displayed a type of dejected brevity in her answers to his questions.

Adozindo didn't try to get any nearer to her. She was a woman whose mentality and education he had not judged properly. She was a wild, nervy

creature, ever on the defensive, ready to run off at the slightest sign of im-
probity. He needed to be patient, very patient. It was all a question of time.
  After the initial pauses, their talk took a course he hadn't planned. What
topic of conversation could there be with a water-seller unless it was about
the goings-on in her neighbourhood, her everyday routine, the well and her
granny, the Tou Tei Temple? But it was a first step. She had talked and that
was something.
  After barely half an hour she got up. She justified her departure. She
had to get an early night, for she would jump out of her cot just as the sun
was rising, and the rest of the day would be spent running backwards and
forwards, delivering water to many houses, and hurrying around until
nightfall. She spoke with emphasis to show that she didn't surrender easily.
She might be ignorant, but she had her honour and her shame. She wasn't
cheap ...
  It was a difficult business trying to arrange another meeting. He heaved
deep sighs to demonstrate his sadness, and begged her not to be bad to him.
He persisted and she ended up agreeing.
  'The day after tomorrow at the same time.'
  Patience, supreme patience, for patience was the secret of victory. In
an instant, her slender shape melted into the gloom. Adozindo chewed over
his disappointment, and took out a cigarette which he smoked slowly. He
prepared his excuse for arriving late at the house of the jealous widow
awaiting him at Baixo Monte.
  A-Leng was more calm and collected on their second meeting. She
arrived punctually, taking the usual precautions. The conversation once again
focused on Cheok Chai Un, but in greater detail. She was poor, very poor,
but didn't aspire to anything else. She was content with her lot. In spite of
everything, she enjoyed her work, for it was something she was good at.
  Adozindo didn't talk about his home so as not to bring to the fore their
contrasting lives, but he was ignorant of the fact that she had already had a
chance to judge it. He sought out facts and events from his school days,
things that amused her. In the darkness where they sat, stifled giggles could
be heard. All was going well. He didn't touch her although the distance
between them was now less. He had to be patient, supremely patient.
  When they saw what time it was, they realised they'd been there for
fifty minutes. A-Leng jumped up in a panic. She had missed the Queen-
Bee's evening meeting. They would find it strange that she hadn't been,
and they would comment on the fact.
  She didn't turn up for the third meeting, but he kept his word and waited
for her on the following evenings. He could hardly contain his irritation.
He had shown unusual patience, not at all in keeping with his habits or
temperament. He wouldn't act like this with other women. It riled him that

he couldn't get beyond that stupid platonic adoration. A water-seller! But he had committed himself to possessing her body and her braid.

He proceeded astutely, and refrained from pursuing her by day. Her route to his house was full of inquisitive eyes and there was talk in the air. The maid, A-Sam, had smelt a rat and was on the alert, watching the girl's comings and goings. So he needed to gain her confidence by not causing her embarrassment. He needed to be patient, supremely patient.

But all this was preying on his nerves. He was obsessed. He took out his frustration on the jealous widow who, for the first time, had demanded he put his cards on the table. Lucrécia didn't want to remain a widow for ever, when there was no reason for it.

Just as he had always believed she would, A-Leng returned to the darkness of the bench at the usual hour. She arrived breathless, she hadn't been able to resist coming, catapulted by some inner fire, some invisible spring. She had made her excuses and left the quarter by a circuitous route, using a network of streets and alleyways to put anyone who might be following off her trail.

She wasn't even wearing clogs so as not to arouse suspicion. But she hated going barefoot and suffered for not being able to put on one of her better *tun-sam-fu*, instead of her everyday working one.

When they came face to face, she didn't explain her absence. Bashfully, she murmured:

'I like talking to you … '

Adozindo impetuously seized her hands. Rough, calloused hands, hands that had been spoilt by the *tam-kon*, ropes, buckets, cold water in winter, and by heavy weights. But that night, they were hot. She didn't withdraw them, feeling his eloquent grip. Oh! They were the soft, refined hands of one who had never had to bear the yoke of a harsh life day after day, from sunrise to sunset.

They sat side by side, forgetting any awkwardness between them, united in their happiness at having met again. The scent of the champac flowers, pinned to the top knot of her braid, mingled with the fragrance of eau de cologne. And her voice was an embracing murmur. Enough to drive him crazy.

Soon, his lips were by the girl's face, as he whispered sweet nothings, while attempting to put his arm round her waist.

'I don't want this. I'm not used to it … '

He, however, had turned into a Casanova. He was extolling her beauty with extravagant sentences she didn't understand or didn't know whether she should believe. But they were making her dizzy.

He advanced yet further, bemoaning their not having anywhere to be alone together, somewhere they could be at ease, far from their fears. She answered in a whisper:

'I'm scared.'

'Scared of what? I wouldn't harm you ... '

'There's nowhere.'

Every solution came to nothing on the grounds of impracticability. But the idea whetted their imagination, making them quiver with excitement at the mere thought of such a possibility.

Adozindo's self-control, which up until then he had managed to keep so firmly, now evaporated. Suddenly, all his lustful urges exploded. Unable to hold himself back, he put his arm forcefully around her while at the same time leaning towards her seeking her lips with his own.

Suddenly trapped, her reaction was instinctive and she struggled. He had assaulted her dignity. Lips, no! That was her last line of defence before total surrender. She had never experienced a kiss, she was ignorant of such a sensation. It was a shameless habit of foreigners, revolting and nauseous.

'No ... '

She was strong and fought with verve, avoiding his face by turning this way and that, while their arms and legs entangled along the garden bench. It wasn't an unequal struggle, for she was healthy and angry, and wasn't one to give in. Eventually, they fell to the ground, with A-Leng on top.

The sudden, painful thump slackened his embrace, and the girl leapt to her feet, brushing the dust from her *tun-sam-fu* and tidying her braid that had loosened and lost its champac flowers.

Indignant and disillusioned, she stood up haughtily against the night's indecisiveness and said:

'You just want to fool around ... all you want is to have your fun with me.'

She turned on her heel and walked serenely away. The meeting had been a fiasco and had lasted less time than the previous two. In one leap, he was back to day one, all because he hadn't been patient.

Still on the ground, Adozindo ground his teeth, furious at the pain in his back and his rumpled clothes. And also infuriated at his injured pride. All prim and proper and playing hard to get, and she was just a barefoot water-seller!

The following day, A-Leng didn't go to the house on the Estrada da Victória. One of her companions had taken her place.

7

t 5.45 on the morning of that fateful day, 13th August 1931, at the end of a radiant dawn, the entire city was shaken from end to end by a horrendous explosion. Doors and windows were blown in by the rush of air, accompanied by the crash of glass as it shattered into thousands of razor sharp splinters.

The population, terrified and gripped by panic, came out into the streets in their underclothes or whatever garment they had to hand. Cries mingled with incoherent exclamations. No one knew what was happening.

It wasn't long, however, before news spread like wildfire. The ammunition dump on the top of the Guia, near the Fonte da Solidão, had exploded. There were dead and injured and the terrifying risk of further explosions, for part of the dump, defended by a thick wall and full of munitions, was still intact.

The devastation was frightful. The Governor's elegant summer palace, better known as the Palacete da Flora, the Barracks and the neighbouring houses were all reduced to rubble, as was the Long Tin quarter.

Collapsed walls, twisted metal, beams, roof tiles, bricks, blocks of stone and masonry, trunks and branches of trees, shards of glass scattered along the streets, all bore witness to the extent of the explosion. The Fonte da Inveja spring, destroyed, bubbled up out of the ground, turning the earth to mud. The wall round the Lu Kao Garden[3] was cracked here and there, but fortunately had protected the little lakeside palace and pavilions, with only a few trees blown down. Half of the Estrada da Victória and the Vasco da Gama Garden were laid waste. In the Campal and Tap-Seac quarter, the damage was also considerable.

Scattered all over this ravaged area, there were thousands of empty cartridge cases from bullets and shells of various types. It was said that

---

3.   Now known as the Lou Lim Iok Garden.

some of them dated from the Great War. Later, the larger ones would be used as umbrella stands and other smaller ones would be turned into household ornaments by the city's jewellers.

It was a day when people lived in a climate of terror, while waiting for fresh explosions, under the heat of an unbearable, scorching sun. The dead amounted to twelve Portuguese, including an African sentry at the dump who had been blown to pulp, and fifty-two Chinese. The injured totalled just over a hundred officially, but many more were treated at home and therefore went unrecorded. A disaster and a tragedy such as the city had never known before.

By the end of the day, the nightmare gradually receded. The danger of more explosions had passed. The following day, the city regained its serenity and life went on. Now, there was just the sad task of burying the dead. Two funerals took place, first that of the Portuguese together, and later, that of the Chinese. The heart-rending scenes witnessed by the townsfolk remained engraved in the memory of those who lived through it, until time, in its implacable way, diluted it and other generations took their place.

But what happened to Adozindo during this sequence of events?

The night before, he had gone to bed bathed in sweat, after a day of pitiless sunshine that had castigated the trees, streets, dwellings and people. Everyone was complaining about that suffocating August, which the typhoon on the first of the month had failed to relieve, bringing with it instead yet more heat.

Even though the windows were open, the air in his room was stifling. Because of the mosquitoes, he had lowered the net, and the artificial breeze produced by the noisy fan couldn't reach him freely through the thin gauze. He was spending yet another night on top of soaking sheets, while his sweat drenched the pillowcase.

He didn't want to think about anything, but he couldn't stop himself. A-Leng had not been back again, she had severed relations with him and disappeared into the labyrinth of Cheok Chai Un. She had vanished from his life, and commonsense told him it was for the best. Anything else was folly and dangerous. But the boy remained frustrated, for he had unfinished business on his hands. Her attitude had been like a whiplash to his pride. The idea of vanquishing her resistance fixated him.

He got up more than once to drink water and relieve himself, cursing his insomnia. Eventually, he fell asleep, but only for three hours.

He was awoken by a crash, as if the ceiling were splitting asunder. He found himself being hurled from the bed by a whirlwind, along with the washstand, the mosquito net and various other flying objects. He was aware of panes of glass shattering and then a violent pain high on the nape of his neck, and then he lost consciousness.

Stumbling amid dust from fallen plaster, shards of glass, objects smashed to smithereens, upturned furniture, the family staggered out into the street. All they had suffered were grazes, but masters and servants were brought to the same level in the fright engraved on their faces.

A high-pitched yell alerted people to Adozindo's absence. He'd been left behind. His father, Aurélio, ashen-faced and overcoming a fit of giddiness, went back into the house and up to his son's room. The voices of the womenfolk accompanied him in his distressing search.

He found the boy lying unconscious between the wall and the chest-of-drawers. There was a purplish bruise on his forehead that had been made by some hard object. His left hand was bleeding, cut by flying glass. The most serious thing was the gash in the back of his neck, which was seeping a profuse amount of bright red blood. He was alive, though inert, his eyes closed.

At the sight of blood, his mother collapsed in the arms of her sister and niece. The women began to sob. Aurélio, irritated, pushed the inquisitive maids aside and bellowed:

'Stop all this crying. He's not dead ... I'm going to take him to the hospital.'

It was a sensible course of action. He didn't have any broken bones, just that one injury. But the worst thing would be if he had suffered some internal trauma. That was why a doctor was needed. Cousin Catarina immediately offered to phone the Central Garage to send its taxi, for it was assumed that doctors would not be able to leave their posts in such an emergency.

To everyone's relief, Adozindo opened his eyes. He looked around him, surprised, and was immediately told what had happened. He complained of a violent pain in his head, which by now had been bandaged, but which continued to ooze blood. He let out a groan when he moved his hand. He asked not to be moved from where he was until the doctor arrived, but no one was listening to him.

Half an hour later, the taxi finally came. He didn't appear to have anything seriously wrong with him upon examination at the hospital, but the doctor decided to keep him in for observation. He had lost some blood.

'You've got a head of stone. Something must have weakened the blow. It could have been worse, but I think you've got away with it this time.'

So he'd been lucky. News of Adozindo's hospitalisation also spread fast, thanks to the women of the house and to the maids. By nightfall, there was talk around the city of a cracked skull, and delicate surgery through the bone. A-Sam made sure she broadcast this even as far as Cheok Chai Un, through the intermediary of the replacement water-seller who, unable to deliver water to the Estrada da Victória because of the evacuation, was anxious for news. Then she, who was a gossip, made sure the sad story was conveyed to A-Leng.

The pretty water-seller had been suffering bouts of melancholy ever since she had broken with the Young Master. The Queen-Bee and the girl's friends had noticed this, although they had no idea of the reason behind it. She just wasn't the same. She was sluggish, with a vacant gaze, and devoid of her usual energy and happy disposition. She carried her water without any enthusiasm, ponderously, absorbed in her own thoughts.

'She needs a husband,' the Queen-Bee mumbled.

Apart from the panic, Cheok Chai Un had hardly suffered any damage from the explosion. Just a few broken windowpanes, some dislodged tiles, one or two beams loosened, but no dead or injured. There were the same hours of anxious waiting for other explosions that luckily never occurred.

Even the shock suffered by her grandmother didn't give her too many worries. A-Leng's fear was of another order, and she couldn't reveal it to anyone. She cried for no reason at all. She'd forgiven him for all his offence, and just wanted to be by his side, to relieve him from the heat with her fan, and cool his face with a damp towel. To tell him afterwards in undertones that she was there to soothe his pain. But she couldn't do anything about it. If only he had gone to the Kiang Wu Chinese hospital ...

At night, she went with a group of friends to the Vasco da Gama Garden. The lighting was very dim and they didn't go further than the bandstand. A 'Moorish'[4] guard barred their way, ordering them to go back. The area that had been struck was bathed in darkness, and had a deserted air. A-Leng looked towards the Young Master's house and didn't even see a light. This merely added to her sadness and concern.

The following day, like so many other people, she went like a pilgrim to see the effects of the damage. She came away deeply moved. Later, with her thoughts on Adozindo, she refused to attend any of the funerals. He could have been one of the dead, and at that time he wasn't yet out of danger, according to the busybody, A-Sam.

Little did she know that the boy was in fine fettle, rapidly recovering from his shock, and was getting impatient with his zealous father for needlessly keeping him in hospital.

There was an incessant coming and going of visitors, which the hospital tolerated because Aurélio and his family were esteemed in the community. Fathers, with their marriageable daughters in tow, demonstrated the respect they still had for the Handsome Adozindo.

---

4.   A local term for Indian policemen who were recruited to work in Macao.

But one visitor outshone all others for the significance implied. The widow Lucrécia, boldly and forcefully pushed her case for membership of the family. She wore the latest dress from the 'Paradis des Dames', which the dressmaker, Mme. Lebon, announced had come straight from Paris. She was frankly stunning, flaunting her opulence and money, accompanied by her Chinese dry-nurse and Florêncio, Adozindo's best friend, while distributing sweet-sounding pleasantries.

'The slut ... '

Such was the verdict of Adozindo's mother, murmured to Cousin Catarina, who was inclined to agree. Aurélio, on the other hand, liked it and stifled any disagreeable tone with a fearsome glare. Their son needed to settle down, and who better to support the boy's idleness and indolence than a woman awash with money?

Adozindo, however, received the visit with dread. It compromised him. He felt an invisible rope coiling itself round his neck and he wasn't ready for it. His conquest, which had been accomplished with such ease in the beginning, was now weighing heavily on him. Lucrécia was a determined woman, who was confident of the power of her charms and her money. And to make matters worse, the obsequious Florêncio was serving as choirboy.

Ignoring the fussiness of his father and family, he returned home. It was where he should have been all the time. There were now almost no signs of the explosion and the household had resumed its normal daily routine.

When he saw the new water-seller, fat and sweating, he suddenly yearned for A-Leng, for the rhythmic movement of her hips, her white teeth and above all, her dark braid. He had no news of her, nor did he know what had happened to her with the explosion. All he did know was that Cheok Chai Un had escaped largely unscathed. And once again, he was troubled by his frustration at his unfinished business.

It was at this point that destiny played its trump card. On turning the corner of the Rua do Brandão, he came face to face with her. She had paused to wipe her sweat away, while the water in her buckets danced gently. If she had a tired air about her, he didn't notice. His joy at seeing her there, slender and in good health, overcame all else. She, surprised and caught unawares, blushed and forgot her old anger, suddenly fragile and vulnerable.

'Are you better now?'

'It was only a scratch. It was the doctor who wanted to keep me in hospital.'

'I was so worried.'

'I was worried about you too.'

'Really?'

'Really.'

As they stood there, they forgot all else. The debonair young gentleman and the pretty water-seller were wooing each other, oblivious to the world.

'When? ... '

Hesitation grew within her and she took time to answer. Her eyes down, she placed the ropes of the buckets at each end of the *tam-kon* and before crouching to hoist them up, she said:

'I'm alone at home. My grandmother went to her village to get over the fright. She suffered shock because of the explosion. Tomorrow night.'

Blushing still more, and in some confusion, she whispered instructions on how to get there. He should take great care so as not to arouse the neighbours' suspicion. And she left in a daze, astonished by her own audacity, conscious that she had broken all taboos, but knowing that there was no way back.

8

he Handsome Adozindo slid like a thief over the cobblestones of the sleeping streets. He had come from the Rua Nova à Guia, avoiding the light from streetlamps, and had come down the last side street, his footsteps muffled by the rubber soles of his gym shoes.

She lived on the very edge of Cheok Chai Un, opposite the back wall of the Santa Rosa de Lima College. In his wanderings round the quarter in search of her, he had never discovered where she lived and now, ironically, it was she who had shown him.

His heart was beating ever faster. It was as if he were going to meet a princess while of course his only victory was that he was going to the arms of an unknown water-seller, an *a-mui* from Cheok Chai Un. It was truly amazing!

At such a late, deserted hour, he was merely some night-owl, walking along unhurriedly so as not to draw attention to himself, his eyes and ears alert, in case he should meet some unexpected obstacle.

He had deliberately put on an old suit and had abandoned the usual care taken in his appearance. But as always, the Handsome Adozindo hadn't gone without a long bath, and his skin and hair smelt of fine soap.

He hesitated when he came to the line of houses, even though she had given him clear directions. One mistake and everything would be lost. He managed to identify the building, but as the door and window were shut, he had a final doubt as to whether it was that one or the one at the end of the row. There was no one in the street. But a dog, sensing a new arrival in its territory, began to bark at the corner.

At this point, the door of the building creaked slightly. He went over and a hand gripped his arm, pulling him inside. He was enveloped in the perfume from champac flowers, as he came close to her.

A single flame from an oil-lamp lit the inside of the hovel. It was indeed very poor. A collection of worm-eaten furniture devoid of any comfort, a smell of old things that not even the champac flowers could mask.

That was where they ate, slept and worked. In a corner, there was a tall pile of empty matchboxes ready to be sent off. The fruit of the grandmother's last piece of toil before leaving. The buckets were by the wall along with the pole. An inner door led to a room that must serve as a kitchen and also a latrine.

The bed was made of boards laid across long narrow benches, and covered with a worn mat, faded to a brown colour from long use and copious amounts of sweat. That was where the two women slept every night. There were no pillows in the European style, but only cubes of china on which to lean their heads, so as not to crush or destroy the arrangement of the braid and the hair on the back of the head respectively. Over the bed, there was a mosquito net in evidence, except that now it was rolled up because of the breeze coming in through a little window at the back and going out through an opening above the front door.

The Handsome Adozindo didn't have the affluence of those who lived in the mansions of Praia Grande and São Lourenço, or in the houses that were beginning to be built along the Avenida da República, but he lived very comfortably, with the lavishness that was typical of those brought up in Santo António.

Upon encountering such blatant poverty, he felt a sudden pang of guilt. Why had he disturbed this girl who had caused no one any offence and who was even content with her situation? But it was too late to relent, for she had welcomed him into her home and it would be despicable of him if he were to slink away now, with victory in sight.

The flame from the lamp lit up A-Leng's face, encircling her smooth, unlined skin, with a halo of freshness. A beautiful, radiant Chinese face, with sparkling eyes under slanting eyelids, her healthy mouth half-open in a bashful smile.

She too had taken a bath, and washed away the grime of her working day, had fixed her hair, bringing order to any rebellious threads, and had changed into a pair of black trousers of light cloth and a red silk *tun-sam*, decorated with little golden flowers, the colours of happiness. Her braid stood out against all this in a sensuous black coil.

The conspiracy of the shadows, the flickering light, the hushed conversation and the enclosed space of the house, all lent the atmosphere a warmth and intimacy that dissipated any awkward feelings they might have had. She was touched at welcoming such a 'wealthy' person into her home. She kept apologising for the lowly appearance of the accommodation. She helped him off with his coat and brought him tea.

That tea can't have been cheap, bought from a specialist shop as a mark of respect. It was aromatic, had a reddish hue and tasted good. As she made him sit down on a bamboo seat in the absence of anything more comfortable, she took his tie for him and said:

'I've prepared some supper.'

A side table had been laid with bowls, chopsticks, little dishes of soy and other condiments. She went to the kitchen and busied herself there. He occupied himself examining the two roses he had once given her, and which were now wizened and dry in a modest little jar.

She returned carrying a steaming earthenware dish, containing bright red crabs in a black bean sauce. The appetizing dish of crabmeat, known for its aphrodisiac qualities, was fitting for the occasion, and a glorious hymn to life.

'They're beautiful.'

'Here, no one cooks them like I do.'

They were just right, the sauce peppery, the meat pale and tender, and full of flavour. A taste that was both special and comforting. It seemed unbelievable that all this could be happening in a miserable hovel, where such luxuries can't have been common.

'Don't you want any more? What about this shell here. It can't be wasted.'

'Wait ... just a minute. I've still got my mouth full' — and she let out her tinkling peal of laughter.

By the time he had finished, he was infatuated by those eyes that observed him, taking care of his hunger, and by the way the light danced on the blackness of her braid. He drank abundant quantities of the perfumed tea, washed his hands in the wash-bowl of plain tea, and dried them with a towel. Immediately, she produced another towel, with which she cleaned first his face and then his lips. With this simple gesture, she was telling him he was her man.

She cleared the table, and took the crockery and chopsticks to the kitchen where she washed them. These domestic sounds reminded him how far he had progressed on his journey, but he sat languidly on his stool, waiting patiently and expectantly, without dwelling anymore on it. He was no longer shocked by the poverty-stricken surroundings.

Then, suddenly, she was by his side, equally expectant and fatalistic, for she could no longer change things. He put his arms round her waist and drew her to him. She complied, shyly recoiling her head to one side. They embraced, moved by the force of the same mutual attraction.

He kissed her cheeks, her eyelids, the base of her neck, excited by the smoothness of the skin at the base of her hair. The champac flowers fell onto the table, leaving traces of their scent in her braid. She murmured inarticulately and instinctively turned and offered him her full, ardent lips. This sudden contact shocked her, and her body weakened at this new, dizzying discovery.

'You know so much ... '

Her braid swayed sensually, as if it had a life of its own. He undid the cloth buttons of her *kebaya*, which also rolled onto the table. He paused to look at the white strip that concealed the contours of her breasts. Timidly, she said:

'I'll take it off ... '

With her back to him, she undid the knot, and the strip of cloth slipped away, and after a moment's hesitation, A-Leng turned to him. Her breasts, rising and falling gently with her breath, were full and round, a vibrant, pagan offering.

Their clothes flew off. Adozindo plunged into the blackness of her braid and its careful arrangement began to loosen, the very same bewitching braid that had been his perdition and that he could at last lay claim to as being very much his. He kissed it, smelt it, dug his hands into its abundant tresses of thick, strong threads that now possessed the magical smoothness of velvet.

The wooden boards of the bed creaked with the weight of their bodies. Like a wild doe tamed and conquered, A-Leng was submissive but active, pulsating and sensual, and suddenly understood his guidance.

'A-Leng ... '

'It's hurting.'

'A-Leng ... '

'It's hurting so much.'

'A-Leng ... '

'But it's so good.'

...

And so she surrendered, groaning and compliant, dominated by her fatalism and the knowledge that there was no going back. If it was so good, so deliciously painful to feel his hardness penetrate her and rouse her most intimate depths, then she must take it to its final consummation.

They made love and made love again. They were young, bursting with primitive energy. Time slipped by without their being aware of it, united as they were in the same rapture.

As the crier of the hours struck his bronze plate, his melodious voice echoed through the early morning, signalling its passing. She raised herself sleepily, concerned about her braid that had come undone. How was she going to show her face at the well, after she had spent precious coppers the previous day on having it combed?

'If you show me, I'll be able to get it ready for you. I have skilled hands.'

'It's not a man's work.'

'I know, but someone must help you.'

She laughed and sat up. A radical change had taken place in her. She didn't conceal her nakedness, and even found it quite natural in the presence of the man who had made a woman of her. Sensuously, and with a flick of her head, she tossed the volume of her hair into his hands. Greatly flattered, she gave him precise instructions. She was having her queue braided by a man, her man.

It wasn't an easy task. His fingers required training and a nimbleness that he didn't have. But he didn't make too many mistakes as he passed the comb again and again down the long black curtain of her hair. He was quick to learn, inspired by a strange sense of pleasure.

The hardest thing was when it came to dividing the hair into tresses in order to plait them. He was clumsy, and had to keep doing and undoing the braid. She was demanding, and would pout as he fumbled with the knots. In the end, she had to satisfy herself with what she saw, and insisted no further. But she wasn't upset. As she had said, it wasn't a man's work. She would fix it herself later, as best as she could.

Flirtatiously, A-Leng brushed the tip of her braid against his face: 'This braid could earn me good money. I've already been told.'

'I'll be very angry if you cut it off.'

'I'll do it the day you stop loving me.'

'That's hardly likely to happen.'

She continued to caress him with the tips of her hair. Suddenly she put her arms around him and drew him to her. Covering him with the curtain of her locks, she whispered words of love to him. When he crept out of her hovel, the first dawn cockerel was crowing.

9

Well, it had been hard, but he had achieved what he set out to do. He had proved worthy of his title and was still the irresistible Handsome Adozindo. He could now perfectly well cast off the defeated water-seller and devote himself completely to the adorable, wealthy widow, for the good of his social standing and pocket. That was what social convention and cold logic dictated.

But he was paralysed by a reluctance to take such a cruel, drastic decision. He told himself that he hadn't yet satiated himself on A-Leng's gentleness or her physical attractions, and he hated the idea of letting her fall into the hands of some ruffian from Cheok Chai Un. Moreover, the braid that burned his hands as he caressed it, would be lost for ever to another woman who wanted more hair for herself, an old face in search of its lost youth.

He returned, taking the same precautions as before, like a thief, cursing the dog on the corner that never failed to detect his presence with its loud bark. And he enjoyed nights of similar pleasure and tenderness. By this time, she received him as would a young wife, all homely and intent on satisfying her man, who was rapidly becoming king in that poverty-stricken house.

She might be illiterate, a barefoot water-seller, but she possessed the female instinct in which, by making him king, she sought to bind him to her dominion and her charm. She thus played on her gentleness, her physical attributes and her braid.

At the same time, Lucrécia went on the offensive, impatient and determined. She couldn't understand the reason for further delay. Her reputation was at stake, in a place where gossip chastised her, with malicious and sarcastic insinuation, invariably behind her back of course, but which those 'upright souls', her friends, then communicated to her with venomous intent.

Florêncio, a diligent confidant with an insatiable desire to please, took

Adozindo to task. Dedicated to his mission, he put pressure on him at the very time when his friend was spending his happiest moments with A-Leng. He would offer him sensible advice:

'If you've got another slipper apart from Lucrécia, you'd better make it clear. You can't possibly have two.'

But Lucrécia didn't rely totally on the comings and goings of Florêncio. She boldly visited Adozindo's papa, Aurélio, and was honest with him. She wasn't a woman who would passively put up with indecision. She didn't have to. Either Adozindo took her seriously — she had already placed herself in a compromising position — or it was all over between them.

With the money she possessed, and as she was no plain jane, she would have no lack of marriage proposals. Her clear preference was for Adozindo, of whom she was very fond, but ... She was asking him to talk to his son, to present him with the facts of the matter, to talk to him man to man.

Papa Aurélio was flabbergasted. Lucrécia's audacity shocked him, but her beauty won him over. And it must be said too, her fortune wasn't to be sniffed at. Adozindo would look a fool if he didn't grab her while he could. She was the daughter of an army corporal and, rumour had it, a country girl from the lowlands of the Portas do Cerco. What did that matter if she was the widow of the wealthy Santerra, who had died a timely death? When it came to property and capital, one's origins were overlooked.

Papa Aurélio pondered. It was time for his son to settle down. Among the repertoire that society could offer at the time, there was no one else who combined the two most important things: money and beauty. His main worries as a father would be thus mitigated once and for all. Lucrécia would satisfy his son's negative tendency towards idleness and the good life, and an aversion to work.

He made a solemn promise to speak to him man to man. Lucrécia thanked him profusely, heaved her ample bosom and wiped away her tears. Once at home, she wrote Adozindo a note, for she hadn't yet mastered that monstrous apparatus, the telephone. She was inviting him to dinner and she wouldn't take no for an answer. The paper crackled like some strident command.

Adozindo blew hot and cold. On the very night he had arranged to meet A-Leng. The noose was tightening. Florêncio wouldn't leave him alone, his father had spoken to him about Lucrécia's visit, but had been interrupted in what he was saying because his mother suddenly entered the room. Whatever the case, he wasn't prepared to surrender his neck to Lucrécia's slip-knot, nor to put a cruel end to his affair with the pretty water-seller.

He struggled with his dilemma, but accepted the invitation. Gone was the time when he would flit between one place and another, the Handsome Adozindo of old. Somewhere along the way he'd got trapped and now he didn't know how to untangle himself, while maintaining his self-control and his reputation.

In spite of his reluctance, he dressed elegantly. He doused himself with eau de cologne and spent an hour in front of the mirror. Here was the Handsome Adozindo in all his glory. The maid, A-Sam, came to announce that the rickshaw was waiting, and lingered more than she should in admiration. Everyone in the house knew about the dinner.

He avoided his mother and the other women of the house who were openly hostile to the invitation. What insolence! Only Aurélio defended Lucrécia and it was his will that prevailed.

His father was waiting for him, framed by the door to his study. As he came down the stairs, Adozindo guessed what the conversation would entail. He could barely conceal his irritation. His love life was his own and no one else's. Having other people interfere was an abuse and they were invading a domain that was strictly private. Lucrécia, by making his father an intermediary, was going too far.

'Today is an important day for you ... '

'Why? I'm only going to a dinner.'

'That's not what Lucrécia expects.'

To refer to her by her forename in such a familiar way was tantamount to saying it was a *fait accompli*.

'Oh! Anything beyond dinner is between me and her, father. We'll see ... '

'I don't know what else there is to see. It's all very clear.'

He interrupted his son and launched into a heated speech. The time had come for him to face up to life coldly and rationally. He couldn't go on playing around and being frivolous, for he was nearly thirty. At that age, he should already have children and be leading a life with a solid material base. He had got to stop being a source of anxiety for his parents.

Blushing with embarrassment, Adozindo interrupted this endless claptrap:

'I'm still ... not sure of my feelings. I don't know whether I could live with her forever.'

He didn't have the courage to say that Lucrécia had been one of his many trifles, and there was nothing serious. Aurélio raised his eyebrows in a severe, patriarchal glare, and answered:

'And you tell me all this after all that time spent sneaking into her home on the sly? What about the poor creature's honour? You don't fool around with a rich woman who's also got the good fortune to be pretty. I have great respect for her and I'm happy for you to marry her.'

His voice had a severe tone. He was a father used to getting his way. But then he realised he'd sounded harsh and continued in a conciliatory manner:

'You're confused, and I can even accept that you may not feel the type of love for her that poets and romantics talk about. But I can't conceive that one would invade a woman's intimacy without at least holding her in some affection.'

Nor did he have the courage to shout out loud that his attraction to Lucrécia had been purely sexual and once tried and often repeated, he had got tired of her. But one couldn't say this type of thing to a patriarch, for the word 'sex' and everything related to it was taboo.

'It's only a short step from affection to love. True love will come with mutual pleasures and a life led together in a comfortable home. Meanwhile, the compensations ... '

In a cynical display of pragmatism, he tried to convince him of the advantages that Lucrécia offered.

He'd found out for himself and listed the girl's assets that Santerra, in timely fashion, had deposited in her lap before giving up the ghost. Real estate, bank accounts in reputable currencies, shares on the Hong Kong stock market, other secure sources of capital.

For him, Adozindo, life would be bliss. He wouldn't even have to worry about finding a fixed job. He would have everything at hand, he would be swimming in a fortune placed at his disposal.

'You'll have new friends ... a higher social bracket. Teas at the Riviera, afternoons in the Tennis Club, invitations to the Palace, holidays in Repulse Bay, Hong Kong, and in Shanghai. Can you imagine travelling first class on the "Asama Maru" or the "Empress of Canada" to Japan, contemplating Mount Fuji in the distance from Yokohama? Or even as far as Portugal on one of the liners of the Royal Dutch Mail? It's all yours for the taking.'

He had taken a cheroot from the mahogany box on his desk, and lit it with relish as he continued to daydream. The paper was open and its news there for all to see, reports of incidents in Manchuria and the major attack by Japanese forces on Chinese defensive positions. But who gave a thought for the eternal wars in China, always waged in remote areas that didn't change the course of world history?

'And we would all be better off too. Your cousin Catarina needs to find a husband and with your money, opportunities would open for her too.'

He couldn't stand the conversation any longer. He cut short his father's digressions, saying:

'Lucrécia doesn't have nice ways ... and she's bossy.'

His father smiled indulgently. He blew smoke rings and replied:

'She can be made to learn ... A caning from time to time and she'll soften up, and love you all the more for it.'

Why was he telling him this, he who had never raised a hand to his mother? He took his leave abruptly, but his father didn't take offence. He'd given him the message and it seemed to have worked.

'I hope you bring back good news ... '

10

He thought it ridiculous to make such a short journey by rickshaw to the Rua do Hospital. But it was at his father's insistence, because it looked chic. At the end of the street, he jumped out, paid the driver, and began to climb unhurriedly the steep gradient of the Calçada do Monte.

He had never found it so difficult to go and meet Lucrécia as on this occasion. His feet felt like lead, and as he approached the barred gate, he felt ever more reluctant to go through it. It would have been much easier if his father hadn't intervened.

At that moment, all he desired was to caress a sparkling braid, but what he was going to have to confront was a face that of late had always been angry. And with petty squabbles that left him exhausted.

From the windows of the houses, people leant out, watching his progress inquisitively. For the first time, he was walking openly towards the front gate and pulling on the bell, which tinkled merrily.

In the sky, there were still some lighter residues of dusk, but the stars were already out. Even so, the outline of the hills was still clear, as if drawn by a pencil, something one only encounters in autumn.

The gate squeaked and the doorman greeted him with a toothless smile. Everyone in the house knew who he was and treated him with due deference. All, that is, except for the governess, a sinister Chinese woman, as lanky as a cypress tree, who immediately appeared in order to take him to where the mistress of the house was. He detested this woman who never showed him any courtesy, suspicious and unyielding in her hostility, ever since he had begun his relationship with the widow. She always made him feel like an intruder, a gold-digger.

He didn't know the house. He usually went in by the back door, up a very narrow spiral staircase that led straight to the terrace, where Lucrécia's late husband had had a wooden gazebo built, which was then converted into a room in which to seek relief when the summer heat was at its most inclement. This room had in turn become the love nest for his trysts with the widow, with the complicity of the governess, and far from the curious gaze of the other servants.

Now the whole house was open to him for there was no need to hide. On the ground floor, on his way towards the double flight of stairs, he peeped into the sitting and dining-rooms as he passed by. They were brightly lit, and he was able to appreciate the sumptuousness of the carpets, the glass and silverware, the furniture and the porcelain jars.

When he reached the first floor, he was led out onto a covered veranda, with its arches supported by columns carved in the Corinthian style, and which ran along the entire front of the house. He saw a table that had been set, and further away, another smaller table with drinks, surrounded by wicker chairs. Next to this was Lucrécia, half reclining on a couch.

She was beautiful, of that there was no doubt, and at first sight, dazzling in her long blue dress, whose low neck discreetly accentuated the whiteness of her neck and the clear fullness of her soothing breasts. Her body was languid, but her face hard.

On closer inspection, there was something faded about her, about the skin round her eyes and her forehead. She wasn't in the best of moods, and the tiring prospect of more arguments exasperated Adozindo. The times were long gone when they would kiss and laugh, and tumble into their love nest.

'You're late.'

He leant over her, kissed her and replied:

'I had one or two things to see to with my father.'

'I watched you coming up from the bottom of the hill. You weren't in any hurry.'

'It's steep and you lose your breath if you hurry too much.'

'I waited the whole afternoon for you. We could have watched the sun go down together. It's so beautiful from this veranda.'

'There'll be other opportunities ... '

Yes indeed, even in the late twilight, the view was peaceful, with the outline of the hills still perfectly visible. One could catch a glimpse of the sea at the Praia Grande. The Guia lighthouse flashed, distributing its rays of light around it. The São Rafael Hospital was bathed in silence, but the cry of the hawkers in the street could already be heard. The palm trees belonging to the house and the foliage in the adjacent gardens murmured in the gentle autumn breeze.

Together on the long veranda, they were exposed to the gaze of the neighbourhood. The peeping toms must have had their binoculars trained on them, keeping a general lookout. One could only guess that Lucrécia's efforts to get him there earlier were to show him off to the whole world, right there in her home, she the Handsome Adozindo's owner. That was why she was so put out by his arriving late.

It wasn't long before her tearful litany of complaints began. It was the usual routine, but a feeling of exhaustion began to weigh even more heavily on the boy. Was this how it was going to be for the rest of his life then? She sang the same song she always did, without any variation, in a tone that no longer inspired his sympathy. The absence of any feelings, his lethargy and lack of interest in seeing her, his yawns and silences, were surely not signs of a loving heart.

He knew all this was true, but he couldn't admit it. He couldn't, for example, confess that he would rather be passing a comb through a long curtain of hair and then dividing it into thick tresses, while breathing in the aroma of wood oils and champac flowers.

He defended himself hypocritically, but sluggishly, without answering in kind. This attitude upset her even more and her voice took on a stridency that was inappropriate for the occasion. What she wanted was for him to throw himself at her feet, to admit to his errors and mollify her with sweet talk.

He would have done all this before, but now he was strangely reluctant. If he threw himself at her feet, he would be placing his neck in the noose, and he wasn't ready to do that. He couldn't bear the thought of eating humble pie, with the governess leaning by the door, as severe looking as a cypress in a graveyard, taking everything in, including the slightest gesture or facial expression.

'I'm not going to put up with a situation that's neither fish nor fowl. I don't need it and it upsets me. I've got everyone gossiping about me unnecessarily. There they are at their windows on the hill or at the back of the hospital. Tomorrow, they'll all be talking about us as they go into church. It's not that it matters to me, but it's unpleasant knowing I'm the subject of slander. I want an answer. Either you take me seriously or we're finished. I've done all I could. It's now up to you to give me a concrete answer.'

It was an ultimatum, and she was laying her love on the line. She had sat up very straight and dignified. She was very pretty, her expression one of intense anxiety, a woman in her prime, whose beauty and grace wouldn't shame any man. But was it enough to commit himself to for ever, when he was unable to stifle an immense feeling of tedium?

He tried to placate her by pretending not to take her seriously. He wanted desperately to avoid answering the question, without hurting her. He assumed an unconcerned air, raising and lowering his eyebrows in a way he hoped was comic, and running his hand through his hair, said:

'Why so angry, Lucrécia? You haven't even offered me a drink ... I'm dying of thirst. Let's drink to our health, and to our harmony. I don't want to see your forehead furrowed with lines. It looks bad when you're wearing such a gorgeous dress. You did put it on for me, didn't you?

Here was the Handsome Adozindo, in action, leaning over her with his irresistible grin. He took her right hand and kissed it, sensing that her skin was no longer like satin. Her expression softened, as if by a miracle, on feeling the suggestive brush of his lips.

'Do you like the dress? I bought it especially at the "Paradis des Dames". It was designed by Mme. Lebon.'

'A work of art in the Parisian style. It looks so good on you ... suits your body perfectly. One of your finest attributes is your good taste.'

'Do you think so?'

He'd touched the right chord. Lucrécia ran her hands down her body, and wriggled this way and that, in a brazen exhibition of vanity. She forgot her anger and lamentations and frivolously recounted the odyssey of the dress that was on the point of going to someone else when she'd snatched it in the nick of time. How the other woman would be hopping mad!

While she was briefly explaining her adventure, she watched Adozindo prepare the drinks. A vermouth for her, whisky and soda for him. She wasn't very used to drinking alcohol, but she wasn't going to refuse his offer. She didn't even notice that the governess had suddenly left her position by the door.

There was a jolly tinkle of glasses and then silence while they took a sip. He smacked his lips in sign of approval and pleasure, she made a little face, but liked it because she took another sip.

'For me, it's rather strong. I'm not used to it. Santerra didn't like to see me drinking. He disapproved of it and I didn't oppose him.'

'There's nothing wrong with it at all. That's just a silly fixation. Knowing how to drink is all part of social life.'

Lucrécia owed her education to her late husband. At the age of fifteen, she was a young tearaway in the area where she lived. Her violent father had a string of women at home. Lucrécia never spoke of her dead mother, but she knew she was the legitimate daughter from a forced marriage. Her father would hit her, egged on by the other women, in a cruel, insane manner.

One day, there was a huge racket, which attracted the attention of Santerra who lived two houses down. He was a rich, solitary man, and was truly annoyed when he saw how badly the girl was being treated. On this occasion, he marched into the corporal's house and threatened to smash all his teeth with his walking cane if he didn't stop beating his daughter in such a way.

Although he was in his own domain, the trooper paused, merely inviting the other to leave. Santerra had a Herculean body that inspired respect. There was no doubt that, whatever the circumstances, he would be true to his word.

Lucrécia was grateful to her saviour, and began to seek him out whenever she could, inviting herself into his house in order to escape her bleak life. One day, she moved in without more ado. The rumour-mongers of the Christian city affirmed that Santerra, by no means indifferent to the waif's tender flesh, had eventually bought the corporal's rebellious offspring. Santerra didn't run the gauntlet of society's disapproval because he was a man of considerable property, whose numerous impulses were legendary.

By then, Lucrécia was sixteen skinny years of age. But Santerra, who knew what he was choosing, saw considerable promise in her. Not only did he take her in, but he aspired to make her his own by marrying her. The thirty-year age gap between them didn't prick the man's conscience as he was gradually seduced by the girl's charm and youth. As for her, she felt relieved and blessed, for her future was now secure.

He was born in Macao, although his grandparents had hailed from the north of Portugal. When he was still a youth, he emigrated to the ports of China, first to Foochow, and later to the great city of Shanghai. He was just another adventurer in search of a place in the sun. During his wanderings, he had benefited from experiences and learnt Mandarin. He would have remained unnoticed and in obscurity had he not won a fortune in a memorable game of baccarat that lasted twenty-four hours in a well-known brothel in the French Concession.

From one day to the next he made a name for himself, not only in bohemian circles but in the select clubs and among the Portuguese community. He aroused interest and curiosity. As a result, he made a number of useful contacts, most notably, with an army general who was a true warlord from the interior of China, a powerful and influential man, always at loggerheads with the central government at Nanking.

He gained the trust of this truculent soldier, became his adviser and confidant, and involved himself in shady dealings. His one weakness was to allow himself to fall for a beautiful woman, who claimed she was a Manchurian princess, and one of the most stunning beauties at the general's court.

He lived a perilous existence in that nest of vipers, which couldn't consent to a 'foreigner' being admitted to a warlord's close circle and entering the affections of an imperial princess. But it was worth it, for those were lucrative years and the warlord a generous man. As he was familiar with sudden changes of fortune in a climate of continual civil war, Santerra was prudent enough to transfer his assets to Shanghai.

A palace revolt put an end to this extraordinary existence. The general was arrested and shot, along with the princess and the rest of the retinue, but Santerra managed to escape with only the clothes on his back, and after six months on the run, he finally reached the coast and the safety of the International Settlement at Shanghai.

His adventure in China was over. As he didn't feel entirely safe from the possibility of falling prey to a bullet on a dark night, he sold up everything in the great metropolis, and shifted his assets, taking refuge in Macao, a promised land for political refugees and prodigal sons, with occasional business trips to Hong Kong.

China had more than satisfied his craving for a life of romance. Now he wanted to enjoy his money and lead a quiet life. But Lucrécia's arrival altered all his plans for 'retirement'. He thought his capacity to love had died with the memory of the Manchurian princess. But she was dead, while this one, though skinny, was alive and nearby, in the flesh and warm, of a warmth that pleased him.

Santerra educated his wife and dominated her completely. In return, she showed him affection, mingled with respect and fear. She'd been told that he had killed people in China.

He might do the same to her if she didn't behave herself.

He was a penny-pincher with others, seldom buying a round of beer or coffee, but when it came to his wife, he was open-handed. He surrounded her with comfort, got her used to luxury, gave her the finest clothes and jewellery, took her to Hong Kong, where she could buy whatever she liked. The only thing was that he confined her to the home, where they both led a withdrawn life.

The skinny waif became a physically superb woman, upon whom men feasted their eyes when she went to the smart mass at the Cathedral at eleven o'clock on Sundays. Santerra fashioned her according to his image while she, clever in spite of her more frivolous tendencies, learnt a lot from him, in particular how to manage money. In this matter, she was an attentive student, for she remembered only too well her childhood poverty in the lowlands around the Portas do Cerco, and she didn't want to return to it.

Santerra died from enteritis picked up goodness knows where, and at a time when he seemed to be in the best of health. Lucrécia was eternally grateful to her dead husband, but she broke out of her solitary life to become mistress of her own destiny and of a vast fortune, given that she was the sole beneficiary of her husband's estate.

She was aware of the power of money that enabled her to be independent and authoritarian, now that she had been released from her gilded cage. She had the power of choice, something she had never had when married to a jealous and feared man, thirty years her senior.

Having become what the gossips called a 'merry widow', she chose the most handsome boy in the land, the Handsome Adozindo, who had the reputation of being a conqueror, while remaining unconquerable himself. It was a challenge.

What she couldn't have bargained for was that, having set out to be the dominant partner, she would end up being seduced by the boy, like all the other women. But she couldn't bear the idea of just being a plaything, she who didn't need to beg for love. Either he came to a decision that satisfied her or, no matter how painful this might be, they went their separate ways. The second vermouth brought colour to her cheeks. There was no sign of any lingering anger she might still harbour against him. She seemed to have forgotten all about the answer she'd been so insistent upon.

In the midst of these trivialities, the gloomy servant came in and asked if she could serve dinner. She looked disapprovingly at her mistress's ruddy complexion. Yes, dinner could be brought in, for the guest must be hungry.

'I'll just finish this last couple of mouthfuls ... '

The dinner service was of fine Japanese porcelain, the cutlery was silver, and the glasses of exquisite crystal. The tablecloth and napkins glowed white. The table itself was now lit up, leaving the rest of the veranda in shadow. It was all very cosy.

The vegetable and chicken giblet soup was delicious and hot, just as he liked it. The dinner was European in style, a 'bread meal'. He would have preferred a 'rice meal', in the Macanese manner. She, however, wanted to show off her glasses, her cutlery and her dishes. But it was good anyway.

'You haven't given me your answer,' she said, but without any apparent concern.

He bowed his head, busying himself with the rest of his soup, and the governess came to take the dish away. He began to look around him, and she asked:

'What are you looking for?'

'Wine ... the occasion demands it.'

'Oh! I'd forgotten ... '

A bottle of white wine was cooling in a silver bucket, still waiting to be opened. He immediately took it upon himself to do this, and she sat admiring his skill. It was a French wine he'd never heard of. But with the air of a connoisseur, he commented:

'It's a good vintage ... '

'I've got lots of bottles of that wine and other ones too. Santerra liked wines and collected them. In the basement, we have a sort of wine-cellar. It's full. No wonder, I don't drink. You'll see it later when I show you the house.'

He took a sip, testing it on his lips and tongue. He didn't know anything about wines, but it tasted good, that was for sure. He filled her glass. Lucrécia objected, saying she didn't know how to drink.

'Ah! But you don't do it every day. And today's special ... '

'Is it?'

'Yes.'

There was a clinking of glasses, before the fish appeared, steaming, a freshly caught sea bream, in a sauce that had a divine taste. One ate well in that house! Santerra, a man with an exigent palate, had taught the cook well.

In spite of his nervousness, Adozindo was sufficiently hungry to honour the kitchen. She, however, seemed more concerned with drinking, The wine began to make her more and more high-spirited. She talked non-stop, about the house, about work planned for the sitting room and the dining-room. She wanted to make them lighter, less sombre, with new furniture and new curtains.

When the casseroled meat was served, meat brought especially from the Dairy Farm in Hong Kong, she had a bottle of red wine opened. Another unknown French name from Santerra's abundant cellar.

'The white wine's enough.'

'No. Santerra wouldn't do without this red wine for the meat course.'

He estimated that she was more than a little tipsy and her face was intensely red. The maid hesitated and there was a flash of petulance from Lucrécia. She wasn't going to be contradicted and all her cheerfulness could easily turn to rage. The governess threw a poisonous glance at Adozindo, silently accusing him of trying to get her mistress drunk.

'Lucrécia, you've eaten so little. Try and put something in your mouth.'

She wasn't listening to him. Her speech was somewhat slurred.

'Santerra wouldn't let me drink. He treated me like a fragile little doll and controlled me. He never gave me a chance to be myself. But all that's finished. Now I'm in charge ... and I'll do what I want. I'm very happy today. Aren't you happy?'

'Yes, I am ... '

Had he said yes? She couldn't remember among all that tangle of conversation. More clinking of glasses, the wine was truly excellent. For no reason at all, she burst out laughing.

The governess cleared the dishes away with obvious abruptness, running the risk of a reprimand. But Lucrécia's eyes were now bloodshot. She continued to let out guffaws, even for things that weren't at all funny. Her laughs rang through the air, and even down the hill, where they were heard by the neighbours and at the back of the hospital. It was a shameless assault on the tranquillity of the area.

He hardly touched the egg pudding, whose sweetness provoked thirst and toothache. The fruit, which consisted of star fruit and persimmon, was ignored. All he wanted now was to control her fits of laughter.

Lucrécia got up from the table to walk over to the sofa. She lost her balance and would have stumbled if Adozindo hadn't grabbed her in time. She laughed more and more hilariously, leaning ever more heavily on him.

Adozindo helped her over to the couch, but barely had she sat down than she sprang up again.

'The coffee? Where's the coffee?'

The maid served it promptly, pouring the aromatic liquid into two small cups belonging to the same service. Adozindo suggested a larger cup, but the maid chose not to hear him. All her attention was directed towards her mistress.

Lucrécia ordered her to bring them brandy. The maid hesitated, and Adozindo shook his head as if to say no, but her decisive order reverberated stridently along the veranda. Carefully pronouncing each syllable, she told him:

'I want you to try a fine old brandy. I've never had any myself. Santerra guarded the bottle closely and only drank it on special occasions. That's what we're going to do. Today is a special occasion ... '

The rare nectar slid from its dusty, half-full bottle, into two balloons that glinted in the light of the lamp. Its fragrance was so strong that it overpowered all the other smells. They touched glasses again, and Adozindo signalled to her to drink it slowly. But happy and red-faced, as if she had taken too much sun, Lucrécia knocked the contents back in one draught.

She screwed her face up in an ugly grimace. She opened her mouth, her tongue hanging out, and coughed violently, while fiery tears sprang from her eyes. The governess, outraged, lost control:

'How could you let her drink it? Do you want to kill her?'

He didn't even try to defend himself. Lucrécia's face turned from red to purple. She was now very worried and she knew how unwise she'd been. Her head and bust began to sway and she murmured, her eyes closed:

'Everything's going round and round ... '

They lay her flat out on the couch. By now she was weak, ill, submissive. The efficient governess gave her some smelling salts, and produced some towels soaked in cold water. Adozindo, unnerved by this sudden change, tried to force her to drink more coffee. She shook her head and pushed the coffee and its contents aside with her hand. There was the sound of shattering china as it hit the floor.

'This would never have happened with the old master.'

If only that disgusting woman would keep her mouth shut. He had a lifelong enemy in her. The dinner had turned into a fiasco.

'I feel ill ... '

Suddenly, she unleashed loud sobs in a drunken woman's weeping fit, while at the same time letting out groans. On a night that had grown quiet and peaceful, it was all clearly audible. Adozindo begged her to control herself, but whether or not she understood what he was saying, she sobbed all the more loudly.

A man who really loved her would have carried her inside, to her bedroom, where she would have been better. But this was beyond his capacity, nor did it even cross his mind, for the only thing he did was to pat her on the arms. The governess pushed him aside scornfully, and although slight and skinny as a cypress, it was she who lifted her mistress up and carried her in her arms across the veranda and into her room. With great care and tenderness, she lay her down on the large double bed.

All this movement made Lucrécia feel even worse. She tried to speak, but her mouth suddenly filled with vomit, and she threw up the dinner, wine and coffee, which fell like a cataract down her dress, onto the quilt and sheets of the bed and then onto the floor, in a trail of stinking spatter. At that moment, she disgusted him, her face covered in sweat, snot and foul-smelling spittle. And she moaned and wept. He stood there rigidly, without comforting her, for fear of getting dirty and being contaminated by the stench. How horrible a drunken woman was!

'You ... you haven't given me an answer yet.'

It was a lamentation and it failed to arouse his pity. He didn't love her and that was the proof, he had to be honest with himself. To say yes was to accept a future hell. If Lucrécia weren't so overbearing, he might come to love her. But bossy as she was, no.

'Take a rest ... when you feel better.'

But it wouldn't get any better. As for the governess, her words were abrupt and severe:

'The best thing you can do is go. You're just getting in the way. Don't delude her any more. You are not a friend to her.'

11

He stalked off, furious with the governess's open disrespect, but at the same time, he felt strangely relieved. He hadn't promised anything, hadn't given an answer and therefore had time to think. He bridled at pressure put on him to take this or that decision. It was, after all, his life that was at stake.

He slipped and slid on the smooth cobblestones, and almost tumbled over. He felt increasingly irritated: the impudence of a common servant showing him the door! It had never happened before!

He'd never taken Lucrécia seriously. She was a plaything, one of the many the Handsome Adozindo had taken a fancy to, in order to live up to his reputation as a philanderer. But Lucrécia hadn't played the game and he had been corralled by her, by his father and by society.

Instinctively, he made for Cheok Chai Un. A-Leng was a plaything too, a whim of his that he would cast aside all in good time. But at the moment he wasn't thinking about this. He just wanted to be near her, to feel her warm and tender body, to forget the depressing picture of a drunken woman and her vomit.

He couldn't guess what was happening to A-Leng in her neighbourhood. Their meetings didn't seem to have attracted attention, and it had led them to lower their guard, and Adozindo to start acting carelessly. The previous night, someone had been seen entering the hovel by a neighbour, put on the alert by the fact that the dog always seemed to bark at the same hour.

The giggles and whispers were no longer so hushed and the loud creaking of the wooden boards had caused the man moral outrage at what he suspected was going on in his neighbour's house. He kept watch, counting the hours without sleeping, until he saw him leave. Although he couldn't recognise him in the darkness, he was left in little doubt that it was a *kwai-lo*.

He didn't keep it to himself, and the astounding news spread swiftly through the quarter. By now, everyone knew, except for the culprit herself who went to the well as calmly as ever, as if there were nothing at all amiss.

Lost in her own thoughts, dead to the world, enjoying the secret of being loved, she wasn't put out by the silence around her. Not even the forbidding expression on the Queen-Bee's face, who simmered with rage at the collapse of her plans while still nursing the hope that they were all mistaken. Not even when they made ironic remarks about her untidy braid, something hitherto unseen, did the water-seller show any concern.

As Adozindo made his way towards the hovel, following the usual route but without paying particular attention, there were already witnesses, hidden in the street's darkened corners. He was recognised and the casualness with which he crossed the doorway only confirmed that it wasn't the first time.

At that instant, A-Leng's good name in her tiny world lay in tatters. No matter what she might do, she was stained. Never again could she be princess of the quarter.

Blinded by her folly, she was far from suspecting what lay in wait outside. She glanced at the watch he had bought her, and merely wondered why it was past the hour of their meeting. She needed him. She had peeped out of the window various times, but hadn't seen anything untoward.

She welcomed him joyously, complained of his lateness but accepted without argument his confused explanation about a meeting with friends. Her slanting eyes displayed a touching glow of trust. She didn't even find it strange that, unlike other days, he was smartly dressed.

'I prepared you some broth.'

'I'd still like some.'

But the broth would have to wait. She went to the kitchen while he took off his coat and stretched out on the boards that made up their bed of love. It was funny how he felt better there than amid all Lucrécia's opulence, with the old stick of a governess watching him.

A stone crashed against the door, followed by others. They were both alarmed, and A-Leng came rushing from the kitchen, while Adozindo jumped up and put on his coat. There was no doubt about it, they'd been discovered, and the angry disapproval of the local inhabitants was being unleashed. They looked at each other, she very pale, he trembling, in growing panic.

His foremost thought was to get out of there. He couldn't be trapped and caught up in the whirlwind of a gigantic scandal. It didn't even occur to him that he wasn't cutting a very enlightening figure. Indeed, he was behaving like a true coward. She didn't take her eyes off him.

They waited a few moments, sure there would be another volley of stones. But outside, there was complete silence. Regaining his courage, with the utmost care he opened the door a crack. Leaning against the wall, she said:

'It's quiet out there. Take your chance ... You're safer in your own house than here ... '

He hesitated for a few more moments. He was devastated by the shame of not being able to overcome his panic. The hovel had suddenly become a gloomy, foul-smelling cave, crumbling in squalor and decay. The further away he got, the better.

'Get out of here now,' she said, pushing him outside.

He ran headlong up the hill as speedily as an Olympic sprinter. He crossed the boundary of Cheok Chai Un, and could hear the sound of stones whizzing through the air behind him. When he caught sight of a policeman calmly pounding his beat in the distance, he knew he was out of danger.

Yet his feeling of shame persisted. He had behaved like a poltroon, abandoning the girl to the wolves, concerned only with his own safety.

A-Leng crouched behind her bolted door, expecting the worst. She heard the hail of stones and then the loud insults, among which the word 'whore' had pride of place.

Never had she felt so isolated, defenceless against the fury of her people. When things quietened down, she climbed onto her bed, her braid unkempt, her tears flowing in abundance.

First thing in the morning, that was the only topic of conversation at the well, water-sellers and washerwomen on one side, braiding-women and street sweepers on the other. The most beautiful, the most accomplished and the most inaccessible girl in Cheok Chai Un, in the unscrupulous arms of a *kwai-lo* and in her own home, the same *kwai-lo* she had showered with insults. Their spirits were brimming with anger and resentment, scorn at her having violated the moral customs of the quarter. There were those who, in the midst of all these diatribes, suggested that the only road open to her was the one that led to the 'flower houses' of the Rua da Felicidade.

'That's too good for her. The Beco das Galinhas is what she deserves.'

Suddenly, they stopped talking, astonished. The slender silhouette of A-Leng was coming towards them, balancing her buckets. She was pale, but her lip jutted out in determination and defiance. She couldn't do anything about what had happened, but she had to work. She wasn't going to accept insults passively, for if she did, they would trample all over her.

It wasn't long before she was on the receiving end of a painful barb from a group of elderly women. They deliberately moved away from her, as if she were poisonous. She put up with it in silence, but she was soon the target of more quivering darts.

Then she reacted. She replied haughtily that it was her life and she could do as she liked, she was free and whatever she did was no one else's business. They retorted that it was their business because she had shamed Cheok Chai Un. The fallen idol kicked out, and hostilities began. She was astounded at her friends who had become vipers, making such coarse comments. They ostracised her, banished her from their midst. In a word, she could count on no one to help her.

Never had she found it so hard to haul up water. Her buckets weighed like lead. A sense of the inevitable descended upon her, that she couldn't restore things to what they had been. Everyone was against her. She had forfeited her self-control for a foreigner who had promised her nothing in return. It had been so foolish, so crazy from beginning to end, but it had been so good.

Suddenly, there was the Queen-Bee blocking her path. She was furious, her mouth foaming at the same time as she shrieked insults at her that echoed all around the well and its immediate vicinity, causing the crowds of passers-by to stop.

Her pole lost its equilibrium and the buckets spilt their water. She didn't move, rooted to the spot by her fear and respect, incapable of justifying that which had no justification. Without the Queen-Bee's support, she was an outcast. She couldn't go back to the well because the old woman, at that moment passed her sentence:

'Never again return to the well. You will poison the water. If you try, we will stone you. Don't go to the market either. No one will sell you anything.'

And so she had even lost the guarantee of a bowl of rice. Tears of shame and despair blurred the former princess's vision. Amid the mockery, she crept back to the hovel, her buckets empty. That was the end of the pretty water-seller of Cheok Chai Un.

12

Shut away in the comfort of his room, Adozindo barely slept a wink. My! What a night! Everything had conspired to make him unlucky. A complication involving women that the Handsome Adozindo hadn't bargained for, and all on the same night! Somewhere along the way, he had lost control of the situation.

He'd behaved abominably with both of them, he had to admit it! His thoughtlessness, up until then unpunished, had exceeded any reasonable limit. He could picture Lucrécia's fury when she recovered from her indisposition and realised that he had disappeared precisely when her suffering was greatest. It had been a mistake, and he should have remained on duty so as to be with her in her anguish, and comfort her with kind words. If he'd done that, he would have saved A-Leng from the dramatic incident in Cheok Chai Un. But he would never escape the widow's clutches. Contemplating that possibility sent a shiver down him. No, without thinking very clearly, he couldn't bear such a prospect yet.

Turning his thoughts to A-Leng, he was tormented with shame, a shame that would stay with him for the rest of his life if he didn't make amends. He had abandoned her like some wretched coward, at the moment of greatest peril, and had escaped, his tail between his legs, unworthily washing his hands and abdicating from responsibility. And she'd been left behind, left to the judgement and punishment of her community. He hadn't behaved like a man, nor would he ever be one, and that was the stain on his dignity that his conscience would never be able to clean. It was enough to recall her startled eyes staring at him, burdened by the fear he had seen in her face.

On the other hand, he knew that this was a chance to end his relationship with the water-seller. He'd had her, he'd satisfied his lust and once again been confirmed in all his glory. No one escaped the Handsome Adozindo's powers of seduction.

Now he could shut himself away at home, stop thinking about the girl and close yet another episode in his life as a philanderer. What could a poor, barefoot water-seller, unnoticed by anyone, do apart from scream and shout, which wouldn't achieve anything beyond some momentary embarrassment for him and his family, and which could be silenced with money anyway?

All this was possible if he were cynical and completely devoid of any feeling. However, he might be selfish, but he wasn't bad at heart. And he wasn't ready to see her disappear from his life. He still hungered for her, her simple gracefulness, her warm, enveloping body and her thick, shiny braid. That trance belonged to him, he couldn't allow it to go to anyone else.

'No, never.'

He got up at the crack of dawn, when the household was still fast asleep. He looked in the mirror and got a fright when he saw the shadows under his eyes and his look of exhaustion after his sleepless night. He wanted at all costs to avoid his father, who would come at him with an indiscreet question about the outcome of the dinner. As if any of that mattered!

Today, he wouldn't go to the agency. He would quite simply go fishing so as to better gather his thoughts and calm down alone by the sea. He needed fresh air, lots of fresh air. He washed and dressed in a hurry, making as little noise as possible. He gathered his fishing equipment, drank a bottle of milk from the fridge, chewed some stale bread kept over from the previous day, and went out. The maids were still asleep.

He remembered he didn't have any bait, but he didn't dare go to the market in Cheok Chai Un. In the Calçada do Gaio, he hailed a rickshaw that took him to the shellfish shop in São Domingos, and then to the area of the São Francisco Fort, at the end of the bay of Praia Grande.

He was so absorbed in his thoughts that he didn't even pause to admire the junks and *lorchas* setting out from the bay for their day's work, nor did he stop on the rocks which were supposed to be good for fishing. He continued along the paved road of the Outer Harbour, which would lead him in the direction of the catwalks and the most isolated areas. He chose a spot by chance and settled down, crushing a sea-beetle as he did so, his fishing rod held aloft after some delay, and fresh bait on the tip of the fish hook.

If he thought he would be able to organise his thoughts, he was mistaken. The void in his mind remained. By mid-morning, the sun began to burn. Thirst caused the back of his throat to tingle, and he would soon begin to feel hungry. He was too distracted to catch anything, and the cunning fish merely stole his bait. All he could see in his mind's eye were Lucrécia and A-Leng. In his overworked imagination, it was mainly the latter he thought of, and of her house desecrated by invading hoodlums, and she without anyone to defend her.

The hut belonging to the net fisherman was fifty metres away. He decided to go over and ask for some tea. The solitary old man was friendly and welcomed all the amateur fishermen, always willing to teach beginners and to show them the best places to fish. Sometimes he would prepare a nice meal for a group of friends. He liked young people and told them tales of his experiences, there in the barren emptiness of the rocks. He led a hard life but he seemed happy.

He gulped his tea eagerly and as the man was preparing his meal, he didn't hesitate to share it. The sea air and a rumbling stomach didn't allow him to stand on ceremony, no matter what the tribulations of his soul. He felt comforted, more hopeful, and a blessed drowsiness descended upon him. He slept for a couple of hours, lulled by the murmur of the waters as they lapped against the huge boulders. The net fisherman went on with his work, respecting the boy's repose. When he woke up, he felt fully refreshed. He stretched his limbs, paid for his lunch, gave his host the rest of his bait, and asked him to take care of his fishing equipment.

The clear, golden afternoon was already advanced, and the sun hovered over the hump of the island of Lapa. The small lighthouse at Pedra de Areca was already flashing. The island of Taipa was a verdant wall, gloomy and lifeless. The ferry from Hong Kong was just rounding the tip of Barra. The muddy sea glimmered with red reflections. A junk glided by, its sails unfurled, leaving behind it a wake of lacy white foam. It was time to go.

He walked along the catwalks and up onto the paved road. The wind had risen and there was a lot of dust about as he crossed the open ground. On the bend by the São Francisco Fort, he stopped. He had two directions to choose from. Either he went past the Grémio Militar, and along the Rua do Campo towards the Calçada do Monte, or he turned right up the Estrada de São Francisco in order to reach the Rua Nova à Guia, and so into Cheok Chai Un.

Lucrécia could wait. It would merely be a repetition of the previous day. Complaints, accusations, a stormy tone of voice followed by calm. He would be able to weather the storm. It was A-Leng who needed him. It was essential that he find out what they had done to her after the stoning. He would never know any peace if he kept his distance. No matter how unlikely it might seem, he didn't want to be branded a coward, even if his judge were an uneducated water-seller.

He walked quickly along the stony road, under the rustling trees. The sun had gone down, but he was still able to see where he was going in the half-light. His heart was racing, for he didn't know what to expect. But he wouldn't turn back, even though he was scared. It was a matter of honour to him.

In the Rua Nova à Guia, his legs were turning to jelly, but he managed to remain haughtily erect. In his dishevelled fishing gear, he must look like a clown. He took a deep breath and turned the corner into the street where her house was. At first sight he didn't see any sign of danger, but then some small boys raced across the road.

He knocked on the door, announcing himself at the same time. The door opened and a hand pulled him inside. It was A-Leng, unharmed, without a scratch, but visibly marked by her ordeal, with her unkempt braid and the deathly pallor of her face.

'You've come back ... '

Her relief touched him. She leant against him, her arms hugging his waist tightly, as if she feared he would run away again.

'You've come back ... I'm not scared anymore. I'll never be scared again.'

'A-Leng.'

Her simple trust moved him still more deeply. The colour was returning to her beautiful face, the strength of her embrace more eloquent. His physical desire for her grew even more acute when he felt the hardness of her nipples against his chest.

'Your braid ... '

'I'll tidy it in a minute ... I'm sorry.'

At that very moment, there was a crash against the door. Kicks and fists beating the wooden panels, angry, threatening shouts challenging him to come outside. It was the whole quarter expressing its indignation at this intruder.

'Don't go outside ... It's dangerous.'

'I must do something ... They'll knock the door down and invade your house. It's an outrage.'

'Let me talk to them.'

'No, I'm the one who's going to talk to them.'

Plucking up courage, he rushed forward like some knight errant defending his lady. He threw open the door angrily. It was then that he saw the extent of his challenge and how reckless he had been.

In front of him was a row of toughs who belonged to the rowdy gangs of Cheok Chai Un, the renowned *a-tais*, always ready for a scrap within the boundaries of their quarter. Behind them was a crowd of onlookers hurling abuse too.

'Go away ... Leave the girl in peace.'

Hardly had he finished speaking than the hoodlums advanced without a further thought. Adozindo had always taken care not to get involved in physical aggression, so as to safeguard his facial integrity. But now, it was a question of fighting for his life. He threw some punches, but he was one against four of them. A violent blow to his back made him double up and stagger forward, and another caught him in the pit of the stomach. He howled with pain, while a monumental toe-poke in the buttocks rounded off the assault. Flung forward like a piece of old rag, he landed in a pile of rubbish that stank of rancid shrimp husks and other leftovers. He floundered about among the dirt, trampled on furiously and under a storm of kicks. He still managed to grab an ankle, but there was little else he could do by way of a reaction, as pain tore through his whole body.

At this point, he heard the shrill cry of a woman. Although badly beaten, he opened his eyes and was greeted by an astonishing scene.

A-Leng had leapt into the middle of the street, her pole held aloft. Her face seemed to have undergone a transformation and she had a murderous look. She had issued her challenge. With a masterful stroke, she swept the legs of the biggest lout from under him, sending him crashing to the ground as if he were little more than a wattle scarecrow. The victim writhed on the floor, howling, his trousers stained with blood.

The other three stopped, caught by surprise. The nimble A-Leng, cutting the air with her hissing pole, hacked a clear circle round her. Then, in one leap, before her aggressors could regroup, she lunged at the nearest one, catching him at the point where the base of his neck met his right shoulder. The man let out a bellow, his collarbone broken, his arm hanging limp, and he too fell over.

The other two, by now scared, beat a retreat. She gave chase, her *tamkon* still whistling furiously. At that point, they decided to make a run for it, but one of them wasn't fast enough and got a resounding thwack on his back.

She turned towards the bewildered spectators who had wisely recoiled. There she was a warlike Amazon, blind with rage, brandishing her pole with unusual skill. Her two victims crawled away on all fours, moaning.

'No one lays a finger on my man ... And you, go home. You're worn out.'

Adozindo staggered to his feet, his clothes torn, his face and body covered in cuts and bruises. A-Leng swung her weapon of war around to give the boy cover, and urged him to go. She was magnificent, inspiring respect, queen of her territory, beautiful, barefoot, her braid twisting like a whip. Adozindo moved off as speedily as his strength would allow. He was safe and it was a heroic display of love that had saved him.

13

*H*e beat on the back door because he had forgotten his key, and A-Sam, perplexed, let out a cry of horror. She had never seen the Young Master looking so dirty and ragged, his hair all ruffled. He spoke to her brusquely, told her to keep quiet and asked where his parents were.

They had all gone out, only the servants were in the house, came her offended reply. He rushed up the outside stairs and insisted categorically that no one should raise the alarm or call the doctor. He knew what to do, he said abruptly.

His body told him he needed his bed. He washed and changed his clothes with painstaking slowness. He would have to make up a story to explain the cuts. But that didn't matter for the moment. What could have happened to A-Leng whom he had abandoned yet again? After the incident with the pole, the situation had taken an entirely new turn. The figure of Lucrécia had disappeared, like smoke that had dispersed.

He couldn't have foreseen that someone would suddenly knock at the back door. It was A-Leng, in a state of heightened agitation, her braid undone, and her *tun-sam-fu* soiled. The maid, the same garrulous maid familiar with all the gossip from Cheok Chai Un, answered the door:

'What do you want?'

'To speak to the Young Master ... '

'He's not receiving anyone.'

'He'll receive me. He's my man.'

She was still carrying her *tam-kon*. One shove, and she pushed A-Sam into the yard. She made another attempt to block her way, but another stronger push was enough to frighten her. A-Leng, with her knowledge of the house, charged up the outside stairs to the first floor in sprightly manner. There was now no reason to hide anything at all.

She turned down the corridor with its shiny floor, and with no fear at all, made straight for his room. Unconsciously, she was acting as if she had acquired a right.

The sound of the door awoke him from the state of apathy that had taken hold of him since he had gone to bed. For the time being, he didn't want his family there with all their questions and shouting. The figure he saw coming towards him wasn't one of his people.

'A-Leng ... ' There she was, leaning over him, her eyes moist and anxious. The brave girl who had saved him from certain death or from suffering broken bones that would have left him lame for life! He exaggerated his pain. She sat on his bed, with a lover's familiarity.

'Does it hurt?'

'A lot.'

'The hooligans!'

'What about them?'

'They ran away.'

'They're your folk.'

'They're not my folk. My folk is you.'

She tried to examine his bruises. The sight of them made her angry and she let out exclamations. He then exaggerated his groans. However the touch of her calloused hands, the proximity of her slender, curvy body that smelt of all the health of the land, the blackness of her braid, unrolling over her breasts, brought about a miraculous recovery.

'You're the best medicine.'

She smiled happily. She turned the tip of her braid into a brush, and with it she tickled his face, his ears, his neck and his chest. The sorcery worked and Adozindo pulled her to lie down by his side.

'Not here. We haven't even locked the door.'

'It doesn't matter. My family have gone to a supper.'

'The maids.'

'They won't come up ... I told them not to.'

'You're very badly bruised.'

'It doesn't matter.'

So daring were they, so foolhardy and gripped by an urgent need to be together that they forgot the most basic precautions. Outside, night had fallen. The voices of the servants and the household noises permeated through to them furtively, as if some major event were about to occur. Up above, they both gasped in ecstasy, without having yet discussed what the future held in store.

Afterwards, she had to tidy her braid. He helped her, just as he had on previous occasions, using a comb that was totally inadequate. He was more skilled by now and she didn't complain, still dizzy with this new demonstration of their love.

They heard a murmur of voices down below. It was the family arriving. Adozindo shivered, knowing how difficult the coming moments were going to be. A-Leng guessed his embarrassment and said:

'It must be your parents. I'm going. I'll look for you tomorrow.'

'Where are you going?'

'Home. I can't abandon it. All my things are there ... At least today, they won't harm me. I've got my *tam-kon* and a whistle to call the police. I'm going to have something to eat now because I haven't had anything since this morning.'

She slipped along the corridor and disappeared down the outside stairs. Adozindo felt childishly insecure. He didn't want to have to face any of his family. The last twenty-four hours had produced one shock after another.

He heard A-Sam calling him from the corridor.

'The master wants to speak to you. He's downstairs in the sitting-room.'

'You told him everything, you witch!' He exclaimed, hurling the door open.

The maid replied, petulant and hostile:

'And why shouldn't I tell him? Who is she to come into this house like that? She's no better than I am.'

He looked at her and suddenly understood. This one too. She was jealous, because he had passed her over for another, whom she considered beneath her. Women!

14

That night, there was much agitation on the Estrada da Victória. An entire family was mired in shame. The mother, grandmother, aunt and cousin Catarina wept and fainted more than once, in dramatic displays of hysteria. Papa was foaming, his eyes popping with fury. Aware that he was incapable of attacking his son physically, he had smashed glasses and ripped up pictures and a chair. His skin had turned a shade of purple. The passers-by stopped in front of the house, alarmed by the thundering voice that filtered through the closed windows.

All this uproar left Adozindo shaken. It was impossible to erase from his family's eyes the evidence of degradation and promiscuity that they had chosen to see in his room and his bed. The maid had described everything too explicitly. How low their son had sunk!

'This is an honourable house and not a den of whores. You gave no thought to your mother, your grandmother ... '

Adozindo apologised. It was one of those things ... It had all happened so suddenly and had been impossible to avoid. He had been deceitful, he had abused the decency of the house, but he wanted to explain things. There was an explanation for it all.

'Disgusting!'

'She's not what you think.'

'Such a lowly creature. A water-seller with bare feet, and from Cheok Chai Un.'

'Her name is A-Leng.'

'A Chinawoman ... An *amuirona*. How disgraceful!'

'And you were doing all this behind Lucrécia's back. What will people say of you?'

'I don't know. This sort of thing happens to the best of people. I seduced her, led her astray. She saved my life.'

This wasn't what her father and the rest of the family wanted to hear. They wanted him to lay the blame fairly and squarely on the girl. And what was more, they wanted him to show remorse for his thoughtlessness, and beg for forgiveness. But they were unable to drag this out of him, any more than they could extract a promise from him that he would sever relations with this gold-digger. By now, his mother was begging them to call Lucrécia. Their son was under the spell of this rustic, barefoot siren. The evidence of this fact was like a knife thrust to his father's heart. He had counted on getting some good news that would fit in with his own plans, and the very opposite had happened, much to his surprise and anguish. He looked at his handsome son and his heart shrank. The boy had an affluent marriage for the taking, which would open up magnificent opportunities for him, and he was throwing it all away in some colossal act of folly. It wasn't as if it were because of another woman of the same social class. There were plenty who would die for him.

But no, he was turning his back on all of this, chasing a 'pigtail', a braided water-seller, to make matters worse from the disreputable Cheok Chai Un, and who didn't seem to be acquainted with the habit of wearing shoes. A woman who could never be presented to society. What a bitter disappointment!

Tiredness overcame all of them, without any solution having been found. One by one, they retired for a night of sad reflection. Few of them got any sleep, except for the Handsome Adozindo, who collapsed onto his bed exhausted, and fell into a deep slumber. His body was in such a bad shape that it was a miracle he had been able to stay on his feet for so long. His last memory of that night was of a braid twirling, as if it had a life of its own.

Further uproar and raised voices woke him up when it was already morning. The clock was striking nine. He leapt out of bed, his heart racing, for he had guessed what was happening. A-Leng had appeared. He could distinguish her voice clearly calling for him, using the Chinese name she had given him out of love and respect, and because she was unable to pronounce his real name in Portuguese:

'A-Kó ... A-Kó ... '

Elder Brother? He was no longer that, he was her man. The girl's determination surprised him. She was certainly no meek lamb surrendering herself fatalistically to slaughter. Not she, who had faced four hoodlums and swept them away with a few blows of her stick.

Her logic was really very simple. A man had interrupted her normal everyday routine, had disturbed her, made her lose her temper, eventually stimulated her interest and then love. She had given herself to him completely, had surrendered her lips, her breasts and her virginity, and had allowed him to comb her braid. She had saved his life and because of that, had become an outcast in her quarter. For her down-to-earth way of thinking, she was his now. Her only duty was to follow him, to share in his happiness or misfortune. And so there she was, at the main entrance and not at the back door, seeking to gain entry in order to claim the place to which she felt she had an irrefutable right.

It was obvious this attitude would never be accepted by his family, proud and shocked by such insolence. Adozindo was overawed. He wasn't expecting such a drastic resolution of the problem on the girl's part, when he appeared, embarrassed, tucking his shirt tails into his trousers and buckling his belt.

'My people no longer want me in their quarter. I can't live there. I've been banished and have closed my home. Your people don't want to let me in.'

So this was the cost of his fooling around, with all the interest added! A-Leng was looking at him serenely, not showing any humility, her braid tied up hurriedly, still barefoot, and with two large flat baskets tied to ropes and hanging at the ends of her pole, one containing her empty buckets and the other her few possessions all tied up in a sheet.

'Oh! Papa, let her come in so we can talk.'

'No.'

'Don't allow the neighbours to ... '

'I've told you. I'm not having this filthy blatherskite crossing my door.'

The women of the house and the servants closed ranks together. Cousin Catarina was letting out high-pitched sobs. The gossipy, resentful maid was upbraiding A-Leng and insulting her.

'I've already told you that she's a good girl. And this is my house too.'

'No it's not, and certainly not for you to do as you like in. You haven't been earning money for that privilege. You've got a choice. Either you go with her, or you are obedient, and come back inside without her. If it's a question of money, we'll pay her off and be done with this shameful situation.'

The needless insult, fruit of an uncontrollable temper, penetrated deep into Adozindo's sensibility. His disregard was too great. On impulse, he replied:

'Then I'm going with her.'

As he spoke, he realised there was no going back. Amid the chorus of horror from the womenfolk, his father raised his voice:

'If you do so, you are no longer my son. Go and fetch your things and get out of here. You've got five minutes.'

Without a drop of blood in his face, but proud, he turned to A-Leng, suddenly ready with her pole in her hands, as if she guessed what was being said:

'I'll be back in a minute. You won't need to use your *tam-kon*.'

In the background, his mother shouted at her husband before falling into a swoon:

'I told you this house was unlucky.'

Adozindo went up to his room, seized the big suitcase he used when he went to Hong Kong, and threw in a few shirts, as many underpants, two suits, two pairs of shoes, his toothbrush, his razor for shaving and one or two other things of immediate use. He went to the drawer and took out all the money he had and other items of value. He filled the case with no particular plan in mind, grabbing this or that by chance and because it happened to be in front of him. He closed it, gasped at its weight and withdrew without a backward glance.

As he made his way to the door into the street, he expected at any moment to hear his father's and grandmother's voices. But only silence greeted him. He too was an outcast.

Out in the street, A-Leng, her *tam-kon* over her shoulders, the baskets swaying, asked:

'Where shall we go?'

'To a friend's house.'

The boy with his heavy case, and the girl a little way behind, with her few belongings, took their first steps towards a new life, expelled from their respective paradises. Behind them, the door slammed shut. There was nothing else to do but go forward. It was the Handsome Adozindo's hardest journey.

15

They struggled across the streets, while the attention of many was attracted by this unusual and unexpected scene. The Handsome Adozindo, without his customary arrogance, lugging his heavy suitcase, followed by the Chinese girl, barefoot, her *tam-kon* over her shoulders, her baskets swaying, blindly following her man through this strange city.

It was their bad luck that there were no empty rickshaws around. On the other hand, this would only have attracted yet more curious stares. Fortunately, most people were at work and Florêncio's house was nearby, in the Rua do Volong. He was hoping that his friend, who was on holiday, would be at home.

He hadn't exchanged a word with A-Leng, nor had he turned round. But she followed his every movement and didn't lose him from sight. If he stepped down from the pavement, so did she, when he stepped up again, she did too, in the same rhythm and cadence. He was her man.

A loud ringing of the doorbell awoke Florêncio, who lived alone, although his parents and brothers lived spread around the city. He was a bachelor and, like Adozindo up until that moment, was accustomed to telling all and sundry that he hadn't found the woman of his dreams with whom to tie the fatal knot. He was the only friend Adozindo could count on, a friend who was happy to 'eat his leftovers'.

He peeped, startled, through the crack of the open door, ready to utter some insult, and was immediately woken from any residual sleepiness. He couldn't believe what he was seeing.

'Don't start mouthing off. At least let us in. There are so many people staring at us.'

'What's happened? Who is this ... '

'Before anything else, give me a glass of water. I'm parched. I'll explain everything.'

They were in a modest room that Florêncio used as a sitting and dining-room. The master of the house took a close look at A-Leng and didn't invite her to sit down. He couldn't cease showing his astonishment at the sight of her baskets, buckets and bare feet. And in the company of the Handsome Adozindo, who looked worried and agitated.

It was Adozindo himself who pulled up a chair and bade her sit down. They went into the kitchen where the glass of water had a refreshing effect on Adozindo. A-Leng, without taking her eyes off them, saw that they were busy talking in undertones. Adozindo, clearly embarrassed, was as brief as possible. He hid nothing, for it wasn't an occasion for half-truths. Florêncio's gaze switched backwards and forwards constantly between him and the girl. His initial surprise was replaced by a solemn look. He was thinking quickly, and there was no sympathy.

'So is this the slipper you've chosen for your foot? After so much picking and choosing between this one and that?'

He didn't conceal his disdain, while at the same time shaking his head. The philanderer's prestige was rolling ingloriously on the floor. Humiliation struck Adozindo like the crack of a whip, but he parried the blow, replying:

'But she's out of the ordinary and has a sweet personality, more so than any of her rivals.'

'Your problem is lack of judgement. Get some sense back in that head of yours. Take an antidote and throw up the effects of that tea she must surely have given you to drink. And go and ask your parents, whom you've offended, to forgive you. I can imagine how upset they must be.'

'I can't do that. I no longer have a home, and nor does she.'

'Nonsense. Tell her to be off. She's not a woman for you. You know that perfectly well, with your education and way of life. A water-seller with a queue, who doesn't even know what shoes are for.'

'Her name is A-Leng. She saved my life ... '

There was no moving him. He was exactly like his father and the rest of the family. Florêncio plunged his hands in his pockets and leaning back slightly, asked petulantly:

'And does Lucrécia know about this ... About your unwise change of heart? Don't tell me you want them both, both in the same trolley ... '

'For the time being, Lucrécia doesn't matter. First, I've got to look after A-Leng. I regret all that happened ... I'll speak to Lucrécia later. I'll explain ... '

He wasn't going to be open to someone who was no longer his friend. After what had happened the previous day, he knew that A-Leng wouldn't resign herself passively to losing him. She would never raise her pole against him, for he was her man for better or worse. But she would smash any rival, whoever that might be, who disputed her place, with the same bravado displayed against the four ruffians, without a thought for the monumental scandal such behaviour might cause. Suddenly, he imagined Lucrécia being subjected to a beating and knocked to the ground, her blood-spattered legs lying bare and exposed ...

It was enough to look at A-Leng's serene, motionless expression, her arms folded, a latently threatening force. She didn't take her eyes off the master of the house through the doorway to the kitchen, sensing that he was an enemy. If she could understand what they were saying, Florêncio might get the fright, not to mention the hiding, of his life.

'Are you so indifferent to Lucrécia, a society woman who received you so generously, and was so giving?'

'I'm deeply grateful for what she gave me. I alone know how much. But life is full of unforeseen surprises.'

'I don't like your cynical attitude. Anyway, what is it you've come to see me about? Is it just to tell me about your adventures? Just one more among so many, and the most shameful of all?'

'I've come to ask you as a friend to put me and the girl up until we can get somewhere permanent. Everything happened so suddenly. I only need a few days and after that we won't trouble you again.'

'No.'

He had put up with censure and disdain as calmly as he could. But the refusal caused his bitterness to overflow. He clenched his fists and would have smashed that face full of acne in an outburst of temper, if he hadn't heard A-Leng stir and get to her feet. The punishment would be worse than the crime if it came to a thrashing. Disappointed, he exclaimed:

'You're my only friend.'

'Not anymore, after what you've done to Lucrécia. Don't shout or threaten me. What would she say if she knew I was giving you and that female lodgings. She would shut her door on me, and rightly so. Well, I value Lucrécia's friendship like a precious jewel. I'm not going to be a party to your degradation and come out of it covered in dirt from your sordid situation.'

His contempt had grown even stronger. Then it dawned upon Adozindo, and he suddenly understood Florêncio's stance. After all, he had always starkly envied his luck, his success in his conquests, his power of seduction over women. Now he could see that the angel had fallen, he was overindulging himself in the heady delight of grinding him into the ground.

Adozindo decided to be ungracious in defeat. The anguish of seeing himself isolated, beginning to be ostracised, bore heavily upon him. He had to have the last word.

'You always ate the crumbs I left. Now, it's a great big chunk you've got. But sooner or later you'll get to know what it really tastes like.'

'Get out of my house.'

'You scoundrel!'

Shown the door without more ado. He made a brief sign to A-Leng that they were leaving, and she, without making any comment, picked up her baskets with the pole over her shoulders. With his heavy case, he was unable to leave that wretched house with the dignity he wanted.

His kneecap hit the sharp edge of a chair leg made of dark wood, and he had to bite his lip in order to contain his pain. Not once did he look back and upon reaching the entrance porch, they heard the door slam shut behind them.

'He didn't even offer me a bowl of tea.'

He didn't answer her. An anger was gnawing away at him in which humiliation mingled with disappointment. Unable to control his fury, he suddenly took it out on A-Leng.

'At least put your clogs on. You only seem to know how to go around barefoot.'

The irritation in his voice shocked his companion. He had never drawn attention to the way she walked. But it wasn't the right time for domestic arguments. She bent over one of the baskets looking for her clogs, her vision blurred by the first tears of their life together.

PART TWO

16

*L*uckily a rickshaw appeared and the driver went to fetch another two, the third to carry the rest of their luggage. It was a caravan that attracted attention, but there was nothing to be done about it. Not knowing where to go, he thought of a hostel in the Rua das Estalagens, where, in more carefree times, he had enjoyed the company of girls from the red-light district. A-Leng, who didn't know the city, didn't say a word. She just followed him.

It wasn't a respectable place, more of a doss-house than anything else. But it was a resting place, where they could gather their thoughts and get their bearings. Quite simply, he couldn't go on walking all over town, with A-Leng following firmly in his footsteps with her baskets and buckets. It wasn't practical and it attracted a morbid curiosity that he wanted to avoid at all costs.

Once in their room at the hostel, he fell into the deepest depression. Florêncio's treachery had been a rude blow. He hadn't taken care to make more friends. On the contrary, he had irritated everyone with his boasting, and all he could expect now was a bellyful of laughter.

More practical and down-to-earth, A-Leng took the helm. She wasn't too fussy, the room at the hostel was even better that her hovel, and she adapted quite easily. Unlike him, she didn't complain about the lack of cleanliness, the smells, in which sandalwood and opium mingled, or about the noisiness of the street and the building itself. She wanted to know how much money they had to take care of their expenses.

She was a survivor from many a calamity. She had always led a hard life, and discomfort and lack of resources were part and parcel of her everyday life. She was used to having little and never dreaming of much.

She took a little bag out of her bundle, from where she produced some silver coins and one or two notes, money saved from carrying water from sunrise to sunset, a few objects made of gold, silver and jade, of little value, but that in happier times had satisfied her woman's vanity.

All together, they would have amounted to only a bit of loose change for a wealthy man, but they were very useful for an emergency. With what he had in his pockets and in the suitcase, which he had packed haphazardly but also out of divine inspiration, they had just about enough to stave off hunger for a while. But before anything else, they would have to leave the hostel, whose daily rate would soon absorb their meagre budget. The unmitigated austerity of their situation overwhelmed Adozindo who fell into a paralysing state of despondency.

'Lying around isn't going to solve the problem and won't feed us ... ' She murmured impatiently.

But he lay on the bed with its grey sheets, his forearm shading his eyes, without moving. He remembered the morning, the way things had happened so fast, the sudden, dramatic change to his day-to-day routine. He felt miserable, ashamed to go out and show his face in public, to run the gauntlet of 'his people's' judgement. The fallen idol.

A-Leng, on the other hand, was a woman of action. She couldn't bear her man's spinelessness. She shook and disturbed him. Didn't he know anyone who could put them on the right track? No, he couldn't remember anyone. Besides, they would treat him as his friend had.

'Well, I'm going out then.'

'Where are you going? You don't know the city.'

'I'm going to find a place to live. There must be some cheap houses around. I can ask. I've got a tongue to talk with and strength to walk. What we can't do is stay here doing nothing. No one's going to harm me for making inquiries.'

She went downstairs, past the staff of the hostel and other men who looked at her inquisitively. She wasn't the type of woman who usually frequented the place. She blushed when she guessed what they might be thinking of her, but she went out into the street without batting an eyelid.

She picked up snatches of conversation from passers-by about a new war between the Chinese and the Japanese in a far-off place called Manchuria. No one seemed to be particularly excited or alarmed, but people were voicing words of hatred against the enemy. A-Leng quickly focused on more urgent thoughts.

She hurried along alleyways, side-streets, lanes, and open ground. She returned downhearted from her long outing, exhausted and dirty, her frustration ready to boil over. All alone, without knowing the right places to go, her efforts had been in vain. She had come across houses, but they were either extremely expensive or they were very poor. She could have got herself fixed up easily, but the problem was him, her man, and his rich habits.

She found him in the same state of stupor, incapable of helping her, intractable and pessimistic. They exchanged their first bitter words and their ill-humour continued the whole night. Not even their evening meal, the only one they had on that day, raised their spirits. For the first time, they went to bed without touching each other. They hardly got any sleep, what with the noises in the doss-house and from the street.

Hardly was it light than she got ready to sally forth again. It was no good counting on him, nor did she try and insist, for he was a dead weight. By this time, she had a plan mulled over during the night. She didn't even bother to discuss it with Adozindo. She quickly tied up her braid and left, still sullen.

She had remembered a friend who no longer lived in Cheok Chai Un, one of the few who had left the quarter to marry the owner of a joss-sticks shop in the Rua da Barca and who supplied the Tou Tei Mio Temple.

They had been close friends and she, A-Leng, had helped her a lot in her marriage plans, giving her a much better prospect. She must feel some gratitude to her, and she was well out of reach of the Queen-Bee's authoritarian rule.

After a few inquiries here and there, she managed to find the joss-sticks shop in the Rua da Barca. Indeed, there was A-Soi behind the counter and her face lit up in a plump girl's smile at the surprise. Only when she began to notice A-Leng's dishevelled state did she display any concern.

Once she'd heard A-Leng's tale, she reproached her friend for her reckless behaviour, she who had seemed so sure of herself and indifferent to the boys of her quarter. But it wasn't worth wallowing in the past. It wouldn't resolve anything, what was done was done and they had to think of the future.

'Is he with you?'

'Yes, he is.'

'That's a good sign at least. *They* usually abandon girls like us. They just want us to pass the time and for a bit of fun.'

'He's not like that. He's very kind and loving. It's just that he's demoralised and I'm going to have to do everything if he's going to go back to being his old self. If not, he'll put the blame on me, and I'll lose him. And then ... I won't have anything. I need a house ... somewhere I can make a home.'

A-Soi hadn't forgotten the past and offered to help her. She knew people who might prove useful. The pressure of A-Leng's hands on her own was an eloquent sign of her gratitude. Half an hour later, she left her sister-in-law in charge of the shop, and the two women went out, their spirits now higher, just as in the days of their girlhood.

This time, the search bore fruit. They didn't have to walk round in circles, but went straight to a woman who earned her living by acting as an agent, taking a cut from the purchase, sale or renting of property. Her talk was honeyed, all sweetness towards the mistress of the joss-sticks shop, hardly casting a glance at A-Leng, who didn't look the type of customer who might have much to offer.

After the water-seller had nervously explained the circumstances, she made a wry face that showed little interest, but she also didn't want to alienate the owner of the joss-sticks shop, where she bought her supplies. If A-Soi were to act as guarantor for payment of the rent, she did indeed have a little house over in the direction of the Kiang Wu Hospital. It only had one floor, but it did have a loft. It wasn't the type of building where a *kwai* would normally live, but given the conditions, they couldn't expect anything more.

The three of them hurried to see the house. A-Leng liked it as soon as she saw it, but kept her happiness to herself so as not to push the rent up. It wasn't an old building and it was clear that it had recently been whitewashed. It caught the sun all day long in the front and the rear, depending on the time of day, and it was well ventilated and light inside. It also benefited from having electric light.

Above all, it was more spacious than the hovel in Cheok Chai Un, with a little patch of yard to dry clothes in, a view towards the uncultivated land that stretched through San Kio, Lamau and Sa Kong, and there was a public well nearby for the local residents. In fact the location of the house which faced towards the position of the sun suggested that the winds of fortune would be propitious.

They then discussed the rent, a wrangle that lasted half an hour, the agent raising the price of the goods, using all sorts of arguments, among which the new war, the two women defending their offer, by pointing out defects in the house and minimizing its value. As for the war, it was taking place so far away that they didn't feel its effects. The price of foodstuffs in the market hadn't gone up, had it?

They both suspected that the agent was also the proprietor, because of the ease with which she negotiated and the fact that she seemed to be in complete charge of everything. But they needed to keep to the custom of not giving way immediately, for otherwise there was no business to be done, only an imposition to accept.

They eventually agreed on a figure for the rent. There was no written agreement because the three of them were illiterate, and they believed in the spoken commitment, especially that of the guarantor.

A-Leng paid in advance and was overjoyed. Then, from a shop selling second-hand furniture, she hired a bed, a table and four chairs. That was all for the time being. She had packed the most important kitchen utensils in one of the baskets, when she had left her hovel. She breathed a sigh of relief. She had her own house and bed and was free of that disgusting hostel.

In her urgent need, she had taken a decision without her man's consent. Now it was done, whether he liked it or not.

She got back to the hostel when night had already fallen, and she had to avoid the heavily painted women who laughed as she walked by. She arrived even dirtier than the day before, her braid loose and covered in dust. Her feet hurt, blistered from not being used to wearing clogs, her body demanded rest, but her heart was beating serenely. Her friend hadn't failed her, like her man's friend had failed him. The situation could have been far worse.

His appearance immediately grieved her, for he was far from the elegant, confident boy she had fallen in love with. His chin was blackened by a growth of beard, his hair was ruffled, and his slovenly air suggested someone who had been vanquished. It wasn't what she wanted to see in him.

He was furious and starving, and he hadn't been out. He had suddenly felt deeply ashamed of his condition, and wanted to escape the mockery of those who knew him. He was sure that Florêncio wouldn't keep his big mouth shut in his effort to ally himself openly with Lucrécia. He looked at A-Leng with the eyes of a caged animal.

'I managed to get us a house. I've paid the rent and hired some furniture. We can sleep there tomorrow already.'

'You didn't even consult me. You do everything as you see fit. And I just agree with you.'

'No, I'm the one who will follow you wherever you go. But you don't move, you're weak like an invalid, and we don't have time. This hostel isn't a home for us. You brought me to a house frequented by whores. I don't want to be taken for one.'

And in a low voice, so as to lessen the harshness of her reply, she slid her hand down her braid and said:

'It wasn't a bad choice, considering what money we have. It's a quiet place, which I'm sure is what you want.'

He was being unfair and she didn't deserve such treatment. Her exhaustion was apparent in her face, dark rings under her eyes making her look older than she was.

'Your braid ... You're not looking after it ... '

She could hardly resist a laugh. So many important matters to see to and all he could think about was her braid, like a spoilt child whose favourite toy has been damaged.

'I'll treat it like a jewel when this is all over. I promise you.'

17

He hadn't adapted at all well to the house, which was short of comforts and far below the standards he was used to, and he couldn't hide his humiliation. On the other hand, he had to admit that it was better than the hostel or the hovel in Cheok Chai Un. Even the trench that served as a latrine was more inviting after it had been thoroughly sluiced with buckets of water. He remembered vividly how he had puked at the sight of the privy in the hostel, a true nightmare for someone who had grown up enjoying the highest standards of hygiene.

Living in the middle of the 'Chinese city', he enjoyed one advantage. No one was going to pry on him in his new way of life, out of curiosity or malice.

But he felt ostracised and his dejection tormented him, affecting his mood. He would explode in fits of temper over the most trivial matter, causing pain to his companion who was working herself to death to try and put some order into their life together. He considered himself a prisoner of circumstances that had gone far beyond what his shallow mind had been able to imagine. In his selfishness, he couldn't accept that there was no return to his carefree existence, with A-Leng firmly clinging to him, conscious of a right she had acquired. The pole, leaning apparently uselessly against the wall behind the door, was an eloquent reminder of the ever-present threat.

The hours crept by slowly, while she wrapped herself in silence, preferring to avoid any altercation that a passing word might provoke. But the brutal truth didn't pity him in his inertia and one night, before they went to bed, she declared:

'The money's disappearing and you've rested for long enough. You must find a job. If you don't, I don't know how I can keep us going.'

She spoke softly, but her reproach was implicit. And she continued in the same tone:

'Are you scared of presenting yourself to people, ever since your father stopped helping you? But we have the strength of our arms and our brain to work ... '

She was getting to the heart of the question, she, an uneducated woman, but with sufficient intelligence and good sense to understand. She used the first person plural to emphasise that they formed a unit, in both happiness and sadness.

He resisted the temptation to rant and rave, and kept quiet. Whatever he might say, she was right. He must work, the money was ebbing away before their eyes. Neither of them wanted to become destitute just because of his obstinacy. That night, not for the first time, they slept side by side, like two strangers.

In the morning, he got ready for his test. He was going to assess the effects of his act of folly. It was now his turn to walk all over town. With considerable inhibition, he knocked on various doors over a number of days. He was received neither well nor badly.

Jobs at a time when there was a crisis looming with the undeclared war between China and Japan? It wasn't worth thinking about. Jobs were not there for the asking, and there were a lot of dogs after one bone. They had queues of applicants on their waiting list, who had more experience and skills than he did. He'd need to be patient and bide his time.

There were vague promises, words, some more and others less well-disposed, and there was a lot of criticism. No one mentioned the water-seller, but they knew. All of 'Christian' Macao knew. Now, he was able to gauge how much antipathy his bragging and his flamboyance had caused, offending some and affecting others.

His malingering ways were common knowledge. And then there was his light-hearted attitude towards the daily routine, with a father who forgave him everything and turned a blind eye to his faults and lapses, ensuring that he remained a big child, even though he'd nearly reached the age of thirty.

Creatures like him didn't deserve to be taken seriously. They were just one more backside on a seat and not efficient. He, personally, had no credibility. It was his father who had that. Up until then, they put up with him because of who his father was. He discovered with horror that his handsome face and his nickname, the Handsome Adozindo, were of no use, and left him empty-handed. It was annoying but true.

He returned home dispirited, a look of despondence on his face after so many embarrassing incidents, and he didn't know how to give A-Leng any fresh hopes. It was enough for her to look at him, to be able to guess the results of the day. He arrived starving, full of irritation, and he never found any food that satisfied him. He was sick of A-Leng's frugal cooking, and hankered after the rich titbits of the Estrada da Victória, and he would lose his temper. It was horrible to be poor and downtrodden, with the prospect of destitution growing, day by day.

Everything made him rancorous. The house, the district, the dusty street of beaten earth, the neighbours, the smell emanating from the rubbish and the vegetable-gardens, the boisterous, grubby children who played on the open ground, screaming until nightfall, the weakness of the power supply that didn't provide enough light to read by. In his atrocious selfishness, he failed even to notice how he was punishing his companion, secretly blaming her for his situation.

Christmas and New Year's Day, which had no meaning for A-Leng, had passed like normal weekdays. He missed the festive period, and his yearning ground him down cruelly, with its burden of depression and sadness.

One night, three months later, his bitterness became even more extreme and vicious. That day, saddened because no one had agreed to see him, he had pawned his precious watch, the only article of any value he had left, with the premonition that he was going to lose it for good. He was in the depths of despair, pacing up and down like a caged animal, and all he could do was to find fault with everything around him, reinforced by sarcastic comments.

She, however, had reached the limits of her patience. Nothing she did seemed right. She had learnt to read her companion's mind, for she wasn't stupid. She couldn't read or write, but she was no fool. They had now got to know each other better. They shared the same bed and meal table, the long hours of silence, punctuated by acidic exchanges of words. They were divided in their habits, mentality, culture, food and tastes. They spoke different languages.

An ever wider abyss was being dug between them, and they were heading inevitably for a stage beyond which they would never find a way back. It was all the sadder for a poverty-stricken water-seller, who had lived so happily in the squalor of her hovel in Cheok Chai Un, a place she could never return to. If only he could try and heal the breach by some small act of generosity, no matter how hard that might be.

'Tomorrow, I'm going to start work ... '

'Lugging water?' He asked ungraciously.

'No, never again. I lost all my customers. I don't know anyone here because I'm a new arrival. I'm going to work in A-Soi's shop.'

'Why?'

'You know why. We can't wait for your job that never comes. I've got arms and legs too.'

The humiliation pricked him painfully, and anger gave him a bitter taste in his mouth. He wanted to hurt her too. He looked at her and at her braid, which was tied without any fuss or care, and he eyed her bare feet, soiled by the dust in the yard, saying:

'You're only happy when you're not wearing shoes.'

She sprung up as if she'd been prodded in the back. She wouldn't give him the satisfaction of losing her temper. After a moment, she replied coldly: 'I've always gone around barefoot and never felt inferior for it. I can't wear out the only pair of clogs I have, for no good reason. It's no shame for someone who's always had so little.'

Then suddenly, she launched forth in the same tone of voice, fixing him with her gaze, her chin raised:

'Why did you make such an effort to disturb me in my life, if you are so ashamed of me that you won't even walk down the street with me? I was happy in the life I led and the work I did, I had friends, I was a princess in my world, and my godmother's heir until I betrayed her trust. I lost everything too, but because I'm a woman, I lost much more than you.'

Yes, indeed, she missed the well and the gossip, her favourite braiding-woman who fixed her braid just as she liked it, unrivalled throughout the quarter. The trips to the market to buy fish and green vegetables, the fried snacks and broth in the little eating-houses. And then there were the evenings in the Queen-Bee's home, resting on her haunches and listening to stories and legends with rapt attention. And it weighed upon her conscience that she was barred from burning joss-sticks and worshipping at the Tou Tei Temple, and asking for the god's protection, as she used to do. What did she have now?

'Like you, I feel out of place here, although I walk barefoot.'

She cleared the table and the rest of the food, cold and wasted, bowls and chopsticks clattering together. She paused at the entrance to the cubicle that was their kitchen, and asked in anguish:

'Why?'

There was no answer. Adozindo lacked the courage to confess his reasons, and they would hurt each other even more if they debated the empty fiction, to which their relationship had sunk.

Adozindo went to the door and looked out at the starry night. He was overcome by tiredness and didn't want any more arguments. The street was deserted, only sparsely lit, and the neighbours had retired to their homes, from where the sound of occasional voices could be heard filtering through windows. Behind him, A-Leng bustled around feverishly. He preferred not to watch her in her domestic tasks.

'I was mistaken when I thought we were made for each other. It was a nice dream. But reality has made me wiser. I was just an object for a rich boy's amusement, and things went wrong. I hadn't thought of it like that, so I must take the blame for being so naïve. We're now so far apart. If we go on, nothing will remain except bitterness and we'll end up hating each other. I wasn't born to be yours.'

The girl spoke in the same flat tone, and she was very pale, holding back any evidence of stronger sentiments. Instead of domestic chores, she had packed her things into what was by now a smaller bundle. This was play-acting, she wouldn't have the nerve to leave, Adozindo thought to himself.

'If I had a rival, I would know what to do. But I'm struggling against lots of things that go beyond women, and I don't know how to describe them. Your being always unhappy, your disdain for this house, the best one I've ever had, your eyes like those of the imprisoned animal I saw, the only time I ever went to the circus. I don't want to be a burden on anyone. That's why I'm going ... '

'Going?'

'Yes, going. I'm taking half of the money we have left. And you don't need to worry about this month's rent and light, they're paid. Or if you prefer — and that would be the natural thing to do — you'll be able to go home to your parents, because I won't interfere. They'll all be very happy to see you free of me.'

'Where are you going?'

'To A-Soi's, where I'll be working from tomorrow. The house has room at the back and there'll be a corner for me. I don't ask for much. I've lived in worse places.'

'And will they take you in?'

'I'm sure A-Soi will. The husband might object. If they don't want to have me, I'll move on. I'll always find work. They say I'm pretty and I know I am, and a pretty woman can always find work. I'll start by cutting my braid off.'

'You won't have the courage.'

'You'll see.'

She was defying him, ironical and petulant, in the way she used to. He advanced towards her, but stopped himself when he saw the pole. She understood and said:

'The *tam-kon* is no use to me anymore. That and the buckets can stay. My days as a water-seller are over. I don't want any more memories.'

She wiped her eyes, shook her braid down her back and added:

'You know, it's useless trying to hold a body, when you don't hold the heart.'

She walked towards the door, very upright, holding her bundle in her arms, without looking at him again. She was leaving barefoot.

18

He didn't stop her leaving for he was sure she would come back. He smoked half a packet of cigarettes, watching the door and listening for the slightest sound, and he began to get worried. She hadn't been play-acting in order to soften him up and awaken his sense of pity. It had been for real.

'If that's how you want it, let's see which of us can last the longest.'

He went to bed somewhat unhappy and feeling rejected. She'd be back the next day, he murmured so as to convince himself. He woke up several times during the night, and found the other side of the bed empty. She'd even taken the porcelain cube she used as a pillow with her.

In the morning, the silence in the house devastated him, as if he had been punched hard. There was no hot water for him to wash or shave. There was no bread for breakfast. There was no one to iron his shirt or the unsightly creases in his trousers.

He was determined not to panic, that would be useless. He did things for himself with disastrous results, lighting the stove and dirtying himself with the burnt firewood, ignorant of how to control the smoke. He washed and shaved with half-cold water, cursing life all the time as he did so. He left home for another round of job hunting, wearing the previous day's shirt and his creased trousers, and hungry for a piece of bread. The decline of the Handsome Adozindo, who had never prepared himself for such emergencies, was obvious.

It was also a day full of frustration and humiliation. There were the same refusals, the same answers, after endless waiting. He envied the Chinese who could accept humbler jobs such as coolies, street-sweepers, bricklayers or carpenters, for no one batted an eyelid. But he, as a Macanese born and bred, was barred from descending to such lowly occupations, even if he were dying of hunger. He couldn't even work as a mechanic or an electrician. It would cause a scandal of gigantic proportions, he would be a laughing-stock, a figure of fun.

By the end of the morning, hunger was making itself heard in his empty stomach. For the first time, he yearned for A-Leng's wholesome cooking, for there was always some broth and a bowl of rice. But there was no one waiting for him at home.

He made up his mind. Ever since he had set foot in the street, he had been pursued by a yearning for fried eggs that had insidiously permeated his nostrils. He was going to Fat Siu Lau's, the most popular restaurant of the time for Portuguese food, to eat them, along with a succulent steak smothered in onions and fried potatoes. He stroked the money from his pawned watch. He would fill his belly for the rest of the day and save on dinner. Tomorrow was another day and, in his dejection, he needed new strength.

No sooner said than done. He sat down at a corner table on the ground floor of the restaurant so as to avoid the noise, and gave the attentive waiter detailed instructions as to what he wanted. He looked at no one, concentrating as he was on his rumbling stomach.

Fried eggs had never tasted so good with their whites crispy round the edge, the steak was thick and huge, with a mountain of onions and potatoes. He sensed he was smacking his lips, but he didn't care. He washed it all down with half a bottle of red that, on this occasion, was better than any of Santerra's fancy French vintages. He only calmed down after he had mopped up the sauce with his last bit of bread. Then, he looked up and around him.

At the next table was Valdemero, an old classmate from primary school, to whom he had never attached any importance beyond the occasional gesture of recognition in the street. He was smiling at him in a timid expression of sympathy. That softened Adozindo who, in recent times, had only encountered hostility among those from whom he had tried to seek help.

Valdemero was the same age as him, short and skinny, an innocuous clerk in the Harbourmaster's Office, a prudent, affable soul, happy in his job and not aspiring to anything more, for in that way he neither threatened nor envied anyone else. He was one of those 'transparent' people no one noticed in the street or at the office. In short he was what the Macanese called a *raspiate*.

As he was so meek and devoid of ambition, people abused him and forgot all about him. Whether he was present or not in a particular place, no one noticed or remembered him, so unassuming was he. But he had one quality folk never forgot when they needed him. He liked to be of help, within his limited range of possibilities. That's why his confessor had guaranteed him a place in Heaven, provided, of course, he didn't change.

In any other circumstances, Adozindo wouldn't have deigned to speak to him. He hated such mild-mannered men, spineless and open to manipulation for any purpose. He didn't express any opinions, and never contradicted anyone. He never caused any ripples.

But now, living as he did in isolation and yearning for some social contact, the pleasant smile had a profound effect on him. He felt an intense craving for company and, in spite of any misgivings, Valdemero at that point was welcome company.

'I was starving, but I feel better now.'

Valdemero, of course, was not aware of the bitter irony. He continued to smile, commenting on the excellent quality of the steak at Fat Siu Lau's. He felt flattered by the unexpected attention.

Adozindo attached himself to this insignificant soul, and loosened his tongue. It was almost a monologue, the other agreeing with everything. It was irritating, but in the absence of anything better, one couldn't be too choosy. At least he was able to become expansive, talking of inconsequentialities, for the pure love of hearing his own voice.

He invited Valdemero to sit at his table for coffee and a glass of Macieira brandy, which the other accepted appreciatively. After much chatter, he confided in him as if he were his best friend, complaining about life and his fellow men, and telling him that he needed a job. He had to get his bitterness and despair off his chest.

Valdemero listened, full of pity and then suddenly, looking somewhat embarrassed, interrupted him:

'Senhor Adozindo, sir, forgive me ... but I can get you some work ... It's not much, and it's lowly for your class of person, but at least it's a job.'

Adozindo's eyes opened wide. A job and from the humble Valdemero? He, with some agitation as he sat there, explained what it involved. At a pier in the Inner Harbour belonging to a Chinese shipping firm, they needed someone to monitor the movement of goods, someone who knew the language, who could deal with the port authorities, informing them what goods were being loaded and unloaded, and removing any difficulties or smoothing over any bureaucratic problems.

The manager of the firm was at his wits' end and had even asked him, Valdemero, to find someone for the job. If Senhor Adozindo wanted, he would go and speak with the person that very afternoon. He apologised for being so forward about it, but if he could contribute in any way to alleviate his current difficulties, he would do his very best.

'You were always very considerate towards me, Senhor Adozindo, sir. At school, you often allowed me to copy your work, and got me out of a caning or two. I haven't forgotten it.'

He certainly wasn't expecting that! He didn't remember ever showing him any consideration whatsoever, much less allowing him to copy his work. And it was that very same creature, despised by everyone, a *raspiate*, who was the first person to unselfishly show him a light in the darkness. He suddenly felt deeply ashamed and the emotion caused his throat to tighten.

'Is it for sure?'

'For sure ... I don't know whether it's for sure. But I'm going to speak to him right away. I've got time because I'm on holiday today.'

Adozindo paid the bill and went home, after giving him his address without the slightest shame. His mood had lightened, but he felt strangely sad when he remembered that A-Leng wasn't at home to receive the good news. He would have liked so much for her to be the first to know.

Within the solitude of his four walls, he whiled away the afternoon, waiting for Valdemero. Without knowing the answer, he wasn't going to subject himself to another round of humiliation. All in good time. He had suffered enough uncertainty for one day. He occupied some time tidying up his modest possessions, swept the floor, did some dusting and one or two other domestic chores. Then he sat down and gazed melancholically at the buckets and *tam-kon*.

He had eaten lunch in order not to have dinner, but his appetite had returned and he felt like chewing on something, knowing that he had no one to prepare a meal for him. In the silence, A-Leng's absence and the human warmth she provided began to weigh upon him.

Abandoned as he was, he could perfectly well have gone home to his parents. They would have taken him in. But he would go back vanquished, a broken man, bearing with him the evidence of his inability to look after himself. And anyway, he would show he had no strength of character, no self-respect. And he would never regain his lost prestige. He would be left with the burden of his annihilation as a man.

No, he couldn't go back under such conditions, after having lived three months of hell. He had learnt more about his fellow men, he had matured and was no longer interested in being the Handsome Adozindo. His beautiful face hadn't been much good to him ever since he had dared to challenge society's values by going to live with a barefoot water-seller from Cheok Chai Un. In the street, high-class girls, when he managed to catch their eye, looked away.

Valdemero didn't turn up as promised. This just meant that another hope had been dashed. He was alone again.

At that point he gave in to a fit of depression. Huge tears welled up and, as there were no witnesses, he sobbed out loud shamelessly. He lay down in bed and hid under the covers, but as a refuge, it proved useless. It didn't solve anything. The bed was infused with a womanly smell that he knew only too well and desired.

He stifled his sobbing, for it was just too absurd. It wasn't a time for weakness, he had to accept things as they were and to face up to his responsibilities. No one would come to his rescue, he had been banished from his paradise because he had dared to covet and possess the abundant tresses of a lustrous braid. How had he allowed himself to lose such a treasure and end up with nothing at all?

He recalled the famous words of one of Macao's clumsier native sons who, in an attempt to abandon the *patois* he normally spoke, tried to demonstrate his knowledge of Portuguese. He altered the original words in order to describe his own predicament and murmured to himself: 'God wish 'cos God he know. We did choose our path and there we goes.'

Yes, it was the only honourable and decent path to take, whether or not he got crucified for doing so. He felt relieved, as if a weight had been lifted from his chest, and he sat up and reached for a cigarette. The womanly smell was more penetrating than ever.

A-Leng.

It was very late, and in the darkness and with everyone behind closed doors, he wouldn't know how to find the joss-sticks shop. He would disturb the peace of the Rua da Barca, and create mayhem among those suspicious folk, who would summon the police with their whistles. Tomorrow, everything would be settled calmly. He urgently needed to find her, for she had said she would cut off her braid. But would she dare to? He didn't believe it. Much less that she would make use of her pretty face for any other profession. And yet he lit another cigarette, with gloomy thoughts on his mind. He grew angry when he imagined someone else caressing her.

He fell asleep and in a deep slumber made up for the tiredness resulting from the previous sleepless nights. He didn't dream, and he would have gone on sleeping well into the morning, if he hadn't been woken by repeated knocks on the door. He opened the door, bewildered and shivering from the January chill. It was Valdemero.

'Good morning, Senhor Adozindo, sir. I've brought some good news. The boss wants to talk to you. If you like it, the job's yours. I caught him very late last night, which is why I couldn't come sooner. Hurry, for it's good to give the impression you're punctual.'

If he were a woman, he would have kissed Valdemero. Then his enthusiasm evaporated as he exclaimed:

'Oh no! My shirt and suit are all creased. I wanted to turn up looking presentable.'

'That's okay, I know how to do the ironing. Where's your iron? It'll only take a minute and then we can go and have a bowl of hot broth. The boss will take another hour yet.'

19

*S*he had gambled everything when, carrying her bundle of things, she had left the house, deliberately treading in the mud and puddles in the street. She was taking a risk by abandoning him, but she couldn't see any better solution.

For three months, she hadn't had a moment of happiness. Only bad moods, silent rancour or unbecoming outbursts of anger. He was quite clearly ashamed of her, blamed her for his misfortune. It was too much!

If he still loved her as he used to, he would know how to find her. She still vaguely harboured such a hope, although he had not stopped her leaving. What she needed was peace of mind, a balm for her nerves, which had been severely tested. Once removed from that hellish existence, she could give more thought to the question of how to start a new life without him and away from Cheok Chai Un.

She chose the shadows, so that people wouldn't see her tear-stained face. For a water-seller also had feelings, in spite of being illiterate and barefoot. And she had pride too, to prevent her from becoming a mat on which all could wipe their feet.

Her friend was already prepared for the outcome, and welcomed her without any surprise. She asked no questions, but led her to the back of the shop where, among the baskets of joss-sticks, there was a canvas camp bed, with some blankets to protect her from the cold. There was a chill that rose from the bare floor, the smell of sandalwood was suffocating, and it was a gloomy corner that only increased her unhappiness.

She was worse off than in the hovel in Cheok Chai Un, but it wasn't a time for complaints. Her friend had already done a lot for her, and the main thing was that she didn't disturb her or the family who lived on the first floor. She was like the poor relative who was fed a bowl of soup in the joss-stick shop, in return for her labours.

Finding some solace in not having to sleep out in the open, she recounted her misfortunes. A-Soi listened to her, shaking her head, but not interrupting her. Only when the other stopped did she take her turn to speak.

She had made a huge mistake by getting involved with a *kwai*. She was a native of Cheok Chai Un and she should have stayed there, among her people, where she enjoyed respect and consideration, a truly favoured daughter. Who was the poor girl who had ever achieved the status of 'princess'? She was well loved among her folk, but she had dared deviate from the line, without any other guarantees. In a fit of madness, she had surrendered to the weaknesses of her heart.

'I know all this, A-Soi. You don't have to go over it again. These things happen ... they are beyond our control. It was all so different from my day-to-day life. I couldn't resist it, and nor could anyone else who had experienced his sweet ways. During all that time, he never made me feel like a water-seller.'

She was overcome with anguish, her head bowed, as she looked at her toes, bare and covered in mud. In a low, resigned voice, her tears welling up once again, she mumbled:

'I'm so fond of him.'

Her friend put an arm round her shoulder and their heads touched. There was nothing more to be said on the matter.

'Stay as long as you want because you don't disturb us at all. In fact, we need someone to look after the shop. My husband has to go out, and I have to look after our three little ones, who are a handful now.'

At least she now had a roof over her head. When she was alone, and before going to bed, she washed her face and arms, and paid particular attention to her feet, cleaning all the incrustations of dirt from them. She took her clogs out of her bundle, put them on and walked up and down. Then, she extinguished the feeble flame from the oil lamp and went to bed. Once again she realised she was worse off than in the cottage, but at least she would never go barefoot again.

The temperature was falling and the blankets were not enough to protect her from the cold. She couldn't get to sleep. She was troubled by the acrid smell of sandalwood coming from the joss-sticks. She missed the warmth of a body next to her, and the sound of manly breathing she had got used to. The only thing she could hear and that filled her with horror was the scurrying of rats in the old house and the persistent gnawing of cockroaches.

Next day was a difficult one. Her first thought, upon waking, was of her man. How was he going to get by alone with his domestic chores, he who didn't even know how to heat water? It would serve him right, and he would learn how important a woman's presence was.

She soon picked up the tasks of her new job, with A-Soi by her side. It was a busy shop, but it wasn't at all taxing. Sitting behind the counter or attending to the occasional customer, time drifted by very slowly. It gave her the chance to do a lot of thinking.

She still harboured the hope that he would turn up, all contrite, and ask her to go back. The hours flowed by, and people passed down the street in their thousands, but the figure she yearned for was not among them. Could he live without her, after all the beautiful declarations he had filled her ears with? Had he in fact gone back to his parents' house? She began to feel angry and resentful.

After the morning meal, which was taken together, the hours stretched before her monotonously. Customers came and went and she couldn't distinguish one from another. They were faceless people whom she attended with an automatic smile, without giving any of them much thought.

Some lingered in conversation with A-Soi, recounting the anxieties and misfortunes that they wanted to see exorcised, with the help of the gods, which is why they bought armfuls of joss-sticks. Others were in a hurry and bought one or two sticks, but all for the same purpose. Their general desire was for happiness, by which all human souls are motivated!

At this point, she became aware of someone staring at her. A heavily made-up woman in her thirties was openly examining her, appraising her face, her body, her feet and hands, as if she were judging an animal. She didn't like the forthright way in which she was being watched and was about to ask why, when the other spoke:

'You've got a beautiful braid. It's a pity it isn't combed in the right way. It's worth money. There are people who would pay a good price for it.'

'I don't want to cut off my hair.'

'Ah! But you've got a beautiful head of hair. It's thick and there's lots of it. The threads are brimming with health. It's worth money, and a lot of it ... I've never seen such abundant hair.'

She was better dressed than the other customers in the shop. She had gold teeth and jade earrings dangled from her lobes. She also wore bracelets of jade. Her *tun-sam-fu* was of shiny black satin, under her padded *min-hap*. She moved with small dainty steps and didn't seem interested in the bundle of joss-sticks she had ordered.

'I buy any head of hair I get offered. Then I treat them and sell them to people who don't have enough hair. You can't imagine the number of people who lack hair. Or at least, who have patches, the weaker threads that get left on a comb or a pillow. It's particularly common among rich people. I'm always getting requests, and their pockets are deep.'

She was circling A-Leng, admiring her braid with greedy eyes, as if it was some heavenly dish. It was irritating and made her feel uncomfortable. A-Soi looked at her friend anxiously, expecting at any moment a rude outburst.

'And the theatres! Impresarios are always asking me for braids so as to make hairpieces and wigs for the actors and actresses. Just recently, I harvested a good number of braids from the interior, in Canton and Hong Kong. Here too, among the fishwives and *tanka* women and the girls from the factories making fire-crackers, cigarettes and matches. It's strange how you come across the finest hair among poor folk. But I've never seen anything like your braid!'

Seeing A-Leng's hostile expression, her friend intervened, and calling her aside whispered:

'Don't treat her badly, she's a good customer. She's always buying joss-sticks for her devotions at the Má Kók Temple.'

The little woman resumed her banter, fascinated by the blackness of her braid. She contemplated it as if it weren't part of A-Leng's head. She spoke in soft tones:

'I've got a client who would pay a fortune for it. You only have to say yes, and she'll pay for it without question. She's very wealthy and will be grateful to you. You can only gain by becoming her friend. If you please her, you'll have a different future from the one you have here.'

Her eagerness for A-Leng's hair was so intense that she was offending the girl's shame. She instinctively held her braid as if to protect what was hers alone.

The little woman leant forward and spoke softly so as not to be heard by A-Soi and added:

'Don't think you'll be ugly without your braid. You're very pretty, with your cute face and that body of yours. You're not the type of girl to be confined to a joss-sticks shop. What hair you have left, I'll get it permed in the modern way and you'll look like a European woman.'

A European woman! Maybe then he wouldn't feel ashamed of her. The suggestion left an impression on her. Would she ever be able to wear dresses that left her legs showing and balance on high heels, when even the clogs she'd been wearing since the previous evening were so uncomfortable?

'Think carefully, little one. I'll come for your answer tomorrow ... '

And she glided towards the door, her purchases under her arm, her steps light and languid, a fragile doll, but full of the experience maturity brings. Once she'd gone, A-Soi rushed over to A-Leng, the nostrils of her flat nose twitching.

'Be careful of her. She procures girls, young pretty ones. She's silver-tongued, but dangerous.'

'I know what I'm doing.'

Lost in her thoughts, she then worked, bargained, haggled and helped her friend with her domestic chores, in a concentrated burst of effort. She toiled tirelessly in order to distract herself. He didn't show up. He could get by perfectly well without her. She was consumed by a man who had lost her and didn't deserve her. She kept passing her hand automatically and stubbornly over her sparkling braid.

As night fell, she was reduced to yet more despair. At that hour, when business had died down, her enforced leisure intensified her torment. Her eyes were dry, sunken, unable to produce a tear. But she didn't want to cry, for crying was a demonstration of weakness. She had to be strong.

She swallowed her evening meal without feeling hungry, then helped close the shop and put A-Soi's children to bed, envying her uncomplicated life. The husband wasn't very much to her taste and the mother-in-law was crabby, but A-Soi was happily putting on weight, and harboured no ambitions for anything more. In any case, although they treated her well, the joss-sticks shop was only a temporary resting place. She would never become an integral part of the family.

As on the previous night, she slept badly and trembled with cold, but she didn't dare complain. He hadn't come or sent any message whatsoever. He was sleeping between sheets and blankets, nice and comfortable in his parents' home.

She jumped out of bed, her mind made up. She would go with the little woman and sell her braid, because she no longer wanted it and it weighed her down like the symbol of a love that had vanished.

A-Soi tried to dissuade her, but she was determined and almost answered back angrily. She washed, put on her best winter *tun-sam-fu* and began her long wait. And by two o'clock in the afternoon, she was already getting irritated, when the woman arrived, waving a perfumed handkerchief, and apologising profusely with sweet words.

'I knew I could count on you and your good sense. You're going to earn good money and you're going to be even prettier.'

They went off together, the little woman insecure on her delicate little feet, A-Leng suddenly shy, unable to maintain a conversation. She didn't know where the other woman was taking her, nor did she ask. She wasn't happy. She was instinctively repelled by such company. Whoever saw them together would have assumed it was a 'madam' and her escort or maid.

They took short cuts by turning into narrow lanes and alleyways, the little woman ever talkative and unctuous. At the entrance to an alley near the Janelas Verdes, they stopped in front of a modest, glass-fronted establishment. It belonged to the braiding-woman.

'She's the best and most skilled in the city. She knows how to increase the value of the product.'

In Cheok Chai Un, she had always had her hair combed and braided on the corner of the street. She glanced round the establishment, admiring its luxuries. There were mirrors, large, comfortable chairs, so that one didn't have to crouch. The tools of the trade that she could recognise, were of the finest quality.

The prices must be high, given that the braider herself, who greeted the little woman with smiles, was dressed in expensive cloth, and had two assistants, who were also very pleasant. There was no one sitting in any of the three chairs. A-Leng was the only one being attended to.

The braider launched into a stream of appreciative exclamations, faced with such an abundant head of hair. In her job, she had braided a thousand women, but had never had such fine hair as this. She wasn't just saying this to please, her enthusiasm was genuine. Without any obligation, and placing her art above the mere idea of profit, she decided to comb the former water-seller as she had never combed anyone before. She drooled with delight, as she plunged her expert hands into that forest of jet-black hair.

For nearly three hours, A-Leng surrendered to extreme discomfort, submissive and delighted at the same time, in the knowledge that she was in good hands. The braider did what the others had done, but with more refinement and considerable care, using copious amounts of soap and the best wood oils, and with a supply of combs the like of which she had never seen.

Her threads of hair were pulled and stretched to meet the requirements of the styling, to the point where she bit her lip to prevent herself from crying out in pain from the pricking of her scalp. The thick knots were rolled and unrolled countless times until achieving the perfection demanded by the braider. Only then, pleased with her work, did she consider she had done justice to her efforts and skill.

'That's it, my young friend. You're very pretty and you'll drive the boys crazy. No one could have done a better job. From now on, I shall take great pleasure in looking after your hair.'

She contemplated herself unhurriedly in the mirror, mesmerized by the braid that filled her with pride. She hadn't felt so beautiful for months and she looked at herself with untiring self-absorption. Would he reject her if he could see her now, her braid swaying in response to the slightest movement, like a serpent of temptation?

The little woman's voice awoke her from her moment of magic and brought her back down to earth. She was in a hurry to leave so as to go and display her product. A-Leng felt her heart miss a beat and resented the loss of her dream. She watched her pay the fat price and followed her out, after thanking the braider.

'If she knew it was going to be cut off, she wouldn't have spent so much time on you. She might even have refused to do the job. But it looks marvellous. You're going to get a good price for it.'

How she hated her! It had taken her years to perfect her braid. She had grown up and become a woman with it. It had been and still was her source of pride. What right did that woman, almost a stranger to her, now have to consider her a mere item of merchandise, albeit a valuable one? And wasn't it the braid that had been the first of her features to fascinate him? If she still loved him, wouldn't she be losing him without further hope and for good, by committing the abominable act that was now being prepared? She remembered the way his lips brushed across the base of her braid and the nape of her neck, and she shuddered.

Her feet, constrained by her clogs, weighed like lead. They were walking slowly, reluctantly, to the point where the woman began to show her impatience. It was already night-time and they were being expected. She couldn't spend the whole day seeing only to her. The note of irritation in her voice silently fed the girl's hostility.

She was vaguely aware that they were in the Rua de Nossa Senhora do Amparo, where she often bought peanuts, which she liked. They stopped in front of a green two-storey building, with a wrought iron balcony along the whole of the front, decorated with pots of dwarf plants. The little woman rang the doorbell and A-Leng, nervous, didn't know whether she should go in or make her escape.

What later remained in her memory was confused and blotted out by later images. She remembered she had climbed a steep flight of stairs and found herself in a room, which was well lit by gas lamps, and which smelt of sandalwood coming from the incense burner on the altar of some heroic god.

It was a place that was predominantly female, for all she could see were women. Half-a-dozen of them, young girls, in satin *tun-sam-fus* of various gaudy colours, their hair short and curly, in tight locks, all of them wearing heavy make-up, which contrasted with the simple modesty of the former water-seller.

Among them, she saw a hideous old woman who got up from a large dark-wood chair, and made her way avidly towards her. Her face was a mask of red and white zinc, with two black lines where her eyebrows should have been, a face that desperately lusted after its faded youth. Neither the earrings that dangled glitteringly from her lobes, nor her other adornments of jade and gold could save her from her sad, inexorable decrepitude.

Moreover, because she was among women, far from any male gaze, she hadn't bothered to cover her head, which was practically bald, possessing only a few greying tufts of dry, brittle hair. One didn't need much intelligence to realise who the recipient of A-Leng's healthy, lustrous braid was going to be.

The girl had a feeling of nausea in the pit of her stomach. Attention turned towards the precious product, while the other women clapped their hands hysterically, as if their landlady's happiness were assured, and the little woman immediately started to negotiate, now oblivious to A-Leng's presence.

The old woman approached, taking tiny steps on her deformed feet, her hands clasping lustfully, ready to feel the braid, as if it were already her property, her eyes wide with amazement, her blood-red lips cracked open. At the same time, she nodded her head, approving the price that had not been agreed with A-Leng, now reduced to nothing more than an object, an amorphous, obedient being, surrounded by a group of harpies besmirched with the sickly syrup of flattery. Another minute and it would be the end.

'No!'

Her cry of protest silenced the murmur of voices. She had instinctively stepped back, clutching her braid as if to defend it, all the more so as at that very moment, the little woman took out an enormous pair of scissors, which glinted feebly in the gaslight.

'What's this?'

'Don't touch me. I don't want my braid cut off. I forbid it ... '

'Now you tell me? After you made your promise and I spent my time and money?'

The old woman let out an angry growl, used as she was to her passive young girls. These threw themselves forward, as if responding to a tacit command, but stopped because of the sudden assertiveness of the girl whom they assumed to be as timid as a meek young lamb.

A-Leng missed her *tam-kon*. In a trice, she threw aside her clogs and she was the same vigorous girl who had given the four hoodlums a good hiding. Let them come for her, for she was ready to get even. She looked scornfully at the scissors, inanimate in the little woman's hand, indifferent in her indignation to the danger she was in.

'Slut! ...'

In response to this vile insult, she unleashed her fury. She ranted and raved. She knew full well what sort of a place this was, who the old woman and the others were. She'd been tricked by a whoremonger. So who was the slut? Magnificent and fearless in her wounded pride, her braid undulating like a whip, she became a true, independent daughter of Cheok Chai Un, pouring forth a litany of oaths and insults, worthy of a rascal from the streets of her own area.

When she had finished cursing them, she took a handful of silver coins from her purse, which she kept inside her *kebaya*, counted them out and placed them on a side table.

'That's the money for the braider and the tip. I don't owe you anything else.'

She turned on her heel in the midst of what was still a stupefied hush, and descended the steep stairs, stamping her clogs as she went. She slammed the door and once in the street, skipped with joy. She had saved her braid and was once more the 'princess' of Cheok Chai Un, albeit in exile.

There were occasions when blunt truths had to be said, in strong, ugly language. Only then could the weight on one's heart be lifted and one's spirit sing, at peace with the world.

She stopped a flower seller who was on her way home with a tired air, and bought three yellow champac flowers. She stuck them in the top of her braid, while she made her way, with a lightness of step, back to the joss-sticks shop, swaying her hips, free like some pagan nymph.

20

The shipping company was situated right on a dilapidated old pier, which was badly in need of repairs. It wasn't very grand, much to Adozindo's disappointment, but then his opinion changed when he saw how busy it was.

Apart from an ancient, tiny cargo boat that travelled the triangular route between Macao, Hong Kong and Canton, there were two sailing ships belonging to the company that served the ports along the shores of the Pearl River delta.

Stevedores and coolies, men and women, all subjected to the same arduous work, were carrying heavy packages on their backs, with rapid steps, and in response to the bellowed commands of the supervising foreman. A strong smell of the sea hovered in the air, bringing back fond memories to Adozindo of mornings spent fishing. On the muddy waters of the river, *tankas* gathered and bobbed around the larger craft.

They went into the office which was a shed built on the wooden planking of the pier, and consisted of two rough desks, one or two chairs and a cupboard, totally lacking in any comfort, and with an unkempt air. On the walls made of thin planks, there were only Chinese calendars and a gaudy print of a famous actress from Canton. The surroundings once again left Adozindo dispirited, although they protected him from the cold wind coming off the river.

Behind the main desk sat a Chinese, wearing an austere winter *kebaya* and fixing him with a penetrating look. He immediately guessed that this was the boss, for Valdemero stepped forward very nervously to introduce him.

The man got up to shake his hand, which was a sign of good manners. He was a well-covered man, with short hair, few signs of a beard on his face, and with the smooth skin of a woman. But his voice was unmistakeably deep and he was above average in height.

For some time, he listened to Valdemero's words, as he sang his friend's praises, in his anxiety to satisfy Adozindo's claim. It was all an exaggeration, but it sounded convincing and even moving. Eventually, he put up his hand to stop the torrent of words and began to ask the applicant direct questions in Cantonese, for he spoke neither Portuguese nor English.

He nodded appreciatively when Adozindo answered his questions fluently in the same language. So they could understand each other, which was a useful discovery for both. And there was more to it than that. He had expected a simpleton, but what he had before him was a refined, educated boy, with the clear facial signs of being from a good family.

'You speak well.'

'When I was at primary school, I had a good teacher who taught me how to speak Chinese ... But as far as the writing is concerned, I've forgotten almost everything.'

They chatted for about twenty minutes. The Chinese didn't ask for references nor did he ask any indiscreet questions. He realised instinctively that the boy would only accept the humble position offered out of extreme need or because of the pressure of some adversity, for it was below his level of skill and education.

He didn't reveal what he was thinking. He could very well test the boy's competence, given that he seemed to know about the work of a shipping agency, over and above the mere recording of goods loaded and unloaded. At the same time, Adozindo avoided any mention of his father's firm, in case Wong Sang (Mr. Wong) knew him, and decided to ask embarrassing questions that might prejudice his chances. It was imperative for him to get a job.

Once the working conditions and the salary had been agreed, Adozindo started his duties immediately and soon learnt the tasks for which he was responsible. These weren't very hard and the only inconvenience was having to be outside in the sun and rain, when the ships were arriving or leaving. A physical effort he would have to put up with. A man in need doesn't argue.

So this was how Adozindo got the job he longed for. He had money guaranteed at the end of the month, which removed the painful sensation of being a parasite. Curiously, he yearned to be able to tell A-Leng his news, to see her smile with happiness. He was no longer ashamed to return home empty-handed. Valdemero was a blessed friend, and he squeezed his fragile bones in a bear hug.

'Senhor Adozindo, sir, I don't deserve it ... I just did my duty as a grateful friend.'

Valdemero was at a loss for words in the face of such a compliment. He wasn't in the habit of receiving them. He was so happy that he invited Adozindo right there, to have lunch at a *fan-tim* near the pier, a place that didn't pay too much attention to hygiene, and that was frequented by sailors.

Adozindo couldn't escape the invitation without offending and anyway, the cold and his renewed hope had given him the appetite of a wolf. He didn't disappoint Valdemero, and ate like a glutton.

The afternoon dragged on unbearably. His patience was running out. As he waited for the arrival of the boat from Ko-Mun. He was grateful for the company of the faithful Valdemero, who hurried to correct or smooth over any problems arising from his first day at work. His initial joy began to wear off, to be replaced by anxiety and foreboding. She must have convinced herself that he wasn't going to come back. Would she then, in an act of rashness, cut her hair as she had threatened to do?

He couldn't imagine her without her braid. She would look like some of those women stevedores or dockside porters, bent double under the weight of their bundles, their hair short and grubby, cut off roughly by the steely harshness of a pair of scissors. This tormenting prospect made him nervous, and he kept glancing at the river, searching for the boat.

Night had fallen when he left the pier. Valdemero was still there, ever-present, constantly reassuring him that everything was going well, that the boss was pleased and the job guaranteed. Surprisingly though, he didn't pester him, he wasn't annoying, and he knew how to take a back-seat when necessary. When all was said and done, he was a good companion.

Adozindo dragged him along, insisting on his presence, for he wanted to introduce him to A-Leng as the bearer of good fortune who had unselfishly contributed to their happiness. He deserved such consideration, another gesture that Valdemero was delighted to accept.

There were still some joss-stick shops open in the Rua da Barca. A question here, an inquiry there, and they found A-Soi's shop easily enough, with its door now half-closed. When Adozindo saw the plump little woman, seated right by the entrance untroubled by the cold, as if she were waiting for someone, he was left in little doubt that she was A-Leng's exalted friend.

The sudden appearance of two *kwais* gave A-Soi a fright, but then she realised who the younger and taller of the two was. In fact, Adozindo asked straightaway for A-Leng. No, she wasn't there, but she'd be back soon. She didn't know where she'd gone, she was waiting for her so that she could close the shop. There was a touch of uncertainty in her voice that he fortunately didn't notice.

'Has she cut her hair?'

'No, when she left, she still had her braid.'

'It's a beautiful feature of hers ... '

'She's got other beautiful things too.'

'I know ... '

A-Soi lent over the counter, to try and control the apprehension that was patent in her face. The boy was attaching too much importance to the braid and she had gone out precisely to have it cut off. What would his attitude towards her be once the damage had been done? What other commitments would she have given the unctuous woman, whose identity she was too inexperienced to have guessed?

She offered them some seats and invited them to sit down, when she came to the conclusion that they were in no hurry to leave. Then she brought them two bowls of tea, as tradition demanded, and the three of them sat in tense silence. A-Soi's husband came down, was told what it was all about, and now there were four of them, sitting there staring at each other.

'She's late. Where can she have gone? She doesn't know her way round this part of town very well.'

A-Soi was impressed by Adozindo's concern. So many bad things were said about *kwais*, but this one at least was very pleasant.

'Macao is a peaceful place. No one will harm a working girl like her,' said A-Soi's husband good-naturedly.

'In China, there's a war that's getting more and more violent. A lot of newcomers have come through the Portas do Cerco into Macao.'

'Those are rumours. China's very big and the war's far away. It's in the north and in Shanghai. It won't get as far as here for a long time, although we're going to suffer the consequences. The price of rice has already gone up in the market. That's the work of speculators.'

'In Hong Kong there have been disturbances ... '

'That's only against the Japanese community. It's natural. Feelings are running high because of the atrocities. Here in Macao, there aren't any Japanese.'

He was wrong. There was the dentist at the beginning of the Rua Central and his family. But Adozindo didn't say anything. The little man was always smiling and had fixed his teeth, just as he had everyone else's in the Christian city.

Criticism of the Japanese continued, but by now addressed only to Valdemero, who as usual agreed with everything. Adozindo came and went, peeping out into the street, his hand shooting automatically to his pocket, feeling for the watch he no longer had. A-Soi watched him, beads of nervous perspiration running down her back, as she pictured her friend with her new European-style hair.

Then suddenly, A-Leng was at the door, gasping for breath, her face red from the effort of her hurried journey, looking at the group in astonishment. A second's pause and A-Soi burst out laughing, guffawing uncontrollably. She leapt up and rushed over to give her a hug, still laughing.

'You didn't ... '

'No, I just couldn't. I would have lost everything ... '

'Just as well. You've regained ... '

Those words escaped Adozindo's understanding, comforted as he was by a feeling of warmth and tenderness. There she was, safe and sound, with her best *tun-sam-fu* hugging her slender shapely body, her beautiful Chinese face gazing at him intensely, her black braid sparkling bluish flashes, the sensual perfume of the champac flowers dispersing from her, and her feet subject to the discipline of her pair of clogs. He felt an intense desire to hug her to his breast, all their disagreements now forgotten, and murmured to himself with deep conviction:

'I'm so fond of her ... I love this girl.'

Valdemero could hardly conceal his surprise. So this was his friend's great 'passion'! He wasn't surprised that his father and the family wouldn't forgive him and that he had been the target of society's disapproval. What foolery! Yet she was attractive, shapely, with curvaceous hips, eyes that pierced with the soft shine of velvet, oh yes, there was no doubt about that. And his esteem for his friend and his generous heart increased still further.

'I've got a job. My friend here got it for me. The salary isn't much, but with a bit of care, we'll get by. Our most urgent worries are over and we can begin to live a life.' He went over to her and added:

'I wanted to tell you before anyone else, but it didn't seem right to ask for time off on the first day. And I couldn't send you a message via my friend here, because he didn't know you, or where you were living.'

He gave more details, sensing that he was gaining her respect. Her expression became gentler as his good news flooded her ears. He had come back to her. So he had come back after all.

Fingering the edge of her sleeve, he said with humility:

'The house is cold without you.'

'It wasn't me who made it cold ... '

'That's true. But you left and took the sunshine with you.'

A-Leng looked at her friend. Wasn't she right? He knew how to say such beautiful things that softened the spirit.

'Shall we go?'

And he gave her a smile, the Handsome Adozindo's irresistible smile. She was showered with words of encouragement and reconciliation by her friend and the husband, but she barely heard them, for she had already been won over. She withdrew to the back of the shop and, minutes later, reappeared with her bundle hanging from her arm.

'Thank you for everything ... Tomorrow I'll be back to help you.'

Once in the street, Valdemero took his leave of them. Two's company, three's a crowd. And off he went, happy with A-Leng's words of thanks ringing in his ears. They set off, alone at last, she three steps behind, according to Chinese custom. He stopped. As he had decided their way ahead was together, things had to change. He spoke as if issuing an order:

'Don't stay back there. Your place is by my side. You must get used to it.'

She welcomed his order with a sweetly bewitching and submissive glint in the eye. She broke the rigid code of behaviour, ignoring the looks of censure from passers-by, as she flaunted her intimacy with him. Her clogs tapped lightly on the shiny cobblestones, as if they were floating along.

Suddenly, Adozindo heard voices ahead, talking in Portuguese and *patois*. It was a group of Macanese folk, women as well as men, who had come from a dinner in some *cou-lau* on that side of town. This was the test he knew he would have to face one day when he was with A-Leng in public. He recognised their faces, for he had been a regular visitor in the old days to the house of one of the women, and had even flirted with one of the girls in the group at a dance.

His heart missed a beat and he felt awkward, but he controlled himself, revealed nothing, and pretended not to notice them as he leant over A-Leng and took her bundle for her. The group said nothing as they passed by, but left in their wake a buzz of gossip. 'We did choose our path and there we goes.'

Then she broke another taboo. She clutched his wrist with both her hands, like a meek and gentle child seeking guidance, passive and vulnerable. And so they walked on.

The house was cold and dark, lacking human warmth. But anyway, it was their home, and as they went inside, it didn't seem as poor to them as it really was. She leant against the door and her first words rippled mildly forth:

'We're together again. Teach me how to live with you and I will teach you how to live with me.'

Then she touched her *tam-kon* and arranged it more securely along with the buckets, relics from the past and from the beginning of their adventure. As she bent over, her braid rolled off her back, revealing its abundance of perfectly formed knots, the glint of wood oil, and its even length.

'I've never seen your braid looking so beautiful! Did you know I would come back?'

'Yes, I knew you wouldn't let anyone else have it. And if you did, I would never be happy again. I've got used to you.'

She would never tell him all that had happened that day, and the risks she had run. She nestled in his arms and offered herself to him in all her vibrant sensuality. While they caressed, he kissed the first knot of her hair, breathing in the scent of the champac flowers concealed on the back of her neck.

With a groan of pleasure, she wound the braid round his neck and drew him to her as she lay down on the bed. Then, with a mischievous smile, she led him to possess her. Adozindo made passionate love to her with such energy that she, unfettered and unashamed, cried out, waking the shocked neighbours.

21

One evening, when he got home from work, he found her singing as she huddled over the board, pressing his white shirts with the wood-burning iron. That same morning, she had woken him with the same catchy song, which left him truly mystified.

An unpleasant experience suffered in the middle of town was still weighing upon him. He had come face to face with his father, who had made a point of stepping away from the pavement so as to avoid passing him, his ungrateful reprobate of a son, who had set up home with that 'whore from Cheok Chai Un'. It was an unnecessary affront, all the more so as it happened in front of bystanders who would relay the incident.

As disaster never strikes once, a few minutes later he encountered Lucrécia and Florêncio, the latter loaded down with packages, like a servant at his mistress's beck and call. It was an exceedingly unpleasant meeting, and one that he was unable to avoid, so sudden was it.

He hadn't seen her since the night he had left her after the dinner fiasco. He had been incapable of giving her any explanation, which she wouldn't have accepted anyway. There was no excuse for his behaviour, and as far as she was concerned, he had slipped and fallen into the mire of filth and slime. Smitten by a sense of revulsion, she had eliminated him from her memory for ever, severing at root any lingering affection for him, so offended was she.

'Let him carry his cross and bear it, the pig!'

She would never forgive him, for his insult had been too great, so much so that she was going to marry Florêncio, that artful scavenger of the Handsome Adozindo's leftovers, and the date had already been fixed. All this he had found out from Valdemero, who told him all the news of the Christian city. It was a scorned woman's revenge.

She looked regal and resplendent, brimming with opulence, enveloped in a cloud of French perfume. She didn't even bother to cast him a glance, laughing and talking to the weary Florêncio, who was having trouble keeping his balance under all those packages, while at the same time forcing himself to smile at his fiancée. The rogue looked well-dressed and well-fed. A bitter taste came to his mouth, not because he envied Florêncio, or because, at one fell swoop he had lost the wealth that was his for the taking. It was merely because he couldn't compete with them in terms of his appearance. He was no longer the dapper young lad of impeccable taste. His shoes were worn and scuffed, and beyond polishing. His suit was second-hand, bought in a junk shop, a suit that had belonged to someone else, and no matter how smart it might be, didn't fit him well. The others, the ones he had brought from his parents' house, were so moth-eaten, so out of fashion, that he was ashamed to wear them. The taste of humiliation accompanied him all the way home.

A-Leng's singing, in imitation of an actress from Chinese opera, revealed a secret joy. What astonished him was that she was satisfied with so little. She said she'd never lived better, she had a proper bed to sleep in instead of wooden boards, a table and chairs for meals and a fully sprung armchair for her man to sit in and read. She didn't mind about the quality of her modest *tun-sam-fus*, but she did care about her braid, her only luxury. She wore flat-heeled cloth slippers adorned with cheap sequins, because that was how she liked them. The quality of the food had improved because there was more money, and she cooked Macanese dishes that Valdemero taught her how to do. She had no complaints about her present life, because she had never known anything better.

He didn't interrupt her. He accepted the hot towel and bowl of tea she handed him, as always, when he arrived home. He sat down in the armchair, opened the newspaper he hadn't yet read, stretching out his legs while she pulled his shoes off and replaced them with slippers. Would Lucrécia one day do this for that rascal Florêncio? He doubted it, and felt any rancour slipping away. This was his compensation.

Nothing had changed in their everyday routine. She had come home early from the joss-stick shop and, busy with her ironing, had not yet got round to making dinner because she hadn't expected him back at that hour. Out in the little yard, she began singing again as she collected in the washing.

If only she would sing a melody he could understand rather than the ones with the screeching, falsetto sounds. She probably wasn't singing at all badly because she varied the tone of her voice with subtlety. The problem was that she had no appreciation whatsoever of western music. She had no ear for it and it didn't appeal to her emotions. She told him he was mad when he warbled tuneful snatches of opera while he was shaving. In this, they agreed to differ.

'What's the matter? You're very jolly ... '

'I am, and I've got reason to be. But I'll only tell you about it when we go to bed.'

The impish expression on her face sharpened his curiosity. He found her beautiful, with a natural grace that made her ever attractive. He held her calloused hands and pulled her towards him, plunging into the warmth of her firm body. He would never tire of her. That was his compensation, he repeated to himself.

'I'm not letting you go until you tell me what it is.' He tickled her and she screamed and wriggled and they ended up in a long smooch. Later, docile and coquettish, she murmured:

'Soon, I won't be able to show my braid in public ... It won't look good ... '

'Why?' He exclaimed, frowning.

She burst out laughing and shook her head at his slowness to understand. And she said:

'I visited the master healer. He confirmed what I suspected. I'm going to have a baby.'

He jumped up. It shouldn't have come as a surprise, but it did all the same. He knew she had taken the necessary precautions at first, drinking certain teas, but then she had naïvely forgotten. It must have happened on the night of their reconciliation. It was not a convenient time to have a child, for all sorts of reasons.

'What ... Aren't you happy?'

'Yes, of course ... but to get the news so suddenly.'

'So suddenly? Don't we live together? I was beginning to get worried. I was so scared I might be sterile. But I'm not ... I'm not. I'm going to have a child and it's yours.'

He realised why she was so happy. Being a mother would reinforce her position with the man she shared her life with. If she were sterile, then according to the logic of her culture, she would have to surrender her place to another woman. That was A-Leng's secret fear and source of anguish. For a couple, the most important thing was the continuation of the family. Everything was different now. Her belly was going to perpetuate her man's name.

A child! For most of the night, Adozindo gazed at the profile of the woman sleeping peacefully next to him, with no concern for questions of honour, for scandal or shame. For her, it was all very simple, the most natural thing in this world, when a man and a woman lived together.

Had it come at an inconvenient time? Well, everything would fall into place later, as was the case with so many couples who were much poorer than them. He had seen it in Cheok Chai Un, where children survived and proliferated, despite all the hardships. One couldn't expect any other thought from an uneducated water-seller.

In the following days, he concealed the anxiety that was afflicting him. There was still time, it was still an undefined foetus, a piece of flesh without a soul. There were plenty of women in town who would carry out an abortion, and Valdemero could help him find the best and cleanest one.

The thought made him disgusted at himself. Then, he lacked courage to suggest such a course of action to the happy mother who sang the same Chinese song over and over again. He wouldn't be able to face her scorn, and she would abandon him, disillusioned, just as she had done before.

He was going to have to bear it, as the widow had affirmed with such supreme disdain. Yet another painful step, along with all the others. No doubt this would be another blow to his family's pride. The concubine, bearing an offspring 'from the filth of the gutter'.

Weeks passed and the ungraceful characteristics of pregnancy began to manifest themselves. She was vomiting all the time, found the smells of the house and the street suffocating, she was peevish and irritable one moment, and flirtatious and loving the next. For the first time, she timidly admitted that they could do with a better ventilated house.

Touching her belly one night, he felt the foetus stir. Whether or not it was his imagination, it was as if he had received an electric shock. He was deeply moved, and a sense of exhilaration rendered him speechless. What she was carrying in her womb was his, very much his, just like the beautiful mother and the braid.

No, his conscience told him he wasn't behaving well. It was not right of him to keep A-Leng in a permanent state of concubinage, much less to turn his child into a bastard or a 'child-behind-the-door' or a 'child-behind-Lapa'.[5] His religious sentiments, which came from a Catholic upbringing devoted to processions and an early introduction to catechism, wouldn't allow such a solution.

'Let's get married.'

'Married? But aren't we already married? Don't we live together?'

'As far as my folk are concerned, we're not married. No one acknowledges you as my wife.'

'What am I then, if I'm not your wife?'

'We need to go through a ceremony.'

'That's not necessary. We'll spend a lot of money and we don't have any to spare.'

'It's not that, A-Leng. For my people, in order to be married, we have to go to church and stand before a priest.'

'But I'm not a Catholic.'

'But I am ... '

---

5.   Both expressions from Macanese Portuguese referring to births out of wedlock. Lapa is an island adjacent to Macao.

She opened her eyes wide in surprise. She hadn't understood very well. He had been rejected by his family and friends, and had no obligations to them or to his world. Exactly like her. Poor people didn't need any ceremonies. They got together and they were married and made children together. When they had more money, the most they did was to throw a dinner for their relatives and friends. And that was that, all very simple. Why did they need to go to a *kwai-lo* church to confirm a fact that everyone knew about?

She had never felt demeaned because she lived and slept with him. Folk were right when they said *kwai-los* were complicated, with obscure laws and customs.

It was more difficult to explain to her that, if they weren't married, their son or daughter would be a bastard. She was appalled. Among the Chinese, there were no illegitimate children, for they were all recognised as their father's children, whoever the natural mother might be. If they were a concubine's children, the mother was always the first wife. They would never be children without parents, that was for sure.

'You will cease to be my lover and become my wife, according to law. And you're complaining? Won't you think of the child?'

It was then that A-Leng missed the Queen-Bee's wisdom. She was a woman of great experience, and would know how to clarify things like no other could, for she had lived so long. But there was no question of going to consult her.

She confided in A-Soi, who advised her to comply with her 'husband's' desire, even though she disapproved of the foreign ritual. There were, on the other hand, advantages. Marriage in a church was a very serious thing and gave her greater guarantees. The man couldn't legally have concubines, while among the Chinese, she could see for herself, a man could have as many concubines as he liked.

'I'll use my pole,' commented A-Leng ferociously.

'When men want to, no manner of pole across their backs will stop them.'

Eventually, her practical sense made her reach a final decision. If he wanted it and the world of the *kwai-los* required it, there was no solution but to agree to it, for the sake of peace and quiet. She shared her life with one of them, wasn't that so? So that was how, with some reluctance, she consented to embrace her man's religion. A-Soi comforted her:

'What's got to be, has got to be. Take some joss-sticks from here and go to the temple to placate the gods. Explain to them why you're doing this and you'll go home at peace with yourself.'

She accepted her friend's words. As she was barred from the Tou Tei Temple, right in the heart of Cheok Chai Un, she walked all the way to

Mong-Há, to the Kun Yam Temple. Before the image of this gentle Goddess of Mercy, she lit the joss-sticks, knelt, touching the floor with her forehead and explained the circumstances, instinctively placing her hands on her belly. Then she felt an inner peace and went home.

The Chinese priest of the church of São Lázaro, known as the church where 'New Christians'[6] worshipped, was persuasive and patient in the conversion of this pagan soul. Adozindo could never be sure whether the basic tenets penetrated A-Leng's spirit and established themselves firmly there, or whether they merely remained skin-deep. He was just in a hurry, and wanted to be at peace with his God, in case she gave birth in a state of sin. He often went and asked the priest about the girl's progress. The priest gave him an amiable smile so characteristic of his race, and answered in the elegant Portuguese of the S. José Seminary: 'Be patient ... Rome wasn't built in a day.'

At this point, he was given a substantial rise at work. He had won the confidence and friendship of his boss. Instead of being out in all weathers and at all hours, depending on the arrival and departure of the boats, Adozindo went to work in the company's office, and had a desk and a typewriter.

His duties were no longer limited to shipping, and extended into other activities that Wong Sang, still a small-time capitalist in the area, was involved in. He was an interpreter and secretary, and at the same time, wrote letters, drew up requests and applications and contacted the authorities. His responsibilities required him to meet individuals who had rejected him, but now in a different position.

The leap in his salary for the better enabled him to think about another house. It was his wedding 'present' to A-Leng, a modest two-storey building, at a reasonable rent, with a small yard and private well, adequate sanitary arrangements and a larger kitchen. A-Leng was dazzled, for she had never known better, and she asked whether they could afford such 'luxury'. They could if they kept a close watch on their coppers, he replied, with a large, magnanimous gesture.

Before finally agreeing to it, she called for the *feng shui* geomancer who, after examining the place patiently, declared himself happy with the propitious winds that the building attracted. Then, A-Leng asked:

'Don't you think we should only move in on the day we get married? It will be a good start.'

'Yes, I think that's a good idea.'

---

6.   Chinese who had embraced Catholicism.

22

heir wedding was a simple affair, devoid of any pomp, and followed straight after A-Leng's baptism, in which she received the name of Ana, which was easier for her to remember. It was eight o'clock, one weekday morning.

He had always dreamt of a stylish wedding, a church brimming with high society, there to catch a glimpse of the Handsome Adozindo's chosen bride, the girl who had managed to drag the eminent Don Juan or Casanova to the altar. And afterwards, a sumptuous reception, with dish after dish of savouries and sweets cooked up in the best culinary tradition of the old parish of Santo António.

Reality, however, was crudely different. There he was kneeling before the priest, marrying a one-time water-seller from Cheok Chai Un, an illiterate girl whom he had seen when she wore no shoes. Life played so many tricks, and had given him the most unlikely slipper for his foot!

It could have been the gloomiest day of his life, the day of his ultimate defeat, but it wasn't. Others might mock and laugh, what did it matter? He was living his own life. He wouldn't have enjoyed such peace of mind or been so serene in his heart if the outcome had been different. And the compensation was self-evident.

A-Leng, hiding her natural nervousness, arrived totally at ease. Her dignity and timidity touched the bridegroom, in particular when, on the arm of her godfather Valdemero, she entered the church, her eyes down, wearing a large pink *tun-sam-fu* to conceal her heavy pregnancy, and walking with short steps, without stumbling, in a pair of white, half-heeled shoes. Dear girl, how hard it must be for her feet, so used to being free!

On the other hand, what delighted him most, was the fact that she was exhibiting her braid in all it abundance and blackness, the braid that was saying farewell to the general public to become the monopoly of one man in the intimacy of domestic life. Once married, she would roll it up into a chignon, as a sign of her new status. She had insisted on this final act, and had summoned the most skilled braider from the Janelas Verdes who, oozing with delight, had agreed to devote herself and her talent entirely to the job. A-Leng was superstitious. The braid had been at the root of it all, and its bewitching power had made this outcome possible. Adozindo had chosen the most discreet hour and day for the ceremony. But the date had been arrived at with her agreement, as it was one of the most propitious in the Chinese lunar calendar. Apart from the bride and groom, her godfather, his best man, and A-Soi were present. His best man was Olímpio, a member of the harbour police, a true son of Macao, who had got to know Adozindo during his work on the pier. Neither the bride nor groom had any member of their family present. They were a poor young couple.

But of course, nothing passed unnoticed in the Christian city. The banns had been published and there were those, anyway, who were curious about the marriage. Not many of them, but enough to spread the news all over town. Above all a group of old busybodies who, between mouthing their prayers, commented:

'It's the work of that insolent moll from Cheok Chai Un. She fed him a special tea, she did. And it made him cross-eyed and crazy.'

'It's a shame! It was witchcraft for sure ... Poor Beba who cried so much.'

'Serves him right, that's what I say! He pinched his lover so much, she's got a pointed backside!'

After the exchange of rings and the peal of church-bells, their fate was sealed. A-Leng, who had practised signing her new name, lingered over the paper as she laboriously wrote out her name in a child's hand. It was the first time she had ever signed a document and she realised the importance of the act. She was happy.

They stepped out into the sunshine. Swirls of white cloud rolled across the sky and swallows fluttered in dizzying circles over the churchyard. In the street, a dray loaded with firewood creaked along. From the Chinese school opposite came the murmur of children's voices reciting the lesson. Grubby kids begging for money surrounded the couple. The priest who accompanied them, deeply moved, shook Adozindo's hand and said:

'Congratulations ... You're a good man.'

The reception he had dreamt of in days gone by, was limited to a wholesome morning broth and some Chinese fried savouries and cakes, in the company of Valdemero, Olímpio and A-Soi, in a tea-room near the Kiang Wu Hospital. They were transported there, without any fuss, in rickshaws and they sat round the table talking animatedly and exchanging impressions.

A-Leng spoke of her nervousness and fear of making a mistake, her laughter tinkling merrily. She was so pretty in her excitement, that she attracted the gaze of all the men in the tea-room. A-Soi found the religious rituals strange, Valdemero gesticulated while he talked and the harbour policeman, more modest, said that he had enjoyed the ceremony. Adozindo didn't say much, stroking the extremity of his wife's braid, his eyes sad for not being able to offer them anything better.

There was no time for them to be alone together. They had to make the final preparations for the move and wait for the cart that would come to collect their bits of furniture and packages, and for which Valdemero had taken responsibility. Love would have to wait till night, in their new home, where time wouldn't matter, she whispered to him mischievously.

Indeed, the day was not over. There was still the wedding dinner, offered them by Adozindo's boss, who was aware of the couple's economic difficulties, and without which the bride would be demeaned. He had taken a liking to his employee and when a Chinese is a friend, he's a real friend, liberal and generous.

For Adozindo, the simple reception would have been enough. To mix a Catholic marriage with a custom that was Buddhist in origin seemed shocking to him. But for A-Leng, it was public recognition of her marital status by her own people. And he had married a Chinese, hadn't he? And it reflected well upon him that he was acknowledging her sensitivities.

The dinner was held in one of the *cou-laus* on the Rua Cinco de Outubro. A table for just twelve people, around which sat the couple, the godparents, Adozindo's boss and his wife, A-Soi and her husband, the braider from the Janelas Verdes and three employees of the shipping company. In spite of this, there was an atmosphere of exuberance and merriment. A-Leng was so radiant in her joy that she communicated her happy mood to everyone else. That tiny banquet had been put on especially for her, who had never enjoyed the honour of so much attention.

Her braid had disappeared, rolled up into an opulent chignon that had altered her appearance, changing the cast of her physical features. The braider had done another magnificent job. Suddenly, she had a more mature look, far from the profile of the carefree water-seller. With her hired Chinese bridal dress that she had put on beforehand, behind a screen, there was nothing to recall the barefoot girl of previous times, who carried buckets of water. He would have preferred her without the heavy mask of rouge and zinc powder with which the braider had covered her face. But even so, she was truly beautiful.

It was a noisy table, the bride answering saucy and sometimes embarrassing questions, the groom drinking to the challenge, as custom demanded. A-Leng acquitted herself well in her ripostes, as did Adozindo. Before the dinner ended, the bride got up to go and change clothes, returning with the *tun-sam-fu* she had worn that morning.

In the street, once their friends had gone their separate ways, they looked at each other without needing to utter a word. They both knew how important the day had been. A new and decisive chapter had opened in their lives, for good or bad, fair weather or foul.

'Lets go on foot. I want to walk with you,' she said.

They began to walk, simultaneously and side by side, her half-heeled shoes clicking on the damp, glistening cobblestones. The strong rice wine that Adozindo had drunk and the fresh night air combined to make him sway a little on his feet. A-Leng, full of care, passed her hand through his arm and steadied him.

'Lean on me and you'll never fall.'

'I know ... With you, I'll always be safe.'

They crossed the Largo de Hong Kong Mio, and went up the Rua das Estalagens, passing the hostel of ill-fated memory, with its fairylike balloons by the entrance. He expected her to make some comment, but A-Leng pretended not to look at the building with its lit up façade.

'My feet are hurting so much that I feel like kicking off my shoes.'

'No.'

Her laughter carried through the night air. They left the Chinese city and entered the Christian city, which was calm and all but asleep along the Rua de São Paulo. No cars, only a few rickshaws, and here and there, passers-by either alone or in pairs. All of them looked at A-Leng's 'scandalous' make-up, but Adozindo didn't get angry.

The ice-cream vendor, A-Loi, plied his trade with his famous cry of 'assi-clim', echoing along the lanes and alleyways. The boy selling noodles passed them, calling his customers by tap-tapping a piece of dried bamboo with a wooden stick. Further on, the hawker of warm fresh bread and butter biscuits cried out his delicacies with his characteristically nasal voice. From the entrance to a flight of steps, his call was answered by that of the man selling *ham-ioc-chong* and *ko-cheng-chong*, the *catupá* cakes, hot cakes of glutinous rice, pork and salted duck's egg, wrapped in banana leaves. These were the sounds that filled the night with nostalgia and evoked the delights of childhood. The heady perfume of night jasmine emanated from behind garden walls.

In the Largo de Camões, he saw the house where he had been born, bathed in darkness except for the faint glow of a light in exactly the room that had been his. They had all been happier there than in the house on the Estrada da Victória. It was also associated with the Handsome Adozindo's halcyon era, when he reigned over the hearts of all the damsels in Macao. He refrained from making any comment, in case his wife noted any hint of nostalgia for the past and sadness at the present, on that, their wedding night. His guiding principle from now on must be to never look back.

On the Estrada do Repouso, the foliage of the great trees huddled together, overwhelming the street-lamps, barely allowing their light to penetrate the thick network of branches. There was a deep silence. The couple stopped outside the dwelling, which was painted red, thus breaking the monotony of the yellow of the other houses in the neighbourhood, while Adozindo felt in his pocket for the key.

'It's nicer than the rest. I should have told Valdemero to leave all the lights on.'

'We're the ones who'll light it up. It's the house where our child will be born.'

Having opened the door and switched on the light in the entrance hall, they were greeted by the smell of fresh polish and the confused jumble of their things. It didn't matter. They smiled at each other. They were home.

23

he months passed slowly and monotonously while they waited for the end of the pregnancy. Adozindo occupied his time by throwing himself heart and soul into his work and the many and varied activities that his boss was involved in. He wasn't an easy boss to put up with. Most of the time he was friendly, but he was conscious of the fact that the boy was his subaltern, and that he was the paymaster. Occasionally, he would be abrupt and rude, mainly when he had lost the previous night at mah-jong or *pai-kao*.

These displays of impatience and angry outbursts offended him. Luckily, the tantrums didn't last long, but they were sufficient to cast a shadow over his naturally good manners. He then began to understand what it was like to have to put up with superiors and accept their discourtesies. What made him mad was not being able to answer in kind, under risk of losing his livelihood and not being able to guarantee his wife their bowl of rice. He didn't have the security of a civil servant. He knew that if he attracted his boss's antipathy, he would be sent packing with a mere click of the fingers.

It was clear that his boss wouldn't do this, because he liked and needed him, and trusted his talent and his nose for business. As the days went by, Adozindo discovered in himself a gift for work that he had thought only belonged to others. It had been dormant, presumed unnecessary, at the time when he was having fun. The money he was bringing home, while not allowing for any flings, was increasing.

He began to make efforts to improve his standard of living that had fallen to such a low level. A-Leng, intelligent as she was, accepted his customs because he was her husband, without losing her Chinese characteristics that he, in turn, respected. They adapted to each other, with mutual sacrifices, the only way to live in peace and harmony together. A-Leng was no spineless, submissive slave, and would answer back when she didn't agree, proffering her own opinions.

When it came down to it, there was a platform of understanding between both of them, achieved not through imposition or brutality, but through patience and a slow process of persuasion that mollified the disputant. As they were both from such different origins and upbringings, there were discoveries and discords that often made everyday life supremely interesting.

'Sometimes, A-Soi, it's really difficult living with a *kwai*. He's got habits and a way of thinking that leave me appalled because they're so stupid. Take eating as just one example ... Is there anything easier and needing less effort than eating with chopsticks? You only have to use one hand and it's much more elegant, delicate and practical. With cutlery you need both hands for the fork, knife, a spoon for soup, a spoon for rice, all so unnecessary and complicated.'

'But you do what he does.'

'What else can I do? He's my husband, I use his name. I get tired of arguing. And I can't avoid it, but one day I'll have to live more among his people. I don't want to embarrass him in front of his friends. I've come from nothing, I was a water-seller, never went to school, but no one's going to laugh at me.'

She arched her body back to contain the weight of her rounded belly, and walked round the sun-soaked room, dragging her slippers with their red sequins, in front of her friend who looked kindly on her in her new life.

'Just imagine, I can't burp anymore after a meal. What's wrong with a burp? It means we're full, satisfied, that the food was good. It's a compliment to the host, to the cook. But as far as the *kwais* are concerned it's bad-mannered. Aren't they strange folk? I've learnt to drink coffee, a bit of wine and to eat bread and butter. But there's one thing I won't accept. That's drinking tea with sugar. It's a disgusting mixture and spoils the tea. The *kwais* are uncivilized, they don't know the virtues of tea. No, certainly not!'

Adozindo had also changed. The hardship he had suffered had affected him deeply. He didn't feel drawn to clubs, bars and parties. He didn't forgive his old friends who had deserted him in his hour of affliction. He preferred his new friends from the dockside, with whom he played cards or mah-jong at home on Saturdays. He refused invitations to play *fan-tan* and High-Low, games of luck where the boss lost small fortunes.

He had become home loving. He spent his leisure time reading, and was a regular visitor to the Municipal Library. Recently, he'd developed a hunger for culture, and was trying to make up for lost time, poring over books, as the most fascinating and safest form of entertainment that didn't interfere with anyone else.

He was still a good-looking young man, but he was no longer the Handsome Adozindo. He'd had a difficult experience, and now he had a slipper on his foot, while his prestige lay shattered. The idea of sentimental adventures filled him with horror, and he didn't want any more scandals.

And there was always A-Leng's pole in a corner of the house to remind him she would use it, not against him, but against any rival who might threaten the happiness of her home. He knew A-Leng was capable of going to any extreme and he didn't take any risks. And of course, she didn't deserve such treatment.

After a long nine months of waiting, the time for the birth was fast approaching. He couldn't understand his wife's fears, her constant preoccupation over who the midwife might be. Both of them dismissed the idea of going to hospital. The only women who went to hospital were those who were poor or had been abandoned, or were in danger of dying. It would have been tantamount to formally accepting a status of unrelenting poverty, and her pride would never allow it. Such was the mentality of the age.

Adozindo suggested some names, and remembered the old midwife who had been present at his own birth, but his wife wouldn't comply. One night, he saw her crying, and when he asked her the reason, she answered quietly:

'I only trust one person ... She promised me years ago that she would be midwife at the birth of my children.'

He guessed who it was immediately. The Queen-Bee, queen of Cheok Chai Un, the shrew who had banished her. She had nimble fingers, many years of practical experience, knowledge of herbs and remedies to help with a healthy birth. No one had ever died in her care. Whole generations had seen the light of day with the help of her hands.

A-Soi, who had come promptly to help her friend, knew the Queen-Bee very well, for she had also benefited from her protection. Her sympathy aroused, she said to Adozindo:

'I beg you, go and find her.'

'And what if she refuses?'

'Try ... '

He was doubtful, especially as she had been the most virulent critic of her favourite pupil's behaviour, sentencing her to be banished from the quarter. Adozindo tried to dissuade his wife from her intention, but A-Leng wasn't to be convinced. Her child's life was at stake.

Recalling the old affection that had united them, she nourished strong hopes that she wouldn't refuse when there was an emergency. If he knew how to put it to her, she would come. With renewed energy, A-Leng told him how to find her if she wasn't at the well, and as he still hesitated, she wailed in despair once more. She was sure she was about to go into labour at any moment.

'Tell her she's the only one I trust and I venerate her.'

Off he hurried to Cheok Chai Un. On turning into the Rua Tomaz da Rosa that led to the well, he felt his legs tremble and turn to jelly. He imagined his mission ending in failure, the stream of insults he would have to put up with, the risk of suffering the revenge of the *lan-chais*, who had been on the receiving end of A-Leng's hiding. But he couldn't go back empty-handed, without at least contacting the terrible woman.

There were a lot of people round the well, women talking and shouting loudly, as always. A-Leng's disappearance hadn't altered the daily routine. It was just that, without her presence, the well was somehow less attractive.

They fell silent, astonished to see him standing nearby, with the air of a person looking for someone. The noisy hubbub stopped for a few seconds to be replaced by rude murmurings. Was he after some other victim? Had he thrown the other one out of the window like an old rag when he'd got tired of her?

Adozindo didn't blink, exercising good self-control, and asked where the Queen-Bee was. He had an urgent message from A-Leng and he wondered whether they would be so kind as to tell him where she was in this maze of lanes and alleyways. The women didn't move, nor did they seem to be chastened by his urgency. Adozindo was about to set off further into the quarter, looking for the street that A-Leng had referred to, when the stentorian voice of the Queen-Bee resounded over and above the noise of the area round the well.

It was the same formidable and menacing woman, apparently as hard as a block of rosewood. Adozindo stammered. A-Leng was calling her, she didn't want anyone else for the birth, because that had been her promise. There was renewed silence. The women crowded round inquisitively in a tight circle, and began to mutter among themselves. The Queen-Bee, erect as a statue, didn't answer. Adozindo added confusedly:

'A-Leng is my wife. I married her.'

More murmurings of surprise and suddenly the vulgar jokes ceased. Even the Queen-Bee's severe expression softened.

'So it's now she comes looking for me? She only remembers me when she's in difficulties?'

'It's only when we're in difficulties that we know who our true friends are and who we can count on.'

The message had been delivered and he wasn't going to wait for her to make up her mind in the middle of all those people. A-Leng's name could be heard as the women muttered to each other. He said:

'I'll be on my way. A-Leng's alone. Please, if you are still fond of her, don't leave it too long,' and he gave directions on how to reach the Estrada do Repouso.

He turned and left Cheok Chai Un. When he was well on his way, he looked back. With a sigh of relief, he saw the Queen-Bee's large bulk plodding along behind him.

———

There was no time to announce the arrival of the formidable woman, because her thundering voice could already be heard before she even crossed the threshold. The tense expression on A-Leng's face dissolved, at the same time as she let out a long sigh, as if some soothing balm were washing over her. For a brief instant, the two women looked at each other, as if neither of them could believe their eyes. A-Leng raised her hand in her distress and murmured:

'Mother ... '

No one had ever called her that before. The stern, furrowed face became milder and her abruptness disappeared. If it wasn't the voice of blood kinship, it was something similar.

'I'm so frightened ... '

'Don't be scared. Everything's going to be alright ... I'm here.'

She took the necessary measures, as if she were the mistress of the house. She reduced A-Soi and a neighbour to the mere status of submissive and obedient assistants with her crushing personality. She sent Adozindo out of the house, declaring that this was a time for women and he was just getting in the way. There was no need to insist, for A-Leng's groans had already begun, impelling him to retreat, horrified.

Having been given the day off by his understanding boss, he wandered the streets aimlessly, as if he were sleepwalking, the hours dragging by as slowly as a tortoise. He returned to the door of the house, but as the groans continued, he walked away again with his nerves in tatters. Valdemero's company lessened his tension by having someone to talk to.

At about nine o'clock in the evening, the Queen-Bee presented him with a healthy, robust youngster, kicking and screaming his lungs out. The continuity of his family was guaranteed. A-Leng was exhausted, but looked very well, and was smiling proudly. It had been a day of supreme importance for her. Apart from giving birth to a boy, she had her Mother once again.

The Queen-Bee rested. She sat down beside the bed until her pupil fell asleep, all ill-feeling forgotten. Then, she visited the whole house from top to bottom, letting out grunts of appreciation. She took a good look at the little yard and the chickens in the coop. So her pupil had defied her gloomy predictions. She hadn't fallen into prostitution, but had got married and had a home and enjoyed a far higher standard of living than that of any other girl from Cheok Chai Un.

She went back and spread the news throughout the quarter, all past misdemeanours forgiven. A-Leng had in fact been astute, had planned her strategy intelligently and all by herself, and it had come off. The man, who had started the affair as mere amusement, had been led by the nose like a buffalo. She was therefore worthy of respect. Whoever doubted it would end up with egg on their face.

During the days that followed, there was a little procession of water-sellers and washerwomen to the Estrada do Repouso. They were all curious about A-Leng's good fortune. The ones who had been quickest to accuse her in her hour of difficulty, were now the most humble and meek. They tempered their envy by admiring the 'luxuries' that surrounded her. The young mother, conscious of the realities of life, accepted their praise, with the generosity of a 'princess' who had returned from exile. She caught up with all the gossip and happenings in Cheok Chai Un since she had left, but curiously, without a great deal of interest. She learnt of the death of her grandmother, the old woman who had brought her up and from whom she had received no news. When she had left the quarter, she had sent her a message, written for her by a street scribe, but had never received an answer. She assumed that she too had condemned her. She wiped away a tear and promised that, as soon as she could, she would carry out the funeral rites, late as they might be, at the Tou Tei Temple.

Then, the question of the baptism was raised. Clearly, the newly-born child would follow the religion of the parents. But the Queen-Bee wasn't impressed. She meddled again and imposed a further duty. A-Leng was Chinese, and the child therefore half-Chinese. They would have to celebrate the *mun-ut*, that is, the thirtieth day after the birth, which, counted on the lunar calendar, meant a banquet. Either that, or she wouldn't consider herself the baby's 'granny'. A solution to the problem was found when it was decided to have the two ceremonies on the same day.

Where was the money for the expense of a banquet? The woman's mighty voice intimidated Adozindo. She wasn't asking him to open his purse strings. She was the one who would pay for everything. She had got her daughter back, and the youngster was like the longed for grandson she had never had. So emphatic was she that Adozindo didn't dare disagree with her.

'I've suddenly got myself one hell of a mother-in-law ... '

———

The banquet took place on the appropriate day, in the open air, right in the heart of Cheok Chai Un, the tables set out in the area round the well, with food provided by a nearby eating-house. The local policeman didn't object to the invasion, and even used his authority to re-direct whatever passers-by there were through the narrow space that was left. Good-natured, he joined in the general revelry, drinking a few glasses of *sam-cheng*, the strong rice wine, at the moment when libations were being made.

In the morning, there had been a very simple baptismal ceremony, with a Chinese Catholic employee of the shipping company and his wife as godparents, and in the presence of both parents, Valdemero, and A-Soi, the latter already godmother through the Buddhist rite. The banquet, however, was noisy, but the child behaved well, eyes closed and fast asleep, indifferent to all the commotion happening because of him.

The best folk in the quarter attended, honoured for having been invited by the Queen-Bee, and the chattering group of washerwomen and water-sellers came. But there was no one prettier than his own A-Leng in that cheerful gathering, Adozindo pondered, all proud of himself. She was as slender as ever, unaffected by the pregnancy and birth, and in this she was typical of her race. She had the same opulent chignon that contained her bewitching braid, and an air of distinction that motherhood had conferred on her, thrown into relief by her splendid *tun-sam-fu* of red silk. Within that society, she indeed had the bearing of a 'princess', addressing the Queen-Bee out loud as mother. As Valdemero and Olímpio couldn't come, Adozindo was the only *kwai-lo* there, seated at the table of honour, among the washerwomen, water-sellers, hawkers, rickshaw pullers, coolies and *a-tais* of Cheok Chai Un. Reconciliation was now complete, and he could boast of having been the only Macanese ever to have been honoured with a banquet in such a very special place.

He didn't feel very much at ease, especially when, among the people passing by, he unexpectedly saw faces he had known in other times. They pretended not to see him or greeted him briefly and hurried on with apparent discretion, but not failing to miss the slightest detail.

The Handsome Adozindo now reduced to reigning over that riff-raff! That's where bad judgement got you! Here was an example with which to warn the flighty and the idle talkers. The man who boasted of his exclusive and carefully selected conquests and dared to complain to God for having been made so beautiful!

And irony of ironies, while this was the judgement of the Christian city, there, in a quarter of ill repute, a banquet was being held in honour of him, his wife and son! It was something of a consolation and one never stopped learning. Between glasses of *sam-cheng* and the food from the eating-house, he amused himself by watching, with some nostalgia, the braids of the single girls dancing and swaying down their backs, adorned with the same champac blossom.

The Queen-Bee, enlivened by her intake of alcohol, launched into an improvised speech, in which she rehabilitated her 'daughter' and 'son-in-law', to the applause of the guests. She made a public show of returning to A-Leng the key to her house, which had been closed up and put under her guard until that day. In reply, A-Leng returned the key to her, with a request that she administer it in her name.

Such a gesture received the approval of the local 'worthy men', who had all eaten well and drunk even better. The banquet finished amid the noise of people expectorating, belching and the extravagant picking of teeth. A-Leng and Adozindo could now go back to Cheok Chai Un whenever they wanted, for they belonged to the quarter's great family.

The honoured guests stayed behind, while the Queen-Bee settled the bill with the owner of the eating-house. As she rocked the baby to sleep, A-Leng felt moved by the welcome she had received, but she had no illusions.

If it weren't for the Queen-Bee's status in the quarter and, above all, for the dogged determination of the man sitting next to her, who had not abandoned her but had even given her a name and family, she would still be a reprobate and ostracised by her people. That was life.

She had discovered another truth. Even if they accepted her for what she was, she could never go back. She had changed a lot, acquired new habits, a different way of thinking, she had ascended the social ladder. She envied her old companions for being able to walk barefoot, free of the torture of shoes, feeling the coolness of the ground. Yet it was a purely childish nostalgia.

But she also knew that she would feel very awkward if she had to show her bare feet in public as she used to. She was another person. And her friends of old no longer accepted her as their equal. The water-seller of old had disappeared, belonged now to the folk legends of Cheok Chai Un as the woman who had knocked four roughnecks to the ground with her stick, in defence of her love.

PART THREE

24

heir son grew up and grew bigger, and a second child came, another robust boy who, in his first months, sucked his mother's breast with a noisy, voracious appetite.

The appearance of two children increased their commitments and responsibilities, tied the couple more closely to their home life, he, in the struggle to achieve a more affluent economic position, she, in her effort to ensure the good health of their offspring and to make the house as attractive as possible. They threw themselves into this task, seemingly without any higher ambitions, or much of a social life beyond that which was strictly necessary, leading a virtually 'insular' existence.

If A-Leng had been accepted back in her old neighbourhood, without on the other hand becoming integrated into it again, Adozindo had adopted a more radical position. He had deliberately removed himself from any contact with his people, for he still resented society's 'disapproval', and deep down, was unsure whether his wife would be accepted as an equal with other women, whether the fact that she had once been a barefoot water-seller with a braid, would be forgotten once and for all. Now that he had given her his name, he couldn't bear the idea of more insults.

They would never go unnoticed, for the couple were too good-looking for that and the scandal too big in what was a small town. But they were no longer the target of ghoulish curiosity. Other facts and dalliances served as fodder for the gossip-mongers. But even so, he knew that comments were still made behind their backs:

'What a pity! Such a good-looking boy for a marriage like that ... '

'What a waste!'

He never talked about his marriage or speculated on whether his life had been a waste. To look back would have been irrelevant and wouldn't change anything. 'We did choose our path and there we goes.' The children had arrived and A-Leng, with all the deficiencies in her educational level and cultural formation, was the same solid and faithful companion in both happiness and misfortune. He would never want to lose her, and clung to the warmth and affection that united them. And she didn't deserve anything less, for the effort she was making to be worthy of his position and to create a home with which they could both identify.

The house was as clean as it could be with two lively children. With the memory of her miserable hovel in Cheok Chai Un and the prevailing order in the house on the Estrada da Victória still fresh, A-Leng went to extremes in her concern for cleanliness. She would complain at the sight of cigarette ash outside the ash-trays, and drops of urine he left on the lavatory floor when he shook himself.

The atmosphere was predominantly western, with arm-chairs in the living-room and curtains on the windows, the sideboard with gleaming Portuguese chinaware and on a simple altar, a statue of Madonna and Child. In the children's bedroom, there was another religious image, that of the Guardian Angel, arms outstretched in protection, in a glass box.

But there were other details that revealed the influence of a Chinese woman. In the household decorations, in the habit of taking tea and the hot towels, in restorative infusions and other home-made remedies, in the collection of dwarf plants in little clay pots on the veranda, and which she tended with devotion.

A-Leng had a great talent for cooking. She could prepare Chinese dishes with no difficulty at all, but she still hadn't perfected her mastery of Macanese and Portuguese cuisine. She lacked the guidance of an experienced cook. Valdemero and her neighbour, Tina, the wife of a fireman, the only Macanese woman she had got to know, were both very limited in their expertise.

When A-Leng served up Chinese food, she would eat with chopsticks, and she would use cutlery if it was Macanese or Portuguese. But he always ate with a knife, fork and spoon. She insisted that much of the harmony in a household came from the meal table. A man with a good lunch or dinner inside him was always good-humoured. She knew it and she also knew her husband's palate.

She placed great emphasis on the *t'ongs*, the Chinese broths that couldn't be classified as soups, given that they were lighter and more watery, but which, according to her, were fortifying, or good for the lungs, or the digestion, or for cooling the hot temperatures that afflicted the blood. Her rice was loose, fluffy, very white and tasty.

She took a long time to get used to bread and butter and milky coffee. Chinese broth for breakfast and accompanying fried delicacies were only served occasionally, to make a change. In the afternoon, she would occasionally have tea, but never with sugar, accompanied by slices of 'house-bread' or Macanese confectionery, bought from the bun and pastry man from Santo António, who would go round the Portuguese houses hawking his wares with a drawn-out cry:

'*Melenta ... melenta.*'

For his part, Adozindo, as a result of living with her, adopted the habit of taking a bath before going to bed. A-Leng would tell him coyly that this was so that his skin would smell nice and would perfume the bed. When he didn't do it, because it was cold or for some other good reason, he would at least wash his feet, as she put it, in order to drive away the humours that had accumulated in them because of the hours spent standing on them during the day's activity. These were habits and customs from two cultures that mingled together without any imposition on either side, as if this was the most natural thing in the world. They didn't go out much, and even then, almost only to the cinema. On Sundays, they would break their voluntary solitude by going to the second morning mass at the São Lázaro church, because Adozindo had promised the priest, a good friend, that he would attend. It was a mass that had also been absorbed into their routine. Afterwards, they would go for a walk in the more bucolic corners of Macao, through the gardens of the Camões Grotto, or across the uncultivated land around Mong-Há, or they would venture as far as Ilha Verde.

They didn't do much entertaining. The group of regular visitors to the Estrada do Repouso was very restricted. Apart from Olímpio and Valdemero, who were by now regarded as family, there was the fireman, Josué and his wife Tina and two or three other Macanese, new friends made down on the pier and within the same professional activity. None of them had the same level of education as Adozindo, and they themselves were aware of it, which is why they subtly kept a distance that was never breached, in spite of the warmth of the hospitality offered.

They would come on Saturday afternoons to play mah-jong and stay there until dinner-time or sometimes, when spirits were especially high, for longer. Other times, they would play enthusiastic games of poker, now that manila was out of fashion. And they would seldom fail to turn up, knowing that they would have the pleasure of being indulged by a beautiful woman, who would serve them and regale them with her charm.

Unlike many Chinese women, A-Leng didn't play mah-jong. She hadn't had time when she was a water-seller and now, with children and domestic responsibilities, much less. But she knew the rules and had an intuitive appreciation for the game, like all those of her race. She had also got to grips easily with the rules of poker and its variants, with just a few explanations from her husband as she sat behind him, when time and the children allowed.

As time went by, another form of entertainment came to light by chance. One day, Adozindo, with some savings, bought a wireless, the great novelty and craze of the age, through which he could pick up radio stations in Hong Kong and Manila, as well as the experimental broadcasts from the CQN station in Macao, from which he sat enraptured by the melodies of the Macanese string combo, Bragazinho.

It was this inspirational group that stimulated his interest in string instruments. All the more so when, one night, Olímpio turned up with a guitar and Valdemero and Josué with their respective mandolins. It was an evening of artistic performance as the three lads played and sang melodies from the films of the moment, Latin American tunes and the scores of popular songs from the Portuguese film, 'Song of Lisbon', which was all the rage in Macao.

Adozindo was so enthusiastic that the following day, he went straight down to the 'Agência Mercantil Limitada' on the Avenida Almeida Ribeiro, a Portuguese shop selling sporting equipment, musical instruments and records, and bought a brand-new guitar, after Olímpio had tried it out first.

Adozindo wasn't a beginner. He was just out of practice because he hadn't played for so many years — his old guitar was probably gathering damp in his parents' house along with so many other things. In the golden age of the Handsome Adozindo, he had strummed away in many musical groups, on park benches in the Vasco da Gama Garden or in the Largo de Camões, round the well in the secondary school or under the rustling shade of the trees along the Praia Grande. Once, along a quiet stretch of the Rua da Penha, he and a number of other romantic balladeers had a bucket of foul-smelling water thrown over them, the act of a furious father set on putting an end to the gallantries directed at his besotted daughter. This adventure still made him laugh.

The group grew, with a further three players of the guitar and ukulele, and they would all meet at least once a week at the house on the Estrada do Repouso. All they did was to imitate other similar groups spread out over the Christian city, which practised, not only for their own amusement, but also with a view to participate in the contests of the *tunas* at carnival time, musical groups that competed with one another in merry but hotly contested rivalries. Adozindo, however, never belonged to a *tuna*.

A-Leng welcomed this circle of friends amiably, and made every effort to be congenial. Unconsciously, she was training herself. She had been shrewd enough to understand that while she had ascended the social scale, he had descended to a lower level, for the simple reason that he had refused to abandon her. None of those friends had been her husband's companions in mischief during his childhood and adolescence. They had nothing in common with him. A brief moment was sufficient to throw into relief the difference between the refined manners of Adozindo and the rough and at times rude language that issued from the mouths of the others.

She still retained in her memory the images of the house on the Estrada da Victória. The waxed wooden floors like a mirror, the curtains billowing at the windows, the furniture in the living-rooms and bedrooms that attested to a solid state of well-being. And then, the perfect clothes that Adozindo wore when she first knew him, the shine of his polished shoes, the pure white shirts and that smell of eau de cologne of a cosseted rich boy. That was the real Adozindo and not the clean but poorly dressed young man, with his cheap shirts and scuffed shoes. She was afflicted by guilt and harboured a secret desire to restore to her husband what he had lost because of her.

She sometimes found him lost in thought, sad, bowed down by loneliness, at moments when he thought there was nobody there to see him. She knew such moments too, for she also suffered them, when the lack of contact with her friends tormented her soul, full of memories of the well and of the braiding-woman and of the evenings in the Queen-Bee's house, a carefree time, albeit one of unremitting poverty. Fortunately, such moments were fleeting and they felt almost ashamed for having betrayed themselves. They would look at each other, say some pleasantry and call the children.

A-Leng lent her support to the mah-jong and music sessions. They helped to distract him, but she wanted more. She wanted him to come out of his hiding-place once and for all, to go and have a beer somewhere and resume old friendships that had cooled or establish new ones. As he had such an engaging manner, she couldn't believe he would be greeted with sticks and stones. He was bringing home more money than before, and there was no reason for penny-pinching. She persisted gently in her purpose but to no avail. She found him stubborn or indifferent. He was proud and had been badly hurt.

Six years had gone by in this way. Had these years been innocuous, empty of meaning, distressingly banal? If you had asked the couple this question they would have denied it categorically. In their silent struggle, these years had been vital to both of them in terms of the experience and knowledge of people that they had gained, and for her, in terms of her learning to live in his world.

Whenever he could, Adozindo read, devouring book after book, either borrowed from the Municipal Library or bought at the 'Oriente Comercial', the well-known bookshop that belonged to Ângelo on the Avenida Almeida Ribeiro. He read novels and shorter fiction, travel literature, history, the classics, works in Portuguese, English and French, a whole breadth of culture that he sought to grasp, regretting his years when he had lacked any awareness and had not done anything worthwhile. He blushed when he recalled the enormity of his words upon completing his secondary education, namely that studying was finished as far as he was concerned.

A-Leng considered her husband the fountain of all knowledge. In her insatiable curiosity, she would ask him about this and that. She was like a child always asking why. Jealous of the concentrated attention he dedicated to his books, she would ask him what he was reading. If it was a novel, he would patiently tell her the plot as he read. It was as if a film were unrolling before them, an episode at a time. But she wasn't a passive listener. She would be critical if the narration clashed with her cultural values. She would give her reasons, and even go so far as to say that the author was stupid. He would then get irritated and she would sulk. When they calmed down, they would both laugh. After all, it was only a book.

The same thing happened when they went to the cinema. If it was a western film, almost invariably American, he would tell her the story in detail from beginning to end when they got home, for she didn't know English, nor could she read the subtitles in Chinese which were projected next to the screen. Criticism would emerge, sometimes favourable, sometimes dismissive. They often disagreed and argued with each other. What she couldn't accept were the scenes of prolonged, passionate kissing. Such things were a fact of life, and were only suitable and highly enjoyable when done in private, without any witnesses. Certainly not in front of hundreds of spectators, for they were an offence to people's sense of propriety. She would compare them to Chinese films. There was no need for kissing, for this was understood by the slightest turn of a cheek. He would burst out laughing or get excited, and she would stick to her views.

For his part, Adozindo had learnt with A-Leng to gain a greater appreciation of the Chinese soul and culture, even though this was less than he desired. He was astonished that although she had never been to school, she was gifted with a prodigious memory, and she understood all the complicated ritual of traditional Chinese theatre in all its most subtle details, its symbols, the suggestions of its scenery, the costume, and the music played on native instruments. She loved the long operas, would listen with rapt attention to the sharp, screeching sounds of the actors' voices, and even shed tears, while he sat blankly and patiently indifferent. At home, gripped and moved, she would repeat the tragic story acted out on the stage and explain the meaning of the mannerisms of the actors and their characterization, their movements and turns, their jumps and gestures with swords and lances, the transposition of time and space. Apart from this and on other occasions, she would recall the legends and ancient odysseys of the heroes of old, from which one could extract lessons in Confucian morality. She would often cite popular sayings, in a classical language and would point out the lucky or inauspicious days on the lunar calendar, the only one she was familiar with.

A-Leng didn't fear robbers. When there was a strange sound at the door or the windows, suspicious steps or murmurings in the street, when the dogs in the neighbourhood barked furiously, she would jump out of bed before him, her *tam-kon* held high, for whatever might befall her, ready to hit out. And yet this same woman, so courageous with those who were alive, went pale at the mention of the dead, would tremble at the idea of wandering ghosts and spirits that inhabited dark places. He would encourage her, saying: 'We're good. They only appear to bad people.'

'How should I know? ... You can never be sure.'

In the early days, when everyone around her spoke in Portuguese, she felt terribly isolated. Especially when Valdemero, Olímpio and the others who were frequent visitors to the house, began a heated discussion or fell about laughing because of some story or piece of gossip. Why so much hilarity or so much shouting, she would ask, full of curiosity. They would sum things up for her, but it wasn't the same.

So she took the only practical step possible: To learn words in the foreign language. She would ask what this or that was, pronouncing them syllable by syllable, one after the other, countless times. Her prodigious memory helped her immensely, and she retained things with ease. She would ask people to correct her when she made a mistake, and never felt embarrassed.

'My own language is the only one I have an obligation to speak well.'

She would pronounce Portuguese in a Chinese way, as she was incapable of saying it without an accent and, between husband and wife, Portuguese words mingled with Chinese ones without any effort, unconsciously. But Adozindo addressed his children only in Portuguese, so that they would get used to their father's language from an early age. Their mother, in turn, introduced Chinese to them naturally, because she wanted them to gain a good knowledge of her language. One of the games the couple played was to show the kids objects and make them identify them in each language. In this way, all four of them learnt at the same time.

As time went by and as a consequence of two cultures trying to understand each other in a common language, the children would talk in Portuguese or in Chinese or in a mixture of Chinese and Portuguese. When they were answering their parents, they would always reply in kind, in one of the two languages.

This was the home, Adozindo thought to himself, that had emerged from what his family and outsiders considered an act of folly. But had it really been one? In the middle of so much heedless living during the frivolous years, when he could have ended up with so many good or bad, rich or poor, blond or dark, round-eyed or slanted-eyed women, he had met A-Leng. It had all been a question of chance, a quirk of fate. It could have been worse or better, but it was with her that he had chosen to stay. And every time he thought of it like that, a wave of tenderness washed over him.

He liked to watch her moving around doing her domestic tasks, her slender, nimble body, though a little thicker now, had remained unaffected by childbirth, in keeping with the women of her race, and she had lost her earlier rustic simplicity, gaining new ways and habits through home life. He liked to listen to her chatting with the neighbour, Tina, from window to window, about women's things or everyday matters, and launching into her wholesome laughter. He liked to listen to her lulling their youngest son, singing a gentle, sad ditty that never changed, and recalled from her orphaned childhood. He liked it when she crouched next to him on a little stool, listening to the music from the wireless to please him, in a silent moment of concentration, while he gently fondled her nape and neck and she fell under the spell of his erogenous caress. He liked to watch her, audaciously naked, her round breasts shaking, as she undid the thick mass of her hair in a sensual movement of her arms, trunk and head, and then asked him to tame her locks in a braid, to recall the spell that had brought them together.

It pained him that his parents, blinded by their rancour, seemed unable to understand that he could be happy, in his own way, with A-Leng. The abyss between them, had remained as wide as ever for all those years. In the beginning, they would turn their back on the couple when they happened to pass each other, wherever it might be and whatever company they might be in. Their skin tingled with shame when they saw the cursed woman, wearing her *tun-sam-fu*, by the boy's side. Later, this behaviour ceased, because it didn't alter anything and merely fed their unwarranted bitterness. The water-seller had held on to him for good, she was his lawful wife and mother of his children. It was a *fait accompli*, and there was nothing that could be done about it.

Adozindo, firm in his pride, made no effort at reconciliation. He knew he would be received with open arms, like the prodigal son in the Bible, if he returned alone and contrite. But such a step did not belong to the realm of the possible. He had emancipated himself, he had his own life, and had survived without his parents. This had been achieved through toil and suffering.

He imagined what the full extent of their disappointment must be. Their only son had not lived up to their hopes and ambitions. He felt for them sufficiently to miss them, the attentions of his grandmother and aunt, the occasionally stifling devotion of his cousin Catarina. The smell of the furniture in the house, the creaking of the old wood, the incense, lavender and benzoin at Christmas, whose smoke both perfumed and rid his suits of their mustiness on days of extreme humidity. The Macanese dishes that were a speciality of his parents house: the pie made of puff pastry with its filling of chicken, mushrooms and chunks of pork, the *capela* flavoured with cheese and black olives, the *sarrabulho* with its peppery sauce. The condiments that accompanied the rice, such as *missó-cristão*, *peixe esmargal*, Timor lemon and Macanese *balichão*.

Everyone had dreamt of a happy future for him, in which success would be assured and everything would be offered to him on a silver plate. But life wasn't a shining path or one lined with soft silk, whose course could be set beforehand. Along the way lay the unexpected, such as tempting short cuts and crossroads, and a detour was enough to change everything. And so a whole melting-pot of situations could occur leading to unforeseen consequences from which one couldn't escape. There was no point in asking why such things happen. They just happen, even to the most saintly and cautious of men.

25

*I*n spite of the isolated life they led, the couple were well informed and didn't need to ask what was going on in town. On her visits to the house, the Queen-Bee brought news of all the goings on in Cheok Chai Un and the Bazaar. In the market and on the pier, the day-to-day happenings in other corners of the Chinese city were relayed. Valdemero, Olímpio and their neighbour, Tina, told them all the latest news and gossip from the Christian city. Romantic attachments, weddings, baptisms, funerals, rivalries within the civil service, abuses of authority, scandals and fisticuffs, cases of adultery, separations, and news of who the latest kept women were. Whether news arrived late or distorted or exaggerated, they knew a little bit about everything. And if they knew about others, then the others certainly knew about them.

Papa Aurélio had been right when he listed the privileges and gains that would accrue to him if he married Lucrécia. In addition to her magnificent body with its full breasts and milky skin, every one of these privileges and gains had been seized by Florêncio, like some bountiful harvest. The selfsame Florêncio, he who had been more than willing to eat his crumbs. And as for her, what better way to humiliate him, Adozindo, than to marry his best friend in a sumptuous wedding ceremony, the same friend who had rejected him in his hour of greatest despair.

It was certainly quite a prize he'd got his teeth into. And with her marriage, Lucrécia had achieved her objective, which was to put an end to her ambiguous situation. As a married woman, she silenced all the gossip-mongers, for the dazzling bride was all very different from the merry widow who had had a fling with a filthy windbag. She won for herself a dignified and respectable status that stopped all the tittle-tattle and gave her a legitimate right to become more toffee-nosed than ever. Full of craving ambition and petulance, she set out to erase once and for all any lingering memory people might still have of 'the girl from the lowlands near the Portas do Cerco'.

Florêncio also underwent a transformation. At first, he was patently embarrassed and even harboured some misgivings, as if he were required to play a role that was not really for him, but this phase didn't last long. Encouraged by the woman, the prospect of a gigantic leap up the social scale went to his head. As often happens in such cases, he distanced himself from his modest family, no longer wishing to be associated with it, and he did the same to his companions of old, lowly clerks with whom he used to play billiards in the 'Aurora Portuguesa' bar on the Rua do Campo, or with whom he would have lunch in the popular 'A-Kuan' or 'A Vencedora', both restaurants known for their mouth-wateringly reasonable prices.

Full of self-importance, in seventh heaven over his new life and appearance, he exuded prosperity. He was well-groomed, reeked of aftershave, his hair smarmed down with an exclusive brand of brilliantine one could only buy in Hong Kong, so as to discipline various obstinate threads of hair that stuck out like a hedgehog's bristles. His new persona would not have been complete without his heavy gold watch-chain, which he always showed off, and his mounted switch that he hardly ever let go of, his weapon of war.

He now enjoyed the use of fine glasses and silverware, of Santerra's wine-cellar, of sofas worthy of a seraglio, of a four-poster bed with canopy, of the splendid view from the terrace and the cool of the veranda at Baixo Monte. Adozindo could do without all the glasses and silver, as well as the languid comfort of the sofas, the beautiful view from the terrace and the cool of the veranda. What he really regretted was the waste of Santerra's wine-cellar, and in particular, that fine old brandy in Florêncio's mouth, for the man would find it very hard to drink without concealing his disgust, and would only do so for the sake of appearances.

Florêncio had got his hands on everything that Adozindo's father had wanted for his son. He frequented the Hotel Riviera at the 'whisky hour', rubbing shoulders with the great and the good, so that he could remain up to date with the palace gossip and intrigues. Or he would accompany his wife to the 'As Delícias' patisserie on the Avenida Almeida Ribeiro, where the cream of society met for five-o'clock tea. He hosted dinner parties at Baixo Monte for the important figures in the Administration, a sign of such events being the bright lights across the ground-floor and the veranda. He went to the Governor's receptions, and Lucrécia, puffing out her impressive bosom, proclaimed out loud that they too belonged to the 'Palace circle'.

He belonged to the board of directors of the Clube de Macau and one day would probably be its president, and he was a member of other recreational and sporting associations. As it was considered smart, he played tennis, and at least developed into quite a good player. He could often be seen, an exhausted, ruddy-faced figure, towel round his neck and racket stuck under his armpit, a tin of tennis balls in one hand, walking in the shade of the trees along the Avenida da República and the Praia Grande, heading towards his blue Pontiac, parked next to the arcades of the Riviera. He justified this long walk as a need for exercise.

In summer, he had his private bathing hut at the 'Tai Pans' Beach' in the Outer Harbour, almost next to the Clube de Macau and not very far from the Grémio Militar. As a member of the hunting club, he would join an exclusive group during the shooting season that would cross into Chinese territory to kill snipe, pigeons, partridges and woodcock, returning through the Portas do Cerco, their belts weighed down with the carcasses of the game they had shot. With his hunting rifle in one hand, and his other controlling two sturdy pointers on a lead, Florêncio cut a convincingly martial figure. At the horse races, which took place in the Hippodrome, he had his own box and would accompany the progress of his horse through a pair of binoculars, while for dog racing, he was the proud owner of a greyhound. He therefore lacked for nothing.

And he would go away on highly publicised holidays, at a time when few people enjoyed such a privilege, travelling first class on the 'Asama Maru' to Shanghai and Japan, the wonders of which he would recount whenever the opportunity arose. Far from his wife, he would cast himself in the role of the man who was familiar with the pleasures of the boudoir, and crossing his leg, would give a mischievous wink in an exaggerated imitation of the Handsome Adozindo, while murmuring with a knowledgeable air, his eyes half-closed:

'Ah! The Russian women in Shanghai ... what smooth white skin, what magnificent breasts! And the geishas of Yokohama, the hot baths and the massages! Heaven ... '

But what price was he paying for all this? Everyone knew and talked about it, for it was fertile pasture for the envious. He was totally dependent on his wife who fed and clothed him and gave him the privileges of a wealthy potentate. He was a humble yes-man, unctuous and servile, next to her. She had forced him to resign his post as clerk in the official pensions department, because the position was unworthy of his present social position. He was now at the head of an import and export firm, of which she was the major stakeholder. Lucrécia managed it with an iron fist and unwavering efficiency and Florêncio parroted her orders and decisions. As they had married with legal separation of estate — Lucrécia was no fool — he didn't possess any material assets that he could really call his own.

His wife had a nose for business, raking in interest on loans she made, and buying and selling property. She escaped unharmed by the effects of the Hong Kong stock market crash, one of the terrible effects of the Sino-Japanese war of 1931–32, preserving her solid fortune intact, while others went to the wall.

All the reservations Adozindo nurtured regarding Lucrécia's personality were confirmed. She had an uneven temper, and would explode in sudden fits of rage, while the neighbours of Baixo Monte grew hardened to her uncontrolled shrieks.

In public, she maintained an appropriate veneer and gushed with elaborate displays of cordiality. But she was a tyrant towards her husband. She often showed it, telling him to keep quiet in front of strangers. It was enough for her to give him a slight frown for him to fidget nervously. And he did a lot of fidgeting. Out of his fear there sprang many jokes of an unflattering sort.

Those who knew the couple well, thought that all her peevishness derived from an intense and permanent feeling of frustration. She had married Florêncio in a bout of hurt pride. He wasn't a man for her, raised and educated under the thumb of Santerra who had known how to tame his wild filly. Now that she had been let loose, she was turning Florêncio's home life into a hell. This was the reverse side of the medal. Not even the arrival of two sons calmed the mother down. They were spoilt, uncontrollable children, inventive in their artful mischief, which constantly played on people's nerves.

To live the type of life Florêncio led, in spite of all the cut glass and Santerra's comforts, in spite of the snipe, the 'Asama Maru' and belonging to the 'Palace circle', was a heavy burden of a reward. And to make matters worse, he had to put up with the sinister governess, as skinny as a cypress in a graveyard, the only one who could rely on the undivided affection and confidence of her mistress.

———

So Florêncio was paying for his infamy, he had his own bitter cross to bear and there was consequently no need to set the matter straight between them personally. Lucrécia's tyranny was sufficient to personify his revenge. But Adozindo was human too, and he felt his flesh creep and he would clench his fists every time they regaled his ears with the rascal's apparent successes.

When he went to live with A-Leng, his old ties were severed and he was ostracised. Adozindo therefore sought to live in obscurity, to disappear, divest himself of the Handsome Adozindo's uniform in order to become a completely new man. He didn't want to feel the past, to become emotionally involved over anything, to have anything to do with anyone else, for in this way no one else would want anything to do with him.

His plan, however, inevitably failed, for it was impossible to create such an isolated, hermetic world. He never resigned himself to disappearing totally. After six years, when the various resentments had died down, he realised that the exile he had banished himself to was too great and utterly senseless. After all, he had nothing to be ashamed off, and no one cared anyway. He was impelled by a need to change his lifestyle. With the money he was saving, there was no justification for his children having to play in the street, learning its vices with a growing group of loudmouthed kids on the loose, simply because there was no room at home. Nor was there any reason why his wife should go on ruining her hands, forever washing clothes, pathetically reclusive, ready to explode, hemmed in by four walls. It wasn't right, and she deserved much more. And what was worse, the day would not long be coming when, losing her patience and fed up with his resignation, she would demand that he assume some other role than that of an eternally passive, innocuous man.

Florêncio was provoking him too with his ever more extreme levels of ostentation. The latest piece of news brought the bile to his mouth. Florêncio had replaced his worn out Pontiac with a Chevrolet that attracted stares of wonderment, with its four doors, its dark grey paintwork, and its silvery, ornately carved chrome. In a place where there were little more than a hundred privately owned cars, Florêncio's vehicle even got on the front page of the local paper.

It wasn't so much the fact that he should change his car, even for a brand-new one. If he had the means, he could do what he liked, and it was nobody else's business. But that he should use the occasion for such a brazen display of self-publicity, that really got one's goat. It was quite common to see him drive by, sometimes alone, other times with his wife and children, along the quiet streets of the city, hooting loudly for no good reason, like some medieval town crier. A thunderous, arrogant horn, with a strident tone, a sign of his importance, announcing his arrival from afar, even before he came into view. It was irritating, unsettling, and attracted unnecessary ill-feeling.

Florêncio had made bad use of the wealth that had fallen into his lap. It had begun with a betrayal and he was now behaving as if he had been born with a silver spoon and with the whole world at his beck and call. The memory, which had long been locked in the depths of Adozindo's heart, of Florêncio's boundless disdain on the day he had rejected him, came bubbling to the surface, making him more and more indignant.

Florêncio thought he had been vanquished and eliminated socially for good. He was wrong. The time had come for Adozindo to assert himself and all it needed was for him to say when.

26

One Saturday, Adozindo decided to devote the afternoon to his wife, who had been insisting on the need to do some shopping in the Bazaar. It was a long time since he had been out with her because he always had some work to do for the firm. So on that day there was no gathering of his friends, except that Valdemero had turned up and decided to join them on their walk.

The children had gone with the Queen-Bee, whom they were very fond of, and would only come home at night. So they would be able to enjoy a quiet walk, without having to contend with restless children.

Was he going to take advantage of the outing to tell his wife? He had discovered, not far from where they lived, an unoccupied house on the Rampa dos Artilheiros, in the direction of the Monte Fort, surrounded by a garden and with a yard at the back. It was a detached, two-storey house, and he had liked its front the moment he set eyes on it, with its veranda and ornamental columns. It would be a huge step up from their little house on the Estrada do Repouso. It would involve a considerable increase in their outlay. He decided not to talk to her about it yet, so as not to delay their shopping in the Bazaar.

They walked down the Estrada Coelho do Amaral, took the Rua de São Paulo as far as the Rua da Palha, and then descended the lane to the Rua dos Mercadores.

As they walked, his mind strayed away from the trivial chatter between A-Leng and Valdemero. His wife would agree to the move. She no longer liked the street where they lived, ever since an ugly building had been put up on the other side of the road, stealing their view, causing trees to be cut down and, according to her beliefs, depriving them of the 'good winds' that they received from a certain direction. But would she accept the Rampa dos Artilheiros, a somewhat deserted area and far from the market and the grocery shops? And wouldn't she consider it a luxury, a drain on the family's budget?

As they were turning into the Rua dos Mercadores, they made their obligatory visit to 'Meng Seng', the well-known general store, where there was always a variety of things to attract the interest of housewives. A-Leng was looking for reels of cotton thread and beads for reasons best known to herself. She took her time over the pleasure of choosing and then haggling over the price. Then, she wanted socks for the children, a pair of slippers for her husband, a thermos for tea, and an elegant, flowery parasol to protect her from the hottest sun of the year.

Outside, the street was still flooded by the bright summer sunlight. The persistent rain of the previous evening had stopped, leaving a clear but oppressively humid day. The punkah, which ran the whole length of the shop, and was turned manually by a sad-faced, skinny urchin, produced a breeze that provided little relief. The two men, waiting patiently, as all men do who accompany the ladies on their shopping expeditions, stood by the door, contemplating the hubbub in the street.

She emerged, at last, with more packets, happy with her new acquisitions and grateful to her husband for not grumbling at her extravagance. But there was more to it than that. She always had a smile on her face when she went out with her husband, and was able to wear her most striking *tun-sam-fu*. It was so seldom that she was able to go out with him at that hour of the day.

They never failed to make a beautiful couple, Valdemero said to himself. Always correct and a little shy, he had felt a platonic love for A-Leng ever since the first day he had met her, and he was more devoted to her than a servant. A request from her was an order for him. How she had transformed the Handsome Adozindo! A man of such a polygamous temperament had been reduced to desiring only one woman! A woman of obscure origins, a unique, luxuriant blossom, raised in the destitute world of Cheok Chai Un, who were her true parents, what ancestral blood flowed through her veins to differentiate her from the others, this once abandoned child, left to her fate in a gloomy alleyway in Macao? In his simple adoration, Valdemero foresaw her future: in another ten years or so, she would be a matriarch, governing her universe.

In his platonic admiration, Valdemero harboured one wish. He had always seen her, whether at home or in the street, wearing a *tun-sam-fu*, whose cut and cloth, whether cotton, satin or silk, had gradually improved, but were still basically the same. What would happen if she were to change to a cheongsam, the long gown which, according to the experts, was the most elegant dress that had ever been produced by the human imagination? She would make a splendid sight in the streets of Macao, with that slender body of hers and her rhythmic, rustling walk that she had not lost, and that came from her days as a water-seller. He couldn't resist it, and broke through the wall of his shyness:

'Why don't you wear a cheongsam?

She arched her eyebrows, surprised, and let out her characteristic peal of laughter. Before her husband could comment, she looked at him and said: 'Oh no ... What ever for? ... I wouldn't have an occasion to wear it. I'm always at home, it would be a waste.'

Adozindo felt his heart go thump. There went Valdemero, with his innocent questions that nevertheless pricked a man's conscience! He had often thought of suggesting this very thing to his wife, but as they weren't going anywhere, he let it pass or decided it wasn't worth it. Could it be that A-Leng now wanted to say more, but hadn't done so in order not to offend him? The Rua dos Mercadores was a hive of noise and activity, even at that hour. Hawkers were obstructing the pavements, competing with the shops. They were displaying the most diverse objects — baubles, second-hand clothes, old iron, little works of art, most of which were fakes, and items of earthenware for all conceivable uses. There were the unmistakable smells of medicinal herbs and teas, all manner of steaming broths and foods, vegetables preserved in vinegar and diverse types of pickle.

People talked, argued, traded in loud voices. Pedestrians were forced off the pavement into the middle of the street, often having to get out of the way of rickshaws and the shouting drivers. There were beggars, dirt-covered urchins jumping around, crying children, shaken by agitated mothers. A few cars and bicycles glided by, hooting or ringing their bells. This was the vitality of the Bazaar in all its restless exuberance.

'I feel like some refreshment,' said A-Leng.

'There's the "United States". They do a good ice-cream,' Valdemero suggested.

Adozindo cut in immediately:

'No, not an ice-cream! I'd rather have a sweet almond broth ... The shop's just over there.'

Valdemero didn't insist, but watched his friend as he hurried off. When would Adozindo decide to mingle with 'his people', an inevitability were they to go to the 'United States of America' restaurant that occupied the ground and mezzanine floors of the Hotel Central, on the side opposite the Victória Cinema? It wasn't as if he'd suggested 'As Delícias' or the Riviera, which were frequented by the elite. On the other hand, he understood: A-Leng was wearing a *tun-sam-fu*.

She said she'd never been to that restaurant, but she was happy to accept her husband's suggestion because it was on the way to the store where she wanted to buy some paper kites that she had promised the children. And if there was any time left, they could even visit A-Soi.

They entered the wide stretch of the Rua das Estalagens, which was as animated and bustling as the street they had left, with its hawkers and little stalls blocking access to the shops, in a permanent fairground atmosphere. The same smells and cries, noisy conversations, bellowing of the rickshaw coolies, creaking drays and mixture of voices. A wandering barber advertised his services, pointing to his customers' chair. At that very moment, the old street dentist was burrowing holes in the teeth of some poor devil who was shrieking, his arms pinned back by a powerful assistant. The storyteller had gathered his audience and was embarking on the eloquent account of the deeds of a legendary hero.

The three of them suddenly paused distractedly almost in the middle of the street, their attention drawn to three young lads playing *chiquia*, each of them in turn kicking a paper ball decorated round the middle with coloured duck feathers. The game involved preventing the ball from falling to the ground. The one who missed his kick lost the bet. These boys were real experts, twisting and turning in order to keep the ball in the air, for which they won applause. A-Leng got carried away. She confessed that when she was about nine, she had competed with the boys in her neighbourhood and had beaten them all, but that she'd been obliged to give up playing that poor folks' game because of the persistent disapproval of the womenfolk.

The honk of a car horn swept through the street, right behind them. This sudden, alarming stridency took them completely by surprise. They leapt to one side, A-Leng's packets went flying and she lost her balance, falling against one of the young boys who, fortunately, was strong enough to steady her.

'Damn you!' shouted Adozindo, quivering with fright and indignation.

'Ah! That was the man who wouldn't give me a bowl of tea,' exclaimed A-Leng, in breathless recognition, while still leaning on the boy.

The dark grey Chevrolet went coldly on its way, its horn honking, while Florêncio and Lucrécia didn't even bother to turn round. Oh! The insolence of those who think they're beyond the law because they have a bit of money!

Valdemero pulled Adozindo away, as he stood rooted to the ground, his blind fury festering inside him. They sat in a corner of the soup shop, listening to the repeated complaints of the passers-by. A-Leng had forgotten all about the paper kites, as she wiped the cold sweat from her brow. Valdemero put the packets on an empty chair and ordered the almond broth from the skinny waitress. He contemplated his friend in his muted anger.

A-Leng broke the silence, saying:

'They had no respect for us.'

'Maybe it wasn't deliberate. We were almost in the middle of the road. It's possible they'd already hooted.' Valdemero tried to play down the incident.

Adozindo took a deep breath and hissed:

'The car was travelling at a reckless speed. And they had room to pass, besides which you don't hoot like that. It's a miracle A-Leng wasn't run over. In any case, they had a duty to stop.'

'The problem is we're not "proper folk" as far as they're concerned. And those who aren't "proper folk" get pushed into the gutter.'

A-Leng's comments came like a whiplash. Adozindo's face darkened, while his hands stiffened, as if he wanted to strangle someone. The broth appeared, the fragrance of the almond hung over the table.

'He still hates you as much as ever.'

'They're old scores ... '

She couldn't contain herself. She was excited and needed to let off steam. She remembered every detail of their visit to Florêncio's house on that sad morning. Only now did Adozindo realise how much she too had suffered. She spoke without their interrupting her and then felt relieved. Having calmed down, she said:

'I never asked you the reason for your hatred and I'm not asking now. We stayed together, that was the important thing. But I never forgot. You asked him for help and he refused to give it. I was always sure it had something to do with me. The way he looked at me, not even inviting me to sit down, not even offering me tea, as good manners demand. I don't know what you were talking about, but it must have involved a lot of insults. I'm just sorry I didn't hit him over the head and round his ribs with my *tam-kon*, which I certainly felt like doing. But anyway, I came out the winner. You left with me, and that was good enough for me.'

The idea of Florêncio getting a beating and howling with pain, and then seeking refuge by crawling under the table, reduced the tension. They all laughed, including A-Leng herself.

She and Valdemero ordered some more broth. Adozindo was drumming his fingers on the table-top, and not paying attention to the conversation. All of a sudden he said:

'Let's go to the silk shop. I want to see you in a cheongsam. I can't get it out of my head.'

'About time too ... '

Valdemero's exclamation was equal in its strength to A-Leng's astonishment. He didn't finish his broth. He would have liked to put in some suitably sweet word, but all he could say was:

'You've made up for the fright with the nicest surprise.'

'Frights sometimes wake us up to reality.'

Adozindo hurriedly paid the bill. He seemed to be in a rush, as if propelled by some hidden spring. They visited a number of shops. He chose the cuts of silk himself, and spent generously. A-Leng, dizzy with affection,

didn't object, for the cloth was so beautiful and she had always trusted his taste. All she said was that she didn't need so much. Four was too much.
'For you, there will never be too much. What happened today won't happen again. I plan to take you to Hong Kong, because you've never been there. As you can see, the time has come for us to be "proper folk".'
'Well, this is a day of surprises ... ' She laughed, putting the parcels of silk under her arm.

He could have told her he had another surprise in store, but he resisted the temptation, and decided to keep it for the following day, after the morning mass at São Lázaro.
'Now you must learn to walk on high-heels, which go very well with a cheongsam.'

Once again, she let out her unique, vigorous laugh:
'And I've got a surprise too. Nearly a year ago, I couldn't resist them and bought a pair of high-heeled shoes. When you were out, I secretly practised walking on them. So don't worry. I don't have any problems with them now. It's just that I knew that one day you'd want to see me in a cheongsam.'

After that, they bought the paper kites and then, without a single comment, passed the hostel where they had once stayed all that time ago, and A-Leng led them towards A-Soi's house. She was moved along by the joyous prospect of being able to tell her friend that a new chapter in her life had begun.

27

fter mass the following day, he did indeed take a detour from his usual route home. He struck out in the direction of the Rampa dos Artilheiros, by descending the steps of the Calçada de São Lázaro. He was more determined than ever, and was still chewing over Florêncio's affront. He answered his wife's puzzled curiosity with a mysterious curl of his lips.

When they got there, he pointed to the house. It was even more graceful at that hour of the morning, with the sunlight on its freshly painted walls. Although it wasn't a new building, it had a welcoming façade. At that point he told her he planned to rent it, given that it was unoccupied, and assuming that she liked it and the owner agreed. His first task was to find out who this might be.

A-Leng was grateful for such a pleasant surprise, and in her excitement, took her husband's arm and asked:

'Have we got enough money for this?'

'I've been thinking about it all night. We can do it, and I'll work all the harder for ... '

There was a resoluteness in his voice and she believed him. Besides, she was taken with the house. It had a yard, a well, a papaya tree, it was exposed to a south westerly breeze, and the air was free of dust. The children could play happily in the street, for apart from the sporadic traffic up to the Monte Fort, few passers-by used the road. The area had the peace and quiet of a village, with Portuguese-style paving and good neighbours. A suitable area for bringing up children.

A question here, an inquiry there, followed by a perusal of the records in the Registry Office, and he managed to identify the proprietor, Dona Capitolina, a lady of property and means, a widow and eminent figure not only in the quarter but among the parishioners of the church of Santo António, and resident in a large town house on the Rua de São Paulo.

Adozindo's enthusiasm faded. She was a friend of his mother, aunt and grandmother, and would have heard all manner of poisonous stories about his marriage. Apart from this, in the more distant past, D. Capitolina had wanted him as a son-in-law, and had tried to lay siege to him on behalf of her ugly daughter, Evelina. He had managed to dodge her skilfully, without offending anyone, but had left both mother and daughter disappointed at their shattered dream.

He thought of giving up, but then how would he explain to A-Leng? She was delighted with the house and had told Tina, the Queen-Bee and A-Soi about it. The four of them had even gone to take a look at it from the outside. They were unanimous in their favourable opinion. The Queen-Bee declared that the house was bathed in good *feng shui*.

———

He decided to go and talk to D. Capitolina's son, Big Fist Joaquim, an employee of the English concessionary, the Macao Electric Company (Melco), whose offices were halfway up the Rua Central. He was a huge, burly man, with a contrastingly piping, feminine voice.

His nickname came from his monumental knockout punch in an amateur boxing match, then very much in fashion, against another monster, a Filipino who went by the *nom-de-guerre* of 'Killer Jack'. It happened about a minute from the end of the second round. The Filipino, who had entered the ring with a lot of threats and much bravado, convinced he was going to win, made the mistake of lowering his guard, at which point Joaquim's ferroconcrete fist smashed into his square jaw. Legend has it that he was unconscious for a good two hours. The winner, amid the tumultuous applause of his fans, shouted at the top of his womanly voice:

'Fuck off out of here, Killer Jack! ... No one can stop this big fist of mine.'

And Big Fist got appended to his name. After that, he couldn't find an opponent to fight in that bloody pastime. So he devoted himself to weightlifting, and loved to admire himself in the mirror, in an almost sickly display of narcissism, in order to keep a close watch on his muscular development. He was a brute, but in front of his mother, he became bashful in his speech, a good, obedient son. He said he would never marry as long as his mother was alive.

'I'm a true son of my mother — but I'm not a son-of-a-bitch because I'm not a scallywag!' he would say.

He also enjoyed fishing as a second sport. He and Adozindo had never been close, although they knew one another. They got on best when they were standing next to each other, fishing rods in the air, bait at the ready. Then they would get quite talkative, and compliment each other on their catch. Afterwards, once they had separated, they returned to their customary formality. Now, after years in the wilderness, he didn't know how he would be received. Had the sister, to whom Joaquim was devoted, made some complaint against Adozindo? But she was married, and her husband had doused the flames of her spinsterhood with a litter of children.

Full of resignation, he entered the offices of Melco, half an hour before they closed for lunch. He waited nervously for ten minutes, seated on an uncomfortable chair, surrounded by the noise of typewriters and exposed to the curiosity of the employees. He had a painful memory of a distant day when he asked them for a job in vain.

Big Fist Joaquim appeared, heaving his huge body, soaked in sweat that not even the ceiling fans could alleviate. There was a look of surprised caution on his damp face. The Handsome Adozindo was looking for him. Did he want to borrow some money? His handshake was cold, and there was no sign of sympathy in the former boxer.

Adozindo hurried to explain what he had come about. The big man's relief was noticeable. He listened and then explained clumsily:

'I can't answer for my mother. I know she'd rather sell it, because she's got too many houses. But I'll speak to her. Maybe she'll change her mind. But the rent will be high.'

He was boorish and didn't know how to treat people in any other way, giving offence without meaning to.

'The last tenant gave her a lot of trouble. He was always late with his rent, and I had to go and give him a shake once or twice. He left the house in an awful state. We had to spend money to repair the floor that was full of holes, and paint inside and out. Drop by this afternoon or phone me. But I can say right away it's not going to be easy to shift my mother.'

He took his leave with the same abrupt manner. He was rude, but otherwise harmless. In the afternoon, Adozindo telephoned. He couldn't get through because the line was permanently engaged. He decided to go and hear the answer in person and set off, tired, on foot, getting there just before the offices closed. He was in a meeting, and they told him he could wait if he wanted. He waited outside in the street for Big Fist Joaquim, who emerged unhurriedly about twenty minutes later. Hardly did he see Adozindo than he shouted:

'My mother says she's not letting it.'

Without uttering any further thoughts on the subject to sweeten the pill, he turned on his heel and walked up the Rua Central, obviously on his way to the Clube de Macau. This time, Adozindo was offended by the treatment. He wasn't 'proper folk'. He was on the point of reprimanding him, but Big Fist Joaquim was far away by now, walking along with his gigantic strides.

His anger clouded his judgement. What sort of opinion did Big Fist

Joaquim and the rest of them have of him? He turned down the Calçada do Governador towards the Praia Grande, where the new land reclamations began. He needed to calm down before returning home and announcing his failure.

He turned the corner by the courthouse and caught sight, about twenty yards ahead, of Florêncio returning from the tennis-courts, racket under his arm, towel round his neck, and the prosperous air of one who didn't need to toil. The rich boy quivered visibly.

The accumulation of anger he felt against him, reinforced by his humiliation at Big Fist's dry, disdainful answer, exploded, not allowing him to consider the consequences. Adozindo walked towards him with such a disturbed look on his face that Florêncio got scared. Looking both ways, he leapt aside, dropping his racket and ran off at speed towards the entrance to the Hotel Riviera. He looked the epitome of a good-for-nothing.

Adozindo gave chase, faster and more threatening than ever before. The sight of his adversary's thick legs, stumbling along the pavement, spurred him on. He caught up with Florêncio just inside the hotel, and grabbed him by the scruff of the neck. There was the sound of cloth ripping, and Florêncio's voice shouting:

'Mind what you're doing ... mind what you're doing ... '

A punch flew through the air, but didn't catch him because he turned his head aside in time. This was followed by a scraping of chairs, running footsteps and excited voices. Arms separated the two contestants.

'Let's have some respect here ... There are foreigners at the tables seeing all this.'

'I didn't do anything ... He assaulted me.'

'Let me go! I'm going to smash that face ... He honked at me, he provoked me, he nearly ran my wife over and he didn't even say sorry. I don't take insults ... '

'I had a feeling it was something to do with women,' said a scornful voice. 'That irritating horn ... '

'It's not going to stop at this ... I'm not letting it stop here,' said Florêncio, whose courage was now returning.

'It's not going to stop here, you can be sure of that ... I'm not leaving here without you making an apology, in front of everyone. If you don't, I'll smash your face wherever and whenever I find you. No one treats my wife with disrespect ... '

'I'm not scared of threats ... '

'And I'll be true to my word because I've got nothing to lose,' and he tried to break free of the arms that were holding him back.

The manager, speaking in English, intervened, upright in his dignity. This was a respectable hotel, the best in the city. The guests deserved respect and this disorder among gentlemen gave a bad impression. If they really wanted to lay into each other, then they should at least go outside to the arcades. But certainly not there, among gentlemen, he repeated. He didn't want to have to call the police, and hoped they understood.

Strangers gathered and began to offer their opinions, along with the waiters, who had been distracted from their work. The news spread like wildfire to 'As Delícias' and the inquisitive rushed over, sniffing scandal. Florêncio and the Handsome Adozindo and that old affair with Lucrécia ... What a juicy titbit! Florêncio's heart began to throb at the sight of these newcomers.

The director of the Post and Telegraph Office, who had witnessed the whole incident, using the weight of his senior rank and his prestige in the pecking order, declared: 'Let's get this over with. We're all adults and gentlemen and not street urchins. Drawing attention to ourselves in this way is unseemly ... Now there's no doubt, Florêncio my friend, that you've got a very strident horn on your car. It's terrible. If you were about to run someone over, then apologise, for it even reflects well on you. And you, Adozindo, give Florêncio the money for a new shirt, and we're quits.'

'I've got more than enough shirts. I don't want a cent from him.'

'You don't need one because you're stinking rich. I want you to look me straight in the eye and apologise to my wife, in a loud voice so that everyone can hear. That's my condition.'

He felt like a hoodlum, ready to go to extremes, such was his hatred. He was also taking the opportunity to purge himself of all past humiliations. He sensed his opponent's cowardice in the way that he began to pulsate even more. Then he heard it:

'I apologise to your wife.'

He had the sensation that his honour had been cleansed. From now on, people would look at him with respect. Hands let go of him, he bowed his head slightly in some vague compliment and went out into the street amid a general hush. Then he heard Florêncio's voice:

'My racket ... What's happened to my racket?'

Years before, his wife had leapt to his defence against four ruffians and had become a legend in Cheok Chai Un. This time, it had been his turn to defend her in public from an abuse and the incident would be talked about all over the city. Nothing else weighed on his conscience, and he had done what had to be done. With this thought, he managed to swallow his disappointment at not getting the house.

28

*S*he had never demanded any revenge or at any time even hinted at anything like it. Everything had happened upon Adozindo's initiative, and the incident could have had more serious consequences. But the knowledge that she had been defended touched her deeply. She had regained her lost face, and the hateful man who had refused to even offer her a drop of tea had apologised in front of witnesses. They were beginning to be 'proper folk', but not yet totally so.

The other fact confirmed this. D. Capitolina's refusal had caused a deep hurt. The feeling that she, A-Leng, was also responsible for that negative answer, gnawed away at her heart. How much easier his life would have been without her. He managed to disguise his disappointment by assuming an air of indifference.

'There are other houses. We just have to keep looking.'

She looked at him hard. She knew her husband, and answered:

'But this is the one I want, and so do you. There must be another way.'

He shrugged his shoulders, told her who D. Capitolina and Big Fist Joaquim were, and didn't mention the Rampa dos Artilheiros again. He spent the rest of the evening listening to the wireless, his thoughts wandering aimlessly. In bed, he took her in his arms and caressed her hair for a long time.

At breakfast the following morning, she said:

'I think I know who the lady is ... the owner of the house. I've seen her in the church of Seng On Tó Nei.'

'In the church of Santo António ... what do you go there for?'

A-Leng bit her lip, blaming herself for having allowed a secret to slip out. Tina, the neighbour, was a devotee of Saint Anthony and had been urging her for a long time to ask for the miracle-making saint to intercede. He answered everyone's prayers. Lovers, spinsters and widows. He resolved marital and family problems, nightmares over money, debts and lost objects. Popular belief in his powers was well established among the Catholic population of Macao.

'Do you have some request to make?'

'Yes, I visit him twice a week. As I don't know how to read the proper prayers, I recite the ones I learnt with our priest at São Lázaro. And then, I speak in silence.'

Adozindo didn't laugh, out of respect for her simple faith, and he didn't ask about the nature of her request. That was his wife's secret. A-Leng hastily changed the subject back to D. Capitolina.

'I think she knows me by sight. Every time she comes into the church, she stops to look at me. I'm going to ask to speak to her.'

As soon as her husband had left, she went to confide in Tina. She couldn't stand her husband's defeated air and she couldn't just fold her arms in resignation. She still nurtured one hope, namely that, with one more try, she might get the owner to change her mind.

Tina didn't show any great enthusiasm. D. Capitolina was a proud old lady who didn't easily change an opinion. When she said no, she meant no. She knew her well from the ladies' meetings at Santo António, and her stubbornness was legendary. She was even physically scared of her, of her long body and her pomposity.

But A-Leng persisted. She wasn't going to knock on her door. That would give the impression she was begging and the owner of the house was always in a superior position. She was going to seek her out in church, on neutral territory, where they would be on equal footing. Then, if the conversation came to nothing, at least it would be less painful. She wouldn't be left with the feeling of having been chased away.

Tina was impressed by her friend's line of thinking. She was intelligent, certainly no dim-wit, and she knew how to plan ahead. Within the church premises, it would be easier to approach her. She would be able to pluck up enough courage to introduce A-Leng to the terrible old woman. That same afternoon, the ladies of the congregation were going to hold a meeting to begin preparations for the annual saint's day festivities. D. Capitolina's certain presence there would provide them with an opportunity. A-Leng, who didn't want to delay matters further, immediately agreed to the suggestion.

'Pray to Seng On Tó Nei to inspire the lady to say yes,' urged Tina in a God-fearing voice.

At the appointed hour, the two women arrived at the church. A-Leng had chosen a *tun-sam-fu* in a discreet tone of deep red — the cheongsams were not ready yet — and had combed her hair very carefully, minimizing its volume by winding into an attractive chignon, in the knowledge that her hairstyle would bring the best out of the simple elegance of her clothes. Devoid of any other accoutrements, wearing half-heeled shoes and carrying a black handbag, she awaited this most difficult of tests.

She had been to the church of Santo António with Tina on a number of occasions, at the insistence of her friend who wanted her to become a devotee of the saint. Whenever the subject came up, she would badger her with a list of his miracles. Now that they were going to speak to D. Capitolina, Tina was encouraging her to pray yet more fervently.

A-Leng, however, still felt a newcomer there, unlike São Lázaro, at the mass conducted by the priest who had baptized and married her, and where nearly all the congregation was Chinese. As she had told her husband, the only prayers she knew were the simple ones in Chinese. She was always doubtful as to whether the saint understood her, although this shocked Tina, who affirmed that God and the saints understood all languages, and that, anyway, the most important thing was intention. In any case, she had kept her request closely guarded in her heart. She had developed an immediate affection for the miraculous image, the gentleness that seemed to emanate from his eyes and hover in the air above.

Having established that D. Capitolina had not yet arrived, A-Leng inisited on staying in the churchyard. In that way, it would be easier to go up to her without wasting any time. She didn't appear nervous as she watched the ladies filing into church. She was sure she knew who Capitolina was, and her assumption was proved correct when Tina pointed to a thin, upstanding figure, somewhat reminiscent of a screw. Her dinner parties at the Rua de São Paulo were well known for their belly-busting qualities, but D. Capitolina never put on weight. How had a great big brute like Big Fist Joaquim been born from such a flat abdomen?

A-Leng, dragging her friend in tow, went over to her. Tina, with her reverential fear of a great lady, walked up to her, her legs quivering.

'Dona Capitolina, if you please, this lady would like to speak with you.'

There was noticeable irritation on her severe face. She said dryly:

'I haven't got time, Tolentina. We're going to begin our meeting.'

'It's only a moment ... five minutes at the most,' interrupted A-Leng with a disarming smile.

A-Leng's slender, elegant posture never went unnoticed. Nor did her attractive face, topped with its abundance of black hair. D. Capitolina stopped, and looked her up and down. She had already seen her in the church, although not at mass.

'I'm Adozindo's wife ... '

Without giving the other time to catch her breath, she explained the situation, the need for a larger house, her children needed fresher air. The Rampa dos Artilheiros was an ideal location. She asked her to reconsider her decision. She would treat the house well and she couldn't ask for better tenants, she promised, in a peculiar speech mingling Portuguese and Chinese that only true Macanese could understand.

'I've already given your husband an answer through my son. I'm not in the habit of going back on my word. I'm only interested in selling the house.'

Couldn't she be gentler in her reply, Tina asked herself anxiously? But bluntness and pride ran in the family. A-Leng wasn't put out and kept her same captivating smile.

'Don't you think it risky to reduce the good fortune you have enjoyed up until now?'

'What do you mean by that?' she exclaimed, bridling with anger.

'Don't misunderstand me. Let me explain ... '

She had been to see the house with a woman she looked upon as her mother and with Tina. Her mother possessed an ancient wisdom and knew many things, the fruit of life's experience. They had examined the house from the outside. Her mother had approved of the position of the house in relation to the sun, the winds and the open country. Even the rampart of the fort up above didn't hinder a slight breeze that was channelled by a particular angle in the wall and descended, like a blessing, directly onto the house. It therefore benefited from good *feng shui*, propitious winds for happiness and good fortune.

'My mother, who knows many geomancers, taught me one should never get rid of a house that has good *feng shui*. It's dicing with one's luck ... '

'I haven't lived there for years.'

'But you are still the owner. I know you have enjoyed good fortune. You have a fine son ... and a daughter who is happily married and grandchildren. And you are held in such high esteem and consideration.'

While Tina was translating, she was profoundly struck by her friend's skill in arguing her case. No one else would have been audacious enough to address the formidable lady like that.

D. Capitolina was completely knocked back by her words and forgot all about the meeting. She had to admit she'd been happy at the house on the Rampa dos Artilheiros, when she moved there after the death of her husband, a good-for-nothing, a person who incarnated stupidity, whom she'd married in a moment of blindness. And if she moved subsequently to the Rua de São Paulo, it was purely because of the obligations of a full social life. But she reacted:

'Your religion doesn't permit superstitions.'

A-Leng broadened her charming smile and answered beguilingly:

'Is there anyone born here, or who has lived in these parts for many years, who doesn't believe in *feng shui*? They must be very few. I'm not an educated person, but I do a lot of thinking. Religion doesn't prejudice *feng shui*. I even believe that *feng shui* is a gift of God.'

She had taken a shot in the dark, for she had nothing to lose, and had hit the bull's eye. D. Capitolina's severe face took on a more benign expression, and as her lips parted, there was just the trace of a smile. A-Leng pressed forward, taking advantage of the moment:

'Could I ask you to grant us, my husband, children and myself, a little of that *feng shui*?'

They were calling D. Capitolina from the side door of the church. Irritated, she signalled them to wait a moment. Her curiosity over A-Leng was rooting her to the ground.

'I've seen you in the church, but never at mass. Don't you go to mass? Aren't you a practising Catholic?'

'Yes, I am. I come to this church to pray to Saint Anthony. But we go to mass at São Lázaro. My husband is a friend of the priest who married us. I follow his wishes.'

'That is very good, for you are an obedient wife. That's what I like to hear. But you should come to mass in our church, because you live in this parish. And apart from that, your husband is a true son of the Santo António quarter.'

'I'll pass on your words to Adozindo.'

She hadn't yet satisfied her curiosity, and her eyes continued to survey this young woman of such sober and all-embracing elegance. She had heard so much about her.

'Tell me, is your beautiful chignon made of your own hair, or is it false?'

Her reply to this piece of impertinence was forceful in tone:

'It's my own hair. My husband won't allow me to cut it. In fact he would rather I went round with a braid all the time. But as you know, I can't do that. I can't show it in public because I'm married.'

'Do you love Adozindo so much?'

She blushed intensely. It was not in her character to talk to an insensitive stranger about such intimate matters as her love. She answered obliquely:

'My husband is a very good man. I have him to thank for all that I am today.'

Nothing more was needed. D. Capitolina seemed satisfied. Once again, she was called. She took a couple of steps and turned.

'I'll think about it. Wait there.'

Although it sounded like an order, it was not said harshly. It was part and parcel of her character to make others wait anxiously. Tina stifled a forlorn moan, but A-Leng, with the patience of her race, declared that she could wait as long as necessary.

'Let's pray to Seng On Tó Nei.'

A-Leng sat down in one of the pews, but didn't copy Tina. She had been making a very secret request ever since the first day she had gone there. Her pragmatic spirit whispered to her that yet another one would be to abuse the saint's generosity.

She went out again into the churchyard in search of some distraction while she waited. The Largo de Camões dozed in the reflection of the still baking heat. Here and there, on the green benches, old men and women enjoyed the last rays of the afternoon sun. A girl's head appeared at one of the windows of Adozindo's former house, peeping out at the street. On the other side, the convent of the Canossian Mothers stood out in its seclusion, its entire façade reclusive and devoid of joy. Hawkers selling noodle soup cried their ditties. There was the whining of a native violin and lute. The distant clacking of mah-jong tiles. From the Rua do Tarrafeiro came the sound of firecrackers exploding. High up in the leafy vegetation of the Poet's garden, there were incandescent flashes of golden sunlight. The chirping of birds was scattered among the branches of the acacia trees.

The figure of D. Capitolina, followed by Tina, suddenly appeared, framed in the side door of the church. The imposing lady bawled:

'The meeting's going to be some while yet. You've got a lot to do at home. I'm going to grant you a little bit of the *feng shui* you asked me for. Tell your husband to talk to my son tomorrow about the lease.'

'It was the good Saint Anthony ... ' murmured Tina, with God-fearing conviction.

29

ig Fist Joaquim didn't approve of his mother's *volte face*. At heart, his opposition came from the antipathy he felt towards Adozindo. Clumsy and coarse, he tried to place obstacles in the way of a lease by imposing ridiculous and unacceptable conditions, before even showing them the house.

His brusqueness irritated Adozindo who almost forgot his good manners. Negotiations ground to a halt and were on the verge of breaking down. Indignant, he withdrew claiming that he didn't know how to talk to a stupid boor. Valdemero agreed, declaring that the employee of Melco was an oaf, an intractable numskull.

A-Leng stepped serenely forward to calm their spirits. She couldn't believe that having conquered D. Capitolina, the son would be an obstacle. They arranged to meet again, this time at the Rampa dos Artilheiros. On this occasion, she accompanied Adozindo and was introduced to Big Fist Joaquim, who was prowling this way and that with an angry expression on his face.

'Let me do the talking ... '

Inside, the house fulfilled all the couple's aspirations. They couldn't possibly let it go. So A-Leng, displaying all her charm, took charge of the negotiations, first casting a balm on Big Fist's initial bad temper, and then leaving him open-mouthed and dazzled. The hare-brained conditions disappeared and the agreement was reduced to a standard two-year renewable contract, the only burden being the monthly rent of eighty patacas. The papers were to be signed in the presence of a lawyer, with the big man representing his mother.

The next day, as they left the lawyer's office, Killer Jack's conqueror was so mild and docile that he invited Adozindo to go fishing the following weekend.

'So I hear you hit that little weasel good and hard.'

'That's a bit of an exaggeration ... '

'I know ... I know. Don't be modest. He'd been asking for it for a long time. That horn ... '

Then he regaled A-Leng with his charm, which was as cloddish as his brimstone fist:

'Don't you have a friend as pretty and shapely as yourself to introduce me to?'

As they went their separate ways, Adozindo murmured: 'What's your secret for turning that stupid mountain of flesh and muscle into a syrupy admirer? You've got him eating out of your hand.'

'It's the way I talk. You let yourself be led by the nose too when I started being nice to you. No man can resist a pretty woman, which is what people say I am. And I am, aren't I?' She answered, screwing up her nose puckishly.

'I don't like people to take such liberties. And I only want you to flirt with me.'

'You're jealous! He didn't treat me with any disrespect. He was just trying to pay me a compliment, in the only way he knows how. You'll have a true friend in him,' and she put her arm coyly through his, the contract, all signed and sealed, held firmly in her hand.

The house on the Rampa dos Artilheiros had more than enough advantages to compensate for D. Capitolina's high rent. It had plenty of space for the whole family, and was endowed with fine views of the Guia and São Jerónimo hills and the valley where the city had developed, and between these two gentle elevations and that of the Monte, one could glimpse a little stretch of sea along the Praia Grande, with Taipa in the distance.

Set in the two-sided roof, there was a small terrace from where one could pick out Santerra's house further down the slope. Adozindo saw this as symbolic of his own social rise, and savoured his new situation with even greater relish.

Prior to finally moving in, and in accordance with time-honoured custom, the interior walls were whitewashed, the floor waxed, and everything that needed to look new was painted or varnished. They waited a few days for the smell of paint and polish to disperse, after which the removal of the furniture from the Estrada do Repouso began. They soon saw that if this had cluttered up their previous home, it was now spread out as if abandoned to itself. There was so much space to fill! But as the good priest from São Lázaro would have said: 'Rome wasn't built in a day.'

The same priest blessed the house at Adozindo's request, and prayed for the family's happiness. At the same time, out in the yard, the Queen-Bee, a committed Buddhist and suspicious of foreign rituals, burnt joss-sticks and votive papers in order to preserve the good *feng shui*. The sanction of two religions augured well for the peace and prosperity of the new home.

They eventually moved in on the same day as the procession of Saint Anthony, which was coincidentally a propitious day in the Chinese lunar calendar. There was an emotional scene as they closed the door of the little house on the Estrada do Repouso. Tina wept openly, even though A-Leng assured her that they would remain friends. But as they approached the Rampa dos Artilheiros, their sadness vanished. A-Leng insisted on their joining the procession, where she would show off her first cheongsam. Adozindo had no objection, for it was time to put her to the test in the Christian city.

They didn't go alone, but with the children, who were all excited in their best Sunday suits. They had their mother's good looks. Her cheongsam, which was for going out and about in, and was therefore not as long as the more formal type, fitted her perfectly, accentuating the curves of her bust and hips. Its tightness limited the wearer's movements, but with her erect body and small, dainty steps, the woman who wore it was given an air of natural distinction. The slit on the sides, revealing the leg and half the thigh, added a discreetly sensual touch.

With a trace of carmine on her lips and a light dusting of powder on her face, and walking rhythmically with a click of her high-heels, A-Leng was the epitome of beauty, instinctively attracting attention. She was graceful and self-assured. And so they arrived at the churchyard.

Unlike the processions of the Good Lord of Passos and Our Lady of Fátima, which brought together all the Catholics of the City of the Name of God, that of Saint Anthony was essentially a local one, limited to the quarter. Lacking the pomp and circumstance of the other processions, and being much shorter, it had a more down-to-earth, genuinely popular character, even though it was followed with the same fervour and piety.

People joined in out of real conviction and genuine faith, each one feeling the magical saint as if he were a member of the family, paternal and protective, generous, predisposed to a little give and take, forgiving of people's little sins, but never failing to call them to account. One didn't try and fool him with false promises, and he always knew how to punish. Such was the belief rooted in his followers.

It was a day of intense activity in the quarter. For a true born-and-bred resident, participation in the procession was obligatory, except in cases of *force majeure*. Commitments were postponed, and invitations to social gatherings avoided, and people dressed in their best clothes. Elaborate drapes were taken out of trunks and boxes to decorate the windows, while in front of the houses, the ground over which the procession was to pass was strewn with flowers and leaves.

The event also attracted the faithful from other parishes, who would come to thank the saint for his intercession or, in their prayers, to implore him once again to answer their harrowing requests. There was no shortage of old women spreading his miraculous powers by word of mouth, girls of a marriageable age or spinsters who didn't want to remain old aunties forever, and married women afraid they were sterile or widows in search of consolation. Indeed, the good Saint Anthony attended everybody, without discrimination.

For those who enjoyed abundant tasty food and plenty of drink, it was also a memorable day. In the big houses along the route the procession took, there was the traditional *chá gordo*, especially in the Largo de Camões, the Rua da Horta da Companhia and the Rua de São Paulo. Lists of guests were drawn up — some would have to visit more than one house — kitchens were filled with the smell of cooking, markets and grocers' shops were stripped of their stock, and the hawkers of snacks and pastries were kept on their feet. Such was the good life of the patriarchal age at the height of its prosperity!

This year, because no expense had been spared, the fair in the churchyard that had begun on the first day of the novena preceding the procession, with games and refreshment stalls, would reach a really spectacular climax on the night of the saint's day, with illuminations, fireworks and the launching of traditional balloons, a monopoly of the Carion family, which would later be carried by the wind and become fleeting stars in the night sky over Macao.

D. Capitolina and the group of ladies who had been so busy, believed in making a success of things, weather permitting. And the weather, with all the sunshine and blue sky, promised precisely that. Another of Saint Anthony's miracles in the middle of the rainy season.

In the churchyard, while waiting for the procession, Adozindo and his family mingled with the crowd. They were the immediate focus of people's curiosity, but they accepted that as inevitable. There was no sign of hostility or scorn. No one turned their face away, as in the old days, and there were those who asked whether that elegant woman was indeed the water-seller of past scandal. There were greetings, handshakes, small talk, gentle pinches of the children's cheeks. The recluse that Adozindo had become was being accepted once again into his social milieu. And she, A-Leng, for the first time surrounded by his folk, felt the weight of guilt at long last being lifted from her shoulders.

The procession began, and a passage was opened for the cortege, headed by the white mass of 'angels', little girls, displaying worthy composure, concentrating diligently on their role, and proud of their immaculate little wings. Then came the seminarists and clerics. When the statue of the saint on its platform passed by in front of them, Adozindo suddenly noticed A-Leng moving her lips slightly. Was she making a request or thanking him? After the Bishop of the Diocese and his retinue came the Municipal Band in full tune. Leaving the churchyard, the wall of people joined the tail of the procession, moving forward to the beat of the music.

So many other processions from the past were revived and mingled in Adozindo's memory. He knew all the faces around him. His school friends were now parents, the girls he had flirted with or wooed were now mothers. Others, their faces lined or their hair greying, reflected their fading youth, their spent beauty. Further on, the young people, open to hope and dreams. There were absentees, and he was distressed not to see his parents, his grandmother and aunt, and Cousin Catarina. How he would have liked them to see A-Leng and their children, and to put their bitterness behind them once and for all.

In the past, he too had eaten *chá gordo* in the big old house on the Largo de Camões. Guests used to gather there from all over the city, drawn there by his father's hospitality, and by the snacks and sweets made by his mother and aunt. He too had taken part in the launching of balloons, along with the other lads lightly singed from jumping over the fires, egged on by the girls shouting at the tops of their voices. He too had joined in games at the fair, the Handsome Adozindo, king of them all. The sensation he had of a time past that would never return filled him with nostalgia, a feeling that was only attenuated by the noise around him.

The windows of the houses along the route, brightly decorated with drapes, were packed with the faces of those who were privileged enough to watch the procession pass by. From that vantage point, people could see who was well or badly dressed and who was romancing whom. Under the wing of godliness and genuine faith, dwelt the poison of the gossipmongers.

In none of the windows did he see his parents or other members of the family, and once again he felt upset. But he caught sight of Florêncio and Lucrécia in D. Capitolina's house. For a few brief moments their eyes met. Florêncio gaped, his drooling mouth hanging open, while Lucrécia frowned. Instinctively, Adozindo looked at A-Leng, who smiled at him knowingly and, as ever, self-assured. She hadn't been a bad slipper after all.

Indeed, he and A-Leng hadn't been invited to any *chá gordo*. They walked the street along with the other commoners, A-Leng's high heels tapping firmly on the Portuguese-style paving stones, without the privilege of 'watching the procession go by'. But what did it matter? 'Rome wasn't built in a day', and it was all a question of time. Hadn't Big Fist Joaquim, after a triumphant day's fishing on the rocks by the Dutch Dock, laughing over their success until he went red in the face, invited the couple to a picnic in the bathing huts of the Outer Harbour on St. John's Day, the city's main festival? There, they would eat the traditional *arroz carregado* and *balichão* pork with tamarind. Many doors would remain closed to them, but this no longer affected them in the slightest. Others too had skeletons in their cupboards.

When the procession was over, they stopped in the churchyard where the fair was livening up with people thronging round the refreshment stalls. The children, exhausted by all the walking, got a new lease of life with all the other children dashing around and shouting. Not having experienced their parents' drama, they mixed easily and made friends. They were joined by Tina and her husband, Valdemero, Olímpio and the musicians from the evening get-togethers at the house on the Estrada do Repouso. They made arrangements for further meetings at the new house.

Valdemero didn't hold back on his praise for A-Leng, and he was joined by the others whose effusiveness was only tempered by their discretion.

'Didn't I say a cheongsam would suit her?'

'Don't spoil my wife with compliments ... '

His old neighbours from the Largo de Camões and his school companions came over too. A-Leng was the novelty, and Cheok Chai Un had been consigned to oblivion or to the domain of folktales, of which the town was full. They strolled around, paused, chatted. It seemed to Adozindo as if he had returned from a long journey.

In the end, tired of running and jumping, the children complained that they felt sleepy. They were finding it difficult to stay on their feet, especially the younger one who wanted to be carried. It was time to go home. They didn't stay for the launching of the balloons and the firework display.

The party was in full swing when they left. They were in something of a hurry because they wanted to enjoy the first evening in their new house. They would have so much to remember that night. The elder son grumbled dozily, led by his mother. The other was carried in his father's arms, already fast asleep.

A-Leng's high heels echoed rhythmically on the ground, with a sound that was so different from her clogs of old. When she thought about this, she smiled to herself happily but nostalgically. She had completed a long, strange journey.

'You've rejoined your people at last.'

'Yes, I think so. And with you too, at my side.' But never completely, he thought to himself. They would always be rebels, because they were independent of the strict canons of two worlds.

———

In the little square at the entrance to the Rampa dos Artilheiros, the clusters of trees rustled, gentle and lulling. The fresh breeze blowing down from the Monte Fort, carried on it the comforting aroma of night jasmine. From a yard came the yapping of a litter of puppies. Far away, there came the faintest of sounds, as someone played a Chinese melody on a harmonica.

On the pavement, next to the door of the house, the diminutive figure of a girl who had been squatting, got to her feet. Surprised, Adozindo asked who she was. A-Leng answered:

'It's the new maid. Mother found her for me in Cheok Chai Un. She's the daughter of an old workmate of mine. She's coming to help me because I can't handle everything.'

She had a short white *kebaya*, black trousers, bare feet and the braid typical of her social class. It was a figure that transported him back to the past. But it wasn't the same. Her braid was scrawny, the girl was skinny, and although she had a pleasant face, she didn't have A-Leng's mystery.

An hour later, after a refreshing shower, Adozindo was on the little terrace lying on the rattan settee, which fitted his body comfortably. He wasn't yet used to the house. It was rather large and there was a lot of empty space. Apart from this he now had to resume habits of old that he had long forsaken.

And what would A-Leng say, she who had never had such a 'palace' as this? He stretched languidly, as he contemplated the shiny beads that glinted in the dark sky. He was vaguely aware of the murmur of women's voices. The boys were already asleep in their new beds. The noises of the city below rose, sparse and indefinable. Somewhere, people were playing mah-jong. From between the tightly packed dwellings of the Baixo Monte, filtered the voice of the man selling fish broth.

Suddenly, there was the sound of light footsteps, and a woman's body smelling of soap curled up next to him on the settee. In the darkness of the night, he couldn't make out her face, but he sensed her pulsating flesh. She had unwound the locks of her hair and improvised a braid, which was permeated with the fragrance of champac flowers.

'I love you. You were so beautiful and elegant that my heart burst with pride. Everyone was looking at you.'

A-Leng's mouth was red-hot and sweet, her tongue vibrant and mischievously active. Her body twisted away as she sought to make herself more comfortable on the settee. They didn't even hear the fireworks being set off.

'I didn't know you were a devotee of Seng On Tó Nei. I saw your lips moving. Were you praying?'

'I was thanking him.'

'For the house?'

'Not only that. I was thanking him for something else too.'

'What? Am I allowed to know?'

Her laughter trilled in the night. She bit the lobe of his ear and placed her hand on his stomach.

'You may and you must know. I'm pregnant, and I've had my first morning sickness. I know ... I'm not mistaken.'

He pulled her closer to him. She melted into coyness and entwined her body with his. She brushed him with the tip of her braid.

'It's going to be a girl ... '

'How can you be so sure?'

'Why not? Seng On Tó Nei has granted so many different types of wish, even the simplest ones. Why should I be an exception, especially as I haven't abused his kindness? He knows how much we yearn for a daughter ... '

High up under the blanket of stars, the red pin-prick of a balloon drew a line of fire.

30

few more years rolled by. Papa Aurélio had aged considerably, and had a marked stoop. His heart was still strong but his knees were full of rheumatism and he found it hard to walk.

He was a man of regular habits, and every afternoon, upon leaving the office to go home, he would sit for at least half an hour on one of the benches in what was left of the Vasco da Gama Garden, around the monument to the great navigator. There was one for which he had a special preference, and he would make his way to it, anxious to rest his legs and enjoy the restorative shade provided by the branches of the St Joseph's tree.

He liked that spot. He was comforted by the hiss of the palm leaves in the breeze, the rustling of the trimmed foliage, forever murmuring vague soliloquies. Then there was the chirping of the sparrows and other birds that provided some relaxing entertainment. He could distinguish the various calls of each species and was fascinated every time he picked up a new twitter amid the usual chorus, and would try his hardest to identify what new bird it might be.

He sat down heavily, massaging his knees. Then, he took his handkerchief out of his pocket and wiped the sweat from his face and neck. The summer was hot and luminous.

He gazed laconically at the further reaches of the old garden, where they had built part of the primary school. What had become of the beautiful flowerbeds and the fountains from the time when he had moved to the Estrada da Victória? Even the bandstand, nowadays silent and abandoned, would soon be demolished. How things had changed during those years!

The anger and disappointment that had seethed in his mind over the years had gradually been replaced by sadness and by a demoralising sense of impotence.

During the initial stages of his estrangement from his son, he had tried hard to lead a normal life. He wanted to show the world that the boy's outrageous behaviour hadn't affected his activity and that he could get on perfectly well without him. But it was just a show, and the constant pretence corroded him, leaving him exhausted. He would frequently explode in fits of rage and pour scorn on the 'trollop from Cheok Chai Un', 'the China girl with her pigtail and bare feet', a woman of the lowest social condition, who had bewitched his flighty son. Secretly, he nurtured the hope, just as the womenfolk did, that Adozindo would come knocking on the door, tail between his legs, begging for forgiveness. In order to make his life still harder, he had forbidden him to collect any of his belongings from the house once he had left. But his son hadn't come back and hadn't even sent anyone to claim so much as a matchstick. And his room, with its collection of elegant clothes, shoes and many personal effects, remained intact and unused, and would have ended up covered in dust were it not for the devotion of his niece, Catarina, who cleaned it once a week.

He accompanied Adozindo's hardships from afar, his struggle to survive with his fateful witch in tow, for people came to tell him about them. A satanic smile danced on his lips when he heard about his fruitless requests for a job. Let him learn to enjoy the bitter taste of his folly. He would come back.

But he didn't come back. The break had been final. This fact upset him. Only then did he realise that underneath his apparent indolence and frivolity, Adozindo possessed a pulsating pride that was as excessive as his own.

He suffered acutely when Florêncio occupied the place that should have been his son's. He felt he had been robbed. Lucrécia's sumptuous wedding, with hundreds of guests, was like an axe-blow to his self-esteem. He shut himself away in his study, where he had last spoken to his son, and cried. Then, later there had been other blows. Foreign travel, whisky sessions at the Riviera, reception's at the Governor's palace and, above all, the Chevrolet, raising clouds of dust from the tarred road, honking stridently as it came along the Estrada da Victória. An impotent rage would then tear away at him, leaving him worn out for the rest of the day. The infamous car horn had long fallen silent, but his wound was as raw as ever.

The family's sorrow took another turn when his niece, Catarina, rebelled against her loneliness and decided to get married. It was an open secret that she had felt passionately attracted to her cousin, for her shyness was scarcely able to disguise it. Adozindo, for his part, had always assumed this to be a question of childishness, a young girl's crush that would wear off in time. The family, of course, had never encouraged such sentiments because if the relationship were to come to anything, it would be tantamount to incest.

Adozindo's departure in the company of the water-seller affected her deeply. She fell ill, shrieked and cried buckets of tears, talked about going to a convent, dressed in mourning, and when she went to early morning mass, she wore a *dó*. Such a display of anguish irritated her uncle. She should stop play-acting, she was wasting her time for no one cared, much less the ungrateful scallywag himself. He was unnecessarily blunt, sick of all the weeping, the moaning and the lamentations in the house.

It took time for her to recover. Then, suddenly, Catarina surprised the family. She was standing by the window one afternoon, when a tall, upright young man walking down the Calçada do Paiol, looked up and enveloped her in an audacious gaze. No man had ever spent so long looking at her. She recoiled, suddenly roused, blushing all over, but she watched him as he walked on from behind the gauze curtain.

The stout young fellow was a sergeant in the artillery, stationed at the Guia Fort. Bored as a caged bird, she noticed, ever alert, that he came down the street at the same hour each day. She fell into the habit of waiting for him. Glances were exchanged, then the first greeting and smile were reciprocated.

The handsome sergeant, however, wasn't prepared to pass under the window every afternoon indefinitely. He began to prowl round the area at night, when he knew she would be in bed, clicking the heels of his shoes hard on the tarred road. She would jump out of bed and peep through the blinds, her heart beating deliriously.

Catarina, who was a true Macanese, sought refuge under the miraculous shadow of Saint Anthony, by praying passionately to him. There was a first meeting in the churchyard, after early mass on Sunday. The soldier went up to her respectfully, twirling his moustache nervously. He apologised for his forwardness, but he couldn't see any other way of getting to speak to her. He was motivated by the very best of intentions and he felt lonely.

Seen at close quarters, Catarina thought him still more handsome. The images of her cousin and the convent became ever fainter and more remote in her mind. She was embarrassed, and the blood heated her cheeks and the core of her body. Far from putting him off, she tacitly accepted his courtship. So that was how this love affair began, she a few years older than him, but gentle and unsophisticated, he a victim of loneliness.

Sergeant Silvério was impatient, and took matters into his own hands. One day, he burst into the agency and walked boldly up to Uncle Aurélio. He explained his feelings, which were sincere and honourable, and asked him for Catarina's hand, given that he was the only man in the house, and head of the family.

Aurélio was flabbergasted. How had such a thing happened without him being aware of anything? Yet another member of the family playing a trick on him behind his back. But he didn't antagonize the suitor. It was true that Catarina needed to get married and this was her first love. If the opportunity were wasted, she might never find anyone else disposed to take her on. He said he would speak to the girl and her mother, and would give him a reply. At home, there was mayhem. If she married a lowly sergeant, a European, sooner or later he would take her back home with him, and she'd end up 'digging potatoes'! The very idea was shameful. Her mother, aunt and grandmother opposed him. Catarina dug her heels in and the other women did too. The girl, always so meek, had turned into a rebel, a demon.

'If you don't agree to it, I'll run away. I'm not going to end my days a dried up, bitter old spinster. I've got a life of my own.'

Aurélio, dumbfounded and at his wits end, banged his fists on the table in anger:

'This house can't stand another scandal. We'll be a laughing-stock again. Stop all this hysteria and marry her off. What she needs is a bed with a man in it!'

'Heavens, Aurélio, what language!'

'But isn't it true?'

'How vulgar you're being!'

'Tomorrow, I'll say yes to the sergeant or whatever the hell he is, and it'll be in God's hands.'

'Thank you, Uncle dear.'

And so the sweet Catarina got married. Aurélio pondered on the matter with sadness. For the family's honour and pedigree, this wasn't what he had dreamt of for his niece. But she hadn't had a chance to fly any higher. Once again, he blamed his son's stubbornness. He was the one responsible for the loss of better opportunities.

Catarina moved away, delighted to escape from her prison and from the control of her mother, who had refused to go and live with her son-in-law. Adozindo's room fell into a state of untidiness. The house on the Estrada da Victória became a mansion inhabited by old people, devoid of joy, where the servants spoke in undertones and walked on tiptoe. A-Sam, the gossiping maid, had long gone and people were vaguely aware that she had married her new boss, for whom she had gone to work and to look after his children after his wife had died.

His train of thought was shattered by the sound of children rushing around, shrieking. The sight of those innocent young creatures reminded him of something else. Aurélio knew he had grandchildren. When the boys appeared, he classified them as the sinful fruit of a concubine. He wanted nothing to do with them, and maintained his initial attitude of indignation. Some years later, the girls arrived, two of them, the youngest still a babe in arms. News dripped steadily into the home of those elderly folk, and people reported that they were very pretty. In their uncompromising obstinacy, no one made any attempt at reconciliation. On the other hand, deep within him, Aurélio had long been curious to see the children, while at the same time, a strange, gushing tenderness enveloped him and cast a balm on his harshness. There was one fact he couldn't deny and it was that they were his grandchildren, his blood coursed through them and they would continue the family name. This feeling had affected him all the more forcefully after an incident at home. Some days before, after dinner and evening prayers, they all gathered in the sitting-room, fulfilling a routine that never changed, the ladies turning to their crochet, and the master of the house reading the evening paper from Hong Kong, which he had bought at Ângelo's bookshop. Reading the day's news was enough to fill one with despair. The European war, which was now two years old, had spread to Russia and to North Africa. In the East, Japanese relations with the United States were hardening and people saw a conflict in the Pacific as inevitable. He cast the newspaper aside, reluctant to continue, tired of bloodshed.

He then noticed that his mother-in-law had become distracted from her needlework, her gaze fixed on the window. She wasn't looking at anything in particular, but was just lost in thought.

If she wasn't yet eighty, she was certainly not far off. She was all wizened and bent, the agility for which she had been known had withered away. She had aged terribly, and her once beautiful face, from which Adozindo had inherited his perfect features, was devastated by wrinkles. It was she who had been the most enraged by her grandson's false step, and had not forgiven him for his mistake. Time, however, had demonstrated the stupidity of her over-reaction, for her grandson had not returned in a state of contrititon. And eight years had passed. Now, at one step from the grave, she was consumed by a yearning for Adozindo, who had always been her favourite grandchild, unlike the morose and awkward Catarina, who taxed her patience. She gave in to her thoughts, resigned and passive.

In the midst of an oppressive silence, she coughed, making the others start. There was a pause, and then she said in a thick, catarrh-laden voice:

'I'd like to see their faces ... People say they're very good-looking.'

'Who?'

'Them ... my great-grandchildren.'

'Oh, mamma, why suddenly start talking about them ... '

'But why not? They're here in my heart. In any case, they are part of my blood and bones. I'll be going to São Miguel[7] before long, without ever having seen them. I'm eighty.'

'Mamma, take some cordial to calm your nerves.'

'It's sad ... so sad.'

She dabbed her eyes with her handkerchief. That was the first time she

---

7.   The Catholic cemetery in Macao.

had wept openly over her great-grandchildren. She staggered to her feet, insisted that no one help her, and slowly left the room. Her unfinished crochet rolled onto the floor.

No one in the room exchanged a word until tea was served. He took a cigarette from the crumpled packet, lit it and coughed immediately. He threw it away because he knew smoking was bad for him.

As he sat glued to the garden bench, the memory of another anxious period came back to him. He, like so many others, had been left poorer as a result of the Hong Kong Stock Market crash of 1932. His salvation had been his shipping agency that had kept him financially afloat, sufficiently not to fall into debt or touch his wife's modest savings. But the old affluence had gone, even though he had managed to maintain a standard of living by keeping a watchful eye on expenses and unnecessary spending. And this state of affairs would have continued indefinitely had it not been for the turbulent climate in international politics.

The first big blow to the agency's income was the second Sino-Japanese war of 1937, an undeclared conflict that continued without an end or solution in sight. The Japanese occupation of the principal ports of China had had a severe effect on merchant shipping in the area. With the exception of Hong Kong, the China Sea was to all intents and purposes Japanese.

Then, war had been declared in Europe, and while at first this had been limited in terms of area, it then turned into a world conflict. The merchant navies of the warring powers, limited to or commandeered for the war effort, had disappeared from the suddenly dangerous and treacherous seas and oceans, with the exception, for the time being, of the Pacific.

In the Far East during that summer of 1941, the clouds of war were gathering ever more menacingly on the horizon. Japan had reacted against the sanctions imposed on it with aggressive posturing against the United States of America and England. Relations between these countries were developing in such a way that there would soon be rupture. It looked as if the Pacific would become another bloodbath.

For Aurélio, war was inevitable. What would happen to Macao? He was surprised that life seemed to be going on calmly, prosperously and buoyantly around him, and people were unconcerned and unconscious of the approaching apocalypse. There were few changes to everyday life, except for the gradual increase in the price of foodstuffs, and the growing number of refugees from across the border in China.

His agency had almost ground to a complete halt, without any freight for the different parts of the world. He was going to have to remodel it, re-direct its activities. But he lacked impetus, new blood, new vigour. He was gripped by lethargy. He was old, his world was going to die and he was alone. How was he going to be able to fight when the great test came?

He shook his head to dispel his anxiety and raised his eyes. He looked at the open stretch of sky, beyond the branches of the trees and watched the movements made by two paper kites, in furious contest, each one trying to sever its adversary's glass-studded line, in the popular game known as 'cut-cut', in which children and adults entertained themselves during long summer afternoons.

He felt a deep yearning for his youth, for the easy years, when there was no sadness, when he was the best kite-flyer, unrivalled in the field, the owner of a sharp, resistant line capable of scything through the others, keeping his kite in the air, the absolute ruler of the skies above the Campal and the Camões Grotto.

He sat up straight, once again wiping the sweat from his face and neck. Why didn't he go to the Campal, which was so near, instead of sitting there wallowing in melancholy and despair? It was only a matter of going down the steps from the garden into the street, walking at his usual pace for five minutes and he would be in the midst of youthful excitement.

As he was wondering whether to go or not, an old friend appeared before him. Sebastião had lived in Macao a good forty years, a retired lieutenant who hailed originally from a little village in the Alentejo. He had married a Macanese woman, and already had grandchildren, and never talked about returning to his native soil.

'What are you doing here, Aurélio my good friend, all alone and glum?'

'I am indeed glum. What did you expect? My life's so empty, the agency is on its last legs, there's a war coming, I see terrible times ahead and I'm all alone. I run to this quiet little spot to escape from my worries ... '

' ... and to think even more. What a pessimist we've got here, dear God! You're unhappy because you want to be. You know very well what I'm talking about.'

He sat down next to him, and took out a Filipino cheroot, whose smoke scattered an aromatic scent. He knew all about Adozindo, for Aurélio had told him the story on various occasions on days when he wanted to get things off his chest. He had always been in favour of reconciliation as the best solution, but his friend was obstinate. And there he was chewing over his same obsessions to the point of tediousness.

' ... I lost my son. He shamed me with his disgraceful behaviour, and I was the butt of gossip and scorn. It's unforgivable! He ignored his duties towards the family and its good name, and towards society. He rejected a wealthy marriage partner to go and wallow in the arms of a promiscuous water-seller, with no manners or education. He surrendered to a life of debauchery, to the base satisfaction of his lust, and poured scorn on the moral precepts that he had been taught with such love and care.'

On and on he went, repeating himself tediously and reciting the same wearisome accusations. Sebastião listened to him, fidgeting nervously, smoking his cheroot to the end and then lighting another. His friend had really gone too far. Raising his index finger, he interrupted the monologue.

'Do you know what you are, Aurélio? You're selfish ... '

'Selfish?'

'Yes, selfish. That's exactly what you are. Throughout this affair, you've only ever thought of yourself, your family's reputation, and how society sees you. You condemn your son because you've always thought, and still do think that he was brought up to serve your plans and interests, bound by obligations decided by you alone. That's unfair. You forget that he's got a mind of his own and that what is good for you isn't necessarily good for him. His life belongs to him alone.'

Aurelio's face went very red. He'd never heard anything like that from anyone.

'Sebastião, mind what you say. I won't accept ... '

'I think the time has come to tell you a few home truths. I don't believe in mincing my words. I've listened to you many times and have never answered you until now in order not to throw more wood on the fire, and because it was a matter between father and son. But this is too much, Aurélio. If it makes you angry, that's too bad. It's the honest opinion of a friend. As far as I'm concerned, Adozindo is one of the most decent and honest men I know. I would be prepared to shake his hand anywhere, and I am honoured to have him as a friend. I've just this moment seen him with his children, flying their kite in the Campal.'

Did he want to hear the truth of what happened, as he himself had verified? Adozindo had rashly disturbed the girl, who lived happily among her own people, accepting her lot, without any greater ambitions. She was held in high esteem by her folk, and was the 'princess' of her quarter. Why did he persist in seeing her as a common fortune-hunter who had taken advantage of his infatuation to trap him in a web he couldn't escape from? Why not accept that the girl really did end up falling in love with him, given Adozindo's undoubted good looks and all his sweet talk and lovey-dovey words?

'Don't defend her ... '

'Let me speak, man! You've made my ears ring with all your reasons until I can't take it anymore. It's my turn now, so don't interrupt.'

Adozindo had been careless enough to take things too far, and had provoked a scandal, not only among his own people, but among hers. For she was a person too and not some little animal. The girl had been banished from her quarter like a leper, insulted and scorned, a fact that flew in the face of any idea that this was all part of some premeditated conspiracy. And the boy, apart from deflowering her, put her in the family way.

Could he abandon her to God's mercy in such a situation? If he were a coward or a cynic, unscrupulous and self-interested, he would have done just that. Would that have been Christian behaviour, merely to maintain his family's reputation, to be rich and obey the rules of society? No, Adozindo felt responsible, refused to keep her as a concubine, and regardless of whether he loved her or not, married her in church, legally accepting paternity of her son. That was his obligation, the duty of an honourable man, a gentleman. Could there ever be such a fine example for all those who vociferated about morality and good customs, who beat their breasts in church, begging for forgiveness and the remission of their sins?

'Aurélio, my friend, believe me, I've found it hard to say these things. But I simply can't go on seeing you divided like this year after year ... Your son lives on the Rampa dos Artilheiros, and I who go to the Monte Fort nearly every day, frequently see him as I pass by. We often talk. I feel for him. I've watched him grow up and you have no idea how much he's changed. He earns well, he has a good house, which is as tidy as any house can be with children. He's never said a word against you or his mother, aunt or grandmother. And Catarina visits him. He asks after your health and doesn't comment further. But he won't give in as long as you refuse to accept his wife. She's the mother of his children.'

'I can't accept her.'

'This is complete madness after so many years ... You are consumed by a bitterness that's sterile, that's not taking you anywhere. And you need him so badly, for he's the only person who can help you. A disunited family is like a broken arm. You are depriving yourself, in the years you have left, of that great gift of God, which are your grandchildren. And your daughter-in-law ... '

'He can't be happy with her ... They have nothing in common ... '

'That's the prejudiced view you cling to in order to justify your resentment. They've lived together for eight years and they've no doubt got used to each other. Maybe he sometimes feels unhappy because she's not the ideal woman he might have dreamt of having. But the same situation could apply to her, for she was torn from her milieu, from her own race, her own customs, in order to follow him. No one knows who made the most sacrifices or suffered the most, and it no longer matters anyway. What I do know is that she's a beautiful woman whom it would be hard to spurn, and who inspires desire in whoever looks at her. When she smiles, she's irresistible. It's not surprising she seduced him. Her beauty was the only weapon she had.'

From what he had been able to see, they got on well, they possessed the same precious gift of harmony and understanding that sweetens and smoothes over the rough patches they may and almost certainly do encounter. And if they could feel comfortable with one another, under the same roof and in the same bed, then that was already plenty to be happy about. And then they had their children, and that was everything.

'Why, Aurélio, are you still chewing over a resentment that is empty and makes no sense at all, when no one out there seems to remember the affair anymore? Let them live as they have chosen to live. The union of their souls, so different in their background and culture, shouldn't surprise anyone. This, after all, is Macao ... '

Aurélio felt chastened and asked for a cheroot. They sat in silence. The sun spread a glittering halo over the pagoda trees and palms, from where there slipped a haze of golden dust. Maids in immaculate white *kebayas* and black trousers crossed the garden paths, taking children back home after their afternoon walk. Butterflies fluttered hectically from flower to flower as if in some frenetic dance. Behind and above them, the birds sang clamorously, in lively dispute for a corner of the nest. A girl's laughter, soothing and clear, scattered in the air.

31

The paper kite was fluttering uncontrollably, veering to the right all the time, and responding only sluggishly to the commands of Adozindo, who held the big reel of line. It was a magnificent Malay, one of half-a-dozen that had been bought in Hong Kong to the delight of the boys, Paulo, aged eight, and Jaime, who was nearly six.

It was an extravagance to buy such expensive kites for such young children, who couldn't make full use of them. But without openly admitting it, he had bought them for himself because he couldn't resist this type of summer sport, in which adolescents and adults took part, filling the open ground there at Tap-Seac, as well as the uncultivated terrain around Flora and Mong-Há and the reclaimed land of the Outer Harbour.

The boys showed their disappointment by whining, after their kite had been the envy of all the others in the field. It was insulting, a waste that a kite of that quality should behave in such an unsteady, unmanageable fashion. If only Valdemero were there! Adozindo was getting irritated with his little daughter of three, who was pulling at his trousers, and shouting that she wanted him to make it go higher.

'There's nothing wrong with the *sarangong*. It's the belly-band that's faulty.'

Adozindo stiffened in astonishment. The voice had come from behind, but he recognised it immediately, in spite of the years. Taken by surprise, he turned round and there was his father a few yards away, standing erect, pale, and making an effort to be natural. He forgot about the kite, while he felt a lump come to his throat and his arms sapped of their strength.

The kite, now out of control, was carried away plunging perilously, and was almost lost. The three children, unaware of the elderly man standing near them, started to panic and scream. Adozindo recovered his self-control, saved the kite at the last moment, and steadied its flight.

'Wind it in and mend the belly-band. When you've done that, you'll find that it flies beautifully. A Malay is one of the best there is.'

He obeyed and his memory was pricked by a scene from his childhood, in which father and son were in an identical situation. He handed the spindle to Paulo, giving him precise instructions.

'Your blessing, Papa.'

'Good afternoon,' he answered, offering his cheek for his son's kiss.

It was as if the gap of years had never existed. Affection seemed to flow between them in their discreet treatment of one another, and neither of them made any reference to the past. In the end, it had all been so easy. The three children looked at them in undisguised astonishment.

'So these are my grandchildren.'

'Yes, Paulo, Jaime and Maria Antónia or Tónia, as her mother calls her. I've got another one at home, Lígia, who is seven months old. Children, kiss your grandfather.'

The boys, still bewildered at having a grandfather suddenly thrust upon them, didn't need any persuading. But Tónia, more timid, hid between her father's legs. Aurélio bent over her pretty little face, in which European and Chinese features mingled in such magnificent harmony.

The kite, once again without anyone to control it, absorbed their attention. They wound it carefully in. The superb *sarangong*, in the shape of a large, graceful diamond, yellow and purple in colour, was identical to the ones commonly seen in the skies over Malaya. Aurélio examined it, touched the sleek wooden spars, and tested the paper.

'I was right. It's a beautiful kite. It's resistant and catches the wind well. The defect is in the belly-band.'

As an expert and former champion, he explained how the belly-band formed a frame made of two lines, which were fastened to two points on the middle spar of the kite and in turn to the spindle line by means of a knot. The skill and the secret lay in the length of the sides of the triangle formed by the knot and the two points to which they were fastened. A sturdy, well-made belly-band enabled the kite to be perfectly manageable and responsive to the spindle in the hands of the flyer.

The boys were fascinated and kept asking questions as they watched their grandfather's hands and gestures as he prepared a new belly-band. Adozindo limited himself to blowing his nose. The little girl, leaving the protection of her father's legs, looked on wide-eyed.

'They speak Portuguese.'

'They speak Portuguese with me and Chinese with their mother.'

Once the belly-band was done and tied to the spindle line, Jaime launched the kite into the air, while Adozindo held the spindle. It soared upwards perfectly and elegantly into the sky, propelled by the stiff breeze. The children yelled enthusiastically.

They weren't the only ones in the field. There were other people entertaining themselves not only by flying kites, but also in cutting their opponents' lines in 'cut-cut' contests. These were genuine dog-fights that galvanised both the participants and onlookers who rushed over especially to watch the spectacle. Even casual passers-by couldn't resist its appeal, as they looked up, head back, oblivious to the traffic, which, fortunately, was quiet.

'There's a kite approaching ours. It belongs to Simão.'

Paulo's warning alarmed Adozindo, who explained. Simão was the terror of the sky over Tap-Seac. His spindle contained a 'razor-thread', that is a glass-studded line that he himself prepared, and which was very sharp, severing his opponents' lines almost at will. He would cause havoc among the other kites and no one was safe when he took to the field. He would take bets and win, his expression one of boastfulness at his own invincibility.

Adozindo knew his own limitations, for he had never excelled in these contests. When Simão launched his kite, he lowered his, knowing that he couldn't match the other for skill. But he seethed with anger and humiliation at the self-confident way in which the champion appraised him with a cheerful, ironic comment. Moreover, his children were there as witnesses to this damage to his prestige.

'I've lost the Malay. It's too high. I can't get it back in time.'

'Don't run away. It's a point of honour. Put up a fight. If you retreat, you'll be a laughing-stock ... a ne'er-do-well. Take up the challenge.'

'I haven't got his experience. He's been doing this for a long time.'

'The arrogant are over-confident, but they make mistakes too. No one's infallible. What's your razor-thread like?'

'I ordered it from Singapore, along with the spindle. They're the best quality.'

'You've got that type of equipment and you're scared?'

'I don't want to disappoint the children. A blow to my dignity ... '

'Such things teach us to be strong. Give me the spindle. Let's see if I can remember the old tricks.'

He felt the line and a slight cut drew blood from his index finger. He whistled knowingly and nodded his approval. In a flash he was a teenager again. He thought he was stiff and slow, but lo and behold, his hands began to gain confidence and speed in their reflexes. No, he hadn't forgotten the favourite summer sport he had abandoned so long ago.

Simão's scornful laugh resounded, but Aurélio didn't even bother to look at him. His attention was focused on the Malay as it fluttered provocatively in response to the dangerous challenge. It was so graceful as it caught the sunlight, that he couldn't bear the prospect of losing it.

The two kites were now very close to each other. There was a hush all over the field as mortal combat was set to begin. Which of them would jump on the other? The line that fell on top of the other always had the advantage, slicing through at the point where they crossed, after a period of friction that could last several minutes laden with emotion. The tactic, then, was to avoid being below, to dodge an opponent's manoeuvre and make one's own kite climb in such a way that its line was above that of one's rival. In this game of cat and mouse, the kites made fascinating twists and turns.

Simão tugged his spindle in a downward movement, the line transmitting a command that caused the kite to plunge in a lethal dive called a 'header', the intention being for it to come down on top of the razor-thread from Singapore. Aurélio was quick to see the lunge and escaped narrowly with another header. Other headers followed, causing the spectators to gasp in admiration.

Father and son joined forces, exchanged brief comments, as if in a council of war, and they were supported by the children. Simão realised that he was up against a powerful enemy. The old-timer was no fool. On the contrary, he was revealing some familiarity with the sport. He began to torment him, switching from defence to attack. Simão got irritated, for his own self-esteem was now at risk.

'The fellow's getting edgy. Losing his calm. That's to our advantage.'

Suddenly, it looked as if Simão's line was going to lie across Aurélio's, but the latter, in the space of what proved to be a vital second, went into a rapid dive and escaped. The Malay then drew a wide, graceful arc and soared upwards, before suddenly falling onto that of his surprised rival, who had been caught in a trap. It had been a classic movement.

The lines crossed at a particular point and began to rub against each other furiously. The spindles spun, paying out generous extra lengths of line and the kites rose higher still in a ruthless 'cut-cut' contest. The razor-thread from Singapore hummed, completely taut, and the children jumped up and down, instilling even greater determination in their grandfather. Adozindo was yelling, and the entire field was mesmerized by this act of revenge.

'Ah! ... '

Everyone shouted in unison. High up above, Simão's kite drifted away out of control, its line ignominiously sliced through, while the triumphant Malay rose serenely and proudly, ruling the skies.

'Didn't I say it was all a question of a good belly-band?'

The two boys spontaneously hugged their grandfather, who was now a hero, and the little girl clapped her hands. Adozindo smiled, wiping the sweat from his brow and the back of his neck, while Aurélio passed him the spindle and, drained by emotion, thought back over the battle.

'I'm not as doddery as I thought. I'm still of some use. But the victory wasn't only mine. It was yours too and the little ones', for they inspired me with their enthusiasm and confidence.'

People walked over and gathered round Aurélio to congratulate him. They discussed the different stages of the fight and recalled other famous occasions that were thought to be buried deep in folk memory. No one seemed surprised to see father and son together. Simão unsportingly left the area to a chorus of jeers.

Once the valiant kite had been wound in and was in Paulo's hands, people began to disperse. After such an emotional event, they said they'd had enough for one day. Father, son and grandchildren left the grass and walked slowly along the street, pausing at the entrance to the road that climbed up towards Monte Hill.

At that moment, the bells of the church of São Lázaro began to gently ring the Angelus, its echoes reaching to the end of Tap-Seac and the Flora and all over the slopes of Guia Hill. They crossed themselves quietly and said an Ave-Maria in accordance with tradition.

'Good night.'

Swirls of white cloud, speckled with traces of red and purple, rolled across the clear sky. On the top of Guia hill, the lighthouse had begun to flash, although its light was still pallid. Cicadas sang among the trees, competing among themselves, for the day was not over for them. Swallows in rapid flight brushed the rooftops of the age-old houses. Higher still, doves fluttered rhythmically, their wings reflecting the last glimmer of sunset.

Aurélio was unsure whether to leave or stay. His elder grandchildren were chattering away asking a thousand and one questions. Tónia, shy as ever, looked at him. Then, Adozindo said in an awkward voice:

'Come with us, Papa. It's still early and night's only just fallen. A-Leng will be so happy. And you'll see Lígia.'

For a moment, he didn't move, as if suddenly blinded by a mist, his throat dry. When the damp veil lifted from his eyes, his granddaughter held out her little hand to him, pure and comforting. He couldn't resist the loving touch of those tiny fingers as he took them in his calloused palm, and he allowed himself to be led like a frightened child.

They all plodded up the road together and Aurélio, before he even realised it, found himself in the Rampa dos Artilheiros. The door of one of the houses opened, and the sleek shape of a woman appeared, holding a baby in her arms.

When A-Leng saw her father-in-law, her heart began to race. Then she remembered the magic words that she had never uttered before and thought would always be forbidden to her. Softly and with great warmth she murmured:

'Come in, Father. This home is your home.'

Outside, the deep red sun was sinking behind the hill of the São Paulo do Monte Fort. The breeze rustled gently and the glass in the windows glittered with golden flashes in the splendour of the dusk.

... *LAST WORDS*

On the eve of my departure to Portugal, where I was going to complete my studies, I ran into Adozindo by chance, sitting on a bench in the São Francisco Garden, in front of the main entrance to the Santa Rosa de Lima College. He was waiting for his elder daughter who was still at her piano lesson. I had been doing the rounds bidding farewell to friends and was soaked in sweat after so much hurrying here and there.

Adozindo was much older than I was, but we knew each other because, during the War of the Pacific, I had been his younger son's teacher at primary school. Being a conscientious father he would appear at school and ask how the little fellow was doing in his work and in his behaviour. The answer was always the same. He was doing well, and there was nothing to worry about with regard to his motivation or discipline.

I walked over to him. The war was over, the seas were open and free, and I was going to fulfil my dream of a university education. He congratulated me warmly and wished me well. I sat down beside him and we talked. I knew his story because I had heard it repeated countless times among the many tales of scandal in Macao.

In looks and physique he was still perfect. He was a man who had won the war, taking advantage of a unique moment, taking the helm of his father's agency and joining it to the one of which he was a partner, to supply the famished city with foodstuffs. One or two white streaks of hair on his temples lent his face a certain distinction and without a doubt helped to justify the continuing use of his nickname, Handsome Adozindo.

Suddenly, my companion fell silent, his eyes fixed on something. I followed the direction of his gaze and noticed a young proletarian Chinese girl, in the flower of her twenty years, walking hurriedly along, her clogs clacking loudly. Aware that she was being watched, she stiffened proudly, raising her chin, and ignoring us completely.

While there was nothing particularly striking about her face, she had a long ink-black braid, neatly tied, its thick knots artfully plaited. This type of hairstyle was no longer very common, destroyed by the war and the winds of modernization. But this girl exhibited it with pride, certain of the effect it produced, and was one of the last defenders of that fashion.

'*What a beautiful braid!' I exclaimed. Adozindo burst out laughing and then sighed.*

'*Take care, lad. That's not just any braid. It's a bewitching braid. The fountain of desire, it seduces us, invites us to caress it, to plunge our hands into it. It has the power to hold us and after that we can no longer escape. I know it.'*

He continued, absorbed in his contemplation of the braid as it got further away, dancing to the swaying rhythm of the girl's hips. It was getting late. I got up, we embraced and I left to go about my business.

I returned eight years later. The City of the Name of God remained structurally intact, without the skyscrapers and motorcars of today. But one thing disappointed and saddened me.

Chinese women of all social positions wore their hair either straight or curly, in accordance with western hairstyles. Nowhere did I catch a glimpse of a bewitching braid, shaking rhythmically like a serpent of temptation.

— *Written after a stroll through Cheok Chai Un on a sunlit morning*

GLOSSARY

a-mui	a young girl in Cantonese.
amuirona	a derogatory Macanese term for a young proletarian girl.
arroz carregado	literally 'loaded rice', it is a type of Macanese risotto, containing chopped meats and vegetables.
balichão	a paste made from ground shrimp, garlic and tamarind used widely in the cuisine of Southeast Asia and Southern China.
capela	a baked dish made from minced pork, onions, olives and cheese, so called because it resembles the golden dome of a chapel when cooked.
chá gordo	literally 'fat tea', this is a Macanese supper at which a wide variety of savouries and sweets are served. Often an occasion for a family or social gathering.
chiquia	a traditional Chinese game, which involves keeping a light ball or shuttlecock in the air for as long as possible, using one's feet.
clu-clu	an onomatopoeic term to describe a gambling table in Cantonese.
cou-lau	a restaurant serving Chinese food.
dó	a dress worn by Macanese women in days gone by, consisting of a black veil and skirt.
fan-tan	a Chinese gambling game, which consists of guessing the correct number of beans in a pot.
fan-tim	a small restaurant or eating house in Cantonese.
kebaya	a short gown traditionally worn by both men and women.
kwai-lo/kwai	a foreigner, foreign devil (Cantonese).
lan-chais	ragamuffins (Cantonese).
lorcha	a light coastal vessel with a hull built on a European model, but with rigging like that of a junk.
melenta	from the Portuguese word 'merenda', meaning tea, or afternoon snack.
min-hap	a Chinese padded jacket widely worn in the cold season.
missó-cristão	a traditional Macanese dish made from a purée of white beans, to which are added finely chopped pork or shrimp, onions, shallots, garlic and saffron.

pai-kao	a type of Chinese dominoes.
patois	derived from French, it refers to the Creole language of Macao, known in Portuguese as *patuá, doce papiaçám* (sweet talk) and *língua maquista* (Macao language). It is no longer spoken widely, but is kept alive by various cultural groups in the city.
peixe esmargal	a variety of soused or pickled sawfish, using dry chilli, cumin, saffron, tamarind, garlic and rice wine.
raspiate	a Macanese term meaning a 'poor devil'.
sarangong	a Macanese word for a kite, deriving from the Malay 'rangong', meaning an adjutant bird.
sarrabulho	a Macanese variant of a dish from Northern Portugal, made with various types of shredded meat, to which cooked pig's blood is added.
siu-tche	a Cantonese form of address meaning 'little miss'.
tam-kon	a pole carried over the shoulders used for transporting buckets and baskets throughout Southeast Asia.
tanka	a small boat derived from an ethnic group of the same name in Southern China that was not allowed to live on land or marry into families living on land.
tau-fu-fá	a type of custard made from tofu.
tuna	a musical group, usually made up of students, in Portugal.
tun-sam-fu	a Chinese tunic worn by women.

SUGGESTED FURTHER READING

The following titles are a brief selection of books in English on Macao:

Brookshaw, David. *Perceptions of China in Modern Portuguese Literature — Border Gates*. Lewiston: The Edwin Mellen Press, 2002. An academic study of depictions of China and Macao in Portuguese literature over the last century.

Brookshaw, David (ed.). *Visions of China: Stories From Macau*. Providence RI/Hong Kong: Gávea-Brown/Hong Kong University Press, 2002. An anthology of short stories by Portuguese and Macanese writers.

Cabral, João de Pina. *Between China and Europe: Person, Culture and Emotion in Macao*. London: Continuum, 2002. A study of the Macanese by a well-known Portuguese anthropologist.

Coates, A. *City of Broken Promises*. Hong Kong: Oxford University Press, 1987. (1967). A historical novel set in Macao in the eighteenth century.

Coates, A. *A Macao Narrative*. Hong Kong: Oxford University Press, 1999. (1978). A brief account of the history of Macao for the general reader.

Cremer, R. D. (ed.). *Macau: City of Commerce and Culture*. Hong Kong: University of East Asia, 1987. A volume of essays on diverse aspects of the history and culture of Macao.

Gunn, Geoffrey C. *Encountering Macau: A Portuguese City-state on the Periphery of China, 1557–1999*. Boulder: Westview Press, 1996. History of Macao from a regional and East Asian perspective.

Pittis, Donald & Henders, Susan J. (eds.). *Macao: Mysterious Decay and Romance*. Hong Kong: Oxford University Press, 1997. A general anthology of writing about Macao.

Porter, Jonathan. *Macau, the Imaginary City: Culture and Society, 1557–the Present*. Boulder: Westview Press, 1996. History and development of the city of Macao.

Willis, Clive (ed.). *China and Macau*. London: Ashgate, 2002. A history of Portuguese relations with China between 1513 and 1650, based on excerpts from travellers and chroniclers.

Visions of China
STORIES FROM MACAU

Selected and Translated by
David Brookshaw

With stories by
Henrique de Senna Fernandes,
Deolinda da Conceição,
Maria Ondina Braga and
Fernanda Dias

Visions of China: Stories from Macau is an anthology of stories translated from the Portuguese, set against the backdrop of that former colony and, to a slightly lesser degree, its close neighbor Hong Kong, during the second half of the twentieth century. Whether the stories take place during the harsh war years of the 1940s, or more recent decades when the city rapidly modernized, they all depict its unique character as a melting pot of Chinese and Portuguese cultures.

2002. Hong Kong University Press

Paperback. ISBN 962–209–592–5

Market Rights: Asia, Australia and New Zealand

For more information or online ordering, please visit:
http://www.hkupress.org